THE CLOCKWORK WITCH

THE CLOCKWORK CHRONICLES BOOK I

Find your magic!

Michelle D. Sonnier

Michelle D. Sonnier

eBooks
Pennsville, NJ

PUBLISHED BY
eSpec Books LLC
Danielle McPhail, Publisher
PO Box 242,
Pennsville, New Jersey 08070
www.especbooks.com

ISBN: 978-1-942990-78-9
ISBN (ebook): 978-1-942990-77-2

Interior Design: Danielle McPhail
Sidhe na Daire Multimedia
www.sidhenadaire.com

Cover Design: Mike McPhail, McP Digital Graphics

Art Credits - www.Shutterstock.com
Woman in Dungeon © By Evgeniia Litovchenko
Steampunk Clock © By Atelier Sommerland
Steampunk Owl © By renikca

For my mother, Mary Gayle.
It's been 16 years and I still miss you every day.
I wish you could have seen this.

CHAPTER I

*In Which We Enter the Witching World
of London Society and Meet Arabella*

T HE HALF-DRUNK GLASS OF LEMONADE IN HER HAND GREW WARM AS
Arabella watched the other guests from a small alcove nearly
completely shrouded by a voluminous potted palm. She was
sure the decorator meant it to be used by discrete young couples, but
Arabella found it just as useful to get away from the uncomfortable
stares and whispers. She watched partygoers swirl and laugh across
marble floors. Brass and crystal chandeliers cast butter-soft candlelight
over the merriment while a string quartet played in the background.
The tall arched windows all around the room appeared black as the
interior light blinded everyone to the more gentle light of the moon and
stars. Arabella sighed as she tugged the low neckline on her lavender
satin evening gown. It didn't fit quite right and the color was just ever
so slightly off, the wrong contrast with her dark brown hair and pale
blue eyes, but it was a hand-me-down from her mother and tailoring
could only do so much.

Arabella may have found the party more exciting, and not tortuous
at all, if she had not thought of herself as barren, completely devoid of
magic. If she could just perform a simple scrying spell, if she could send
or receive a thought, she might not feel like an outcast. Her eyes drifted
half shut as one of her fondest recurring fantasies flitted through her
mind's eye. In it she stepped out from behind the potted palm and

plucked a fan from a nearby lady's hand with her telekinesis. Her imaginary self fanned her warm cheeks with the gaily-colored feathers while she discussed the intricacies of levitation with the other young scions of the London Houses. But she could do none of these things. She felt surrounded by people who either pitied her or were disgusted by her. At least she imagined it so and suppressed a shudder. She was a daughter of Blackstone House, seventh daughter of Minerva Vivienne Sortilege, the Lady Blackstone herself and Grande Dame of the English Council of Witches. Her other six sisters were all accomplished witches in their own right. In fact, the Sortilege bloodline of Blackstone House had not produced a Cassus, a woman born into a witch family with no talent for magic, in over 300 years. That is until she, Arabella Helene Sortilege, the humiliation of the Sortilege line and Blackstone House itself, was born.

"Someone might mistake you for a jungle cat, peeking out from behind those fronds like that," came a voice from behind her.

Arabella jumped, but relaxed when she realized it was her elder sister Rowena, the fifth-born daughter and the only real friend she had in her constrained little world. Rowena's coloring—rich auburn hair and deep brown eyes—was a near perfect echo of their mother, right down to her creamy porcelain skin. The deep hunter green of her plush velvet gown suited her perfectly and set off her witches' robes with flair, but then Rowena could afford to buy her own gowns. She was already drawing her stipend as an active member of the Council.

"You shouldn't scare people like that, Ro," Arabella laughed as she sipped from her glass. "I don't think your healing spells are up to restarting my heart yet."

"How would you know, Ari? I've been studying hard." Rowena jostled her sister's shoulder with her own and began to scrutinize the crowd herself. "Anything interesting?"

Arabella shrugged. "Just the usual, as far as I can tell. You?"

Rowena scanned the assembly with eyes half shut and the tip of her tongue tracing her bottom lip. "All the witches are shielding," she sighed. "Except Lady Wentworth, but she's in her cups anyway, so just the usual."

"Picking up anything from her?" Arabella tried to sound casual.

Rowena blushed. "Nothing you want to hear."

"Very much just the usual." Arabella's mouth thinned out to a hard line.

"Ari, don't take it so hard. Lady Wentworth is a lush and a gossip. Her opinion isn't worth much of anything." Rowena stroked her sister's arm from shoulder to elbow.

"Her opinion might not be worth much, but she's thinking the same thing everyone else is thinking. 'Poor little brown bud, such a disgrace, a stunted vine spoiling an otherwise lovely garden,'" Arabella's voice mocked in a sing-song tone.

"Ari..."

"What about the ordinary people?" Arabella interrupted her. "Can you hear anything from them?"

Rowena looked over the crowd for a moment and then pointed out an older, heavy woman in more lace than anyone but a very young girl should wear. "She's practically shouting."

"What is she thinking?"

Rowena shrugged. "She's trying to figure out who she can get to marry her daughters, who snubbed her and who she should snub, what she should order up from her cook for breakfast. Do mundane women ever think of anything else?"

"What else can they think of, Ro? They're not supposed to have jobs and their husbands rule everything, even their children. What else do they have to think about but marriages and snubs and menus?"

"They're almost as useless as I am," Arabella's voice was soft and nearly lost in the chatter of the party.

Rowena sighed as she crossed her arms over her stomach and held her elbows close. Both sisters looked out over the room in silence. The colors of the gay party whirled around them, but never touched them with their merriment. Every witch who was worth her broom was there, as well as most of the more important alchemists, Lords from Parliament, and their wives.

"I wonder if Father is here," Arabella broke the silence.

"Probably not," said Rowena. "You know he avoids any event that Mother even might attend."

"Yes, but this is so special," said Arabella.

Bartholomew Westerfeld had gathered them all together to preview what he claimed was a great wonder before he showed it at The Great Exhibition. No one knew precisely what he was going to show and the gossip was running rampant. Would it be something to calm the growing unrest overseas, especially in the Crimea? Or perhaps it would be something to finally lift the horrible famine that had gripped the Irish people for so long. Mr. Westerfeld would not drop the slightest hint, and seemed to revel in the attention as everyone continued to guess.

Rowena shrugged. "Father's given his regrets for more important events before. He might have sent Henry or John in his stead. It would be nice to see our brothers again." Rowena craned her neck to observe every corner of the room.

Arabella opened her mouth to say something, but snapped it shut again as she saw Jessamine and Josephine approaching.

"It's time," Jessamine began.

"Mother wants you to come now," Josephine finished for her.

The twins regarded Arabella and Rowena with the bright blue eyes they had inherited from their father, faces unreadable. The twins were always inscrutable. They were absolutely alike in all ways, from their curly brown locks to their unnerving silences, except for one thing. Jessamine showed an affinity for fire magic while Josephine had more talent for the water magic arts. Even the wisest of crones could not explain the differences in the girls' magic. Twins were rare enough, but when they came their magic was usually linked in some way, not diametrically opposite, as it was with Jessamine and Josephine, the third- and fourth-born daughters to the Lady Blackstone. Even their Aunts, the twins Leanore and Lorena just one generation prior, had shared magical proclivities. Both had been talented earth witches.

"Well, I suppose we shouldn't dally now that we've been summoned," Arabella sighed. "Let's go."

"It'll be fine, Ari." Rowena squeezed her hand. "In fact, it might even be fun."

Arabella raised an eyebrow. "I'd settle for not a disaster."

As the girls started to make their way across the room to where their mother held court, along with Arabella's eldest sisters, Vivienne, Amelia, and Elizabeth, Jessamine and Josephine clasped hands together and grinned at each other. "It's time!" they chimed together.

"You said that already," Rowena frowned. "We're going, we're going."

Jessamine and Josephine simply put their heads together and giggled, unseemly behavior at their age and in a public venue.

Rowena leaned in and whispered into Arabella's ear as they walked arm and arm, "I swear, sometimes I think they're just trying to make everyone cross out of sheer perversity."

Arabella had to stifle a giggle, biting her lower lip, as they arrived at where their mother was standing. All four girls sank into neatly executed curtseys and bowed their heads to their mother.

"Is there something humorous you'd like to share with the rest of us, Arabella?" Minerva Sortilege asked.

"No, ma'am," said Arabella, curtseying again. "It was just a stray thought, unsuitable for such company."

"I see," said her mother. "Perhaps you should work harder at focusing on more appropriate thoughts in public, give me *something* to be proud about."

Arabella bowed her head, trying to hide her flaming cheeks. "Yes, Mother," she murmured.

Her eldest sister, Vivienne, presumed heir to both Blackstone House and the position of the Grande Dame, echoed their mother's frown at Arabella. Amelia, the next eldest, glanced at Vivienne and schooled her features in a perfect imitation. Elizabeth, the sixth-born sister, just one year older than Arabella, covered the lower half of her face with her fan and tittered, her eyes gleaming.

"That will be quite enough, Elizabeth." Minerva quieted her daughter with a single frosty glance. "Gather around, ladies, we will go in together."

Minerva Sortilege turned from her daughters to face the ballroom, sweeping her burgundy satin skirts about with the practiced twitch of one hand. Her black velvet robes, open at the front and gathered at the shoulders, as all witches' robes were, showed the cunning cut of her ball gown and shimmered in a graceful fall from her shoulders to the floor, ending in a small, tasteful train. The arcane and esoteric symbols of the proud vocation of witchery were stitched all over the fabric, glowing and glimmering in response to the power the Lady Blackstone held. She was the most powerful witch in all of England, quite possibly the world. All eyes turned to her; every witch in the room envied her power. Minerva Sortilege kept her face schooled in the pleasant neutrality that such social situations required, but those who knew her could see the tell-tale downward tug at the corners of her lips.

Vivienne aligned herself at her mother's right shoulder, one respectful step back. Her ball gown of cobalt blue complimented her robes of deep charcoal velvet, which were not as elaborate as her mother's, nor did they shimmer and glow as much, but her robes still outshone most of the witches in the room. She would not assume her mother's mantle simply because of preference or birth, Vivienne was powerful enough in her own right to earn it. In another move only noticed by the Sortilege women, Vivienne's hand fluttered for a moment over her stomach before she dropped it by her side. This would probably be the last social event she would attend before sequestering herself at the family home in Boscastle to await the birth of her first child. Her husband, Nathanial Moreland, was already there making sure that everything was ready for her return. At thirty-one, she would be considered old for a first child if she were an ordinary woman, but since witches lived longer than most, hers was a very appropriate age.

Amelia settled herself at her sister's shoulder, arranging her dove gray robes with a less graceful hand than her sister or her mother, but she still drew her shoulders up and lifted her chin with pride. Josephine and Jessamine arrayed themselves to their mother's left, still holding hands and watching Arabella with their unnerving stare. Josephine's red velvet robes gave off the banked heat of her not insignificant power in fire magic, while Jessamine's blue velvet gave off the soothing cool of water. Between them the air bent and warped, sending up fitful gouts of steam, but the twins appeared unconcerned even as the party guests closest to them took a step back. Minerva glanced at them and sighed, and Arabella noticed a slight furrow in her brow that she imagined was her mother sending her wayward daughters a shielded thought to tamp down their emotions and get a hold of themselves. The Sortilege name might allow them latitudes not granted to other witches, and much more freedom than the average woman, but scalding their host's guests would almost certainly require significant apologies. The twins broke off staring at Arabella, the heat and steam subsiding, and nodded to their mother, lips twitching around the words of the unspoken apology they thought to her.

Elizabeth, Rowena, and Arabella stood shoulder to shoulder in a line behind their older and more powerful sisters. Rowena's purple velvet robes announced that she was still undecided about where to focus her talents, much to her mother's consternation, while Elizabeth's very pale gray velvet showed a low level of magical power and control, at least compared to her mother and sisters. In most other witch families, she would have been considered average. If Arabella had not been standing there, in only a ball gown and no robes at all, Elizabeth would be viewed as the embarrassment of the Sortilege line. But given that Elizabeth was only eighteen, there was at least some hope that her powers might yet grow with practice and hard work. Arabella had no such hope. The most powerful witches manifested their power at a very early age, Vivienne was levitating her toys before she could walk, and even the most average of witches began to manifest her powers with the onset of puberty. At seventeen, Arabella was well past hope that she would suddenly bloom into the witch her mother always wanted her to be.

All eyes in the room focused on the most important witches in the land. Minerva looked back to ensure all of her daughters were in their proper places. She gave each of her eldest four a slight nod while her youngest three received a barely perceptible frown. The frown deepened when her eyes fell on Arabella, becoming noticeable to even those outside of the Sortilege women. From the corners of her eyes, Arabella could see fans lift in front of ladies' lips and she imagined she could feel their whispers crawl up and down her spine. Hidden in the folds of her robe, Rowena reached out and twined her fingers around Arabella's and squeezed.

Eyes front and shoulders back, Minerva began to stride across the ballroom to where Bartholomew Westerfeld stood in front of the locked door to another ballroom that held what he swore was a wonder for the ages. Her daughters followed behind in tight formation. As they passed, witches and alchemists alike bowed and curtseyed. Even members of Parliament inclined their heads in respect.

Halfway across the room, three witches stepped into the path of Lady Blackstone and her daughters. The room seemed to gasp with one voice. Their robes were clean, but worn thin and only shining dully. The lead witch wore the deep blue of strong water magic, while the two that flanked her wore paler grays for middling general magic. Their ball gowns were of a fashion that had come and passed at least ten years ago. Each one was slender to the point of being sickly, with bright red hair and freckles dusted across ivory skin—Irish witches, all.

Minerva raised an eyebrow and looked pointedly past them. The lead witch raised her chin and kept her fists balled by her side, standing her ground.

"Sister," sighed Minerva. "If you do not mind, I have an appointment to keep."

"Sister," said the lead witch. "I have come to ask your favor and I will not move until I hear your answer."

Minerva's jaw tightened. "This is not the place to discuss such matters. There will be a session of the Council next month and you can address any concerns to me then."

"Grande Dame," the witch's voice cracked. "I have been trying to be heard at the Council for over a year now. I have been given no choice but to seek you here."

Minerva frowned and her eyebrows pinched together. "Remind me to speak to the Secretary about hearing petitions in a timely manner," she murmured to Vivienne, who nodded.

"Well, Sister," Minerva said. "Tell me who you are and what you are about so we can get on with the festivities of the evening."

The water witch took a deep breath and shut her eyes for a moment. Behind her, the other two clasped hands and bit their lips, exchanging glances.

"I am Shannon O'Reilley and I have come to speak for all the Irish witches, well, for all of Ireland, really. We're starving, Sister. Even though our fields grow, our children die from hunger. The English landlords require all but our potatoes, and those crops are failing from blight. Every earth witch we have has failed to cure the blight, and died in the trying. We have no one with earth powers left. Please, aid us so we can feed our families again. Or use your influence to convince the landlords to let us keep enough of what we grow for them to feed our children and old people." All three witches had tears in their eyes.

"Perhaps you are overstating the problem. I have heard recent reports of the blight easing," said Minerva with a frown. "However it stands, there are no earth witches to spare. I am sorry, but you will have to find some other way to deal with the blight."

"Please, Grande Dame," Shannon pleaded. "We've tried everything, we need your help. We have managed to stave off some of its ravages, but the disease refuses to be cured. We fall under the rule of the English Council of Witches, should we not also get help from that same council?"

"Mother," said Vivienne as she touched Minerva's elbow. "My earth magic is strong. I could take some new initiates who show talent in that area and seed the country anew. Some members of the council would be eager to start new Houses in less crowded conditions."

The three Irish witches gasped with joy and clutched each other. "Thank you," began Shannon.

"No," Minerva cut her off and turned to Vivienne. "I'm surprised you would suggest such a thing. You are vitally needed here, especially in the next year." Her eyes were hard and Vivienne blushed.

"I am sorry for your plight, Sister, but the Council can offer you no help at this time."

The blood drained from Shannon's face and she dropped to her knees, her dress and robes puddling around her, her hands clasped together. Tears streamed down her cheeks openly. "Please, please, Grande Dame, I have watched my own children starve. My people would die of shame instead of empty bellies if they knew I was here to plead our case. This is our last resort. You don't understand the sacrifices we've made."

"Sacrifice?" Minerva's voice rose, along with the color in her cheeks. "You dare to lecture me on sacrifice? You Irish witches seem to have very short memories. It was not so long ago that my own beloved blood sisters went to you and gave their lives trying to save your precious potatoes. Do not presume to lecture me on the subject of sacrifice!"

A murmur surged through the crowd as the party guests whispered behind their hands and fans at the show of emotion from Lady Blackstone. Such a thing was unheard of. Even her daughters glanced at each other with wide eyes and tight lips.

Shannon sank further down, pressing her forehead to the floor. "I meant no disrespect, Sister, we on the Isle are well aware of the sacrifices of the Sortilege line and Blackstone House."

"I find that hard to believe given your temerity, approaching us at such an event with such a request." Even scowling Minerva Sortilege remained beautiful.

"Please, Lady Blackstone," wept the broken water witch. "If there is an ounce of compassion within you, please, help us. We have nowhere else to turn."

"The audacity," gasped Minerva. "You have the nerve to question my love for my sisters in magic? Do you not think it pains me to deny my sisters aid?"

Shannon lifted her tear-streaked face from the floor and shook her head, her mouth opening and closing on no sound. Her sister witches sank to the floor behind her, clutching each other and weeping.

"I have to think of the entire United Kingdom," Minerva's strident voice rose and she raised her right hand, power shimmering around long fingers. "Indeed, given that we are the strongest and most talented witches Mother Earth has seen fit to provide, we must be leaders to the entirety of the world! I have more concerns than just one starving island who cannot manage their resources better than the mundane." Minerva cast forth a wave of magical force with her right hand that shoved all three of the Irish witches into the crowd, knocking over several party guests. Minerva showed no strain at all. She raised her hand again, but Vivienne stepped to her ear and whispered. Lowering her hand, Minerva gave a sharp nod to her eldest, who stepped back into line.

Footmen of the Westerfeld estate came forward and helped the party guests and Irish witches to their feet. The room was utterly silent but for the rustle of fabric. Minerva fixed the invading witches with a frosty glare.

"You would do well to leave now, my Sisters," she said. "Before I become angry and forget my temper. You push me too far and it does your cause no good."

The pale-faced footmen hustled the women from the room with the minimum of courtesy demanded of a witch. The Irish problem would see no resolution this night.

Minerva lifted her chin and schooled her features. "Now, let us continue with the evening's entertainments." She swept up to a profusely sweating Westerfeld in front of the locked door with her daughters in tow. "I do hope you can lighten the mood of the evening, Master Westerfeld." She favored him with an icy smile.

"Indeed," said Westerfeld as he executed a deep bow to the powerful witch. "I do hope that I can amuse you, my lady." He turned and unlocked the pair of gilt doors, sweeping them wide open and leading the guests into a ballroom that glittered in brass, crystal, and mirrors.

CHAPTER II

*In Which Minerva Is Further Insulted
and Arabella Finds Unexpected Joy*

A RABELLA FIDGETED IN HER CHAIR AGAINST THE MIRRORED WALL, glancing down the row to her right at her sisters, all arranged in age order, and on to her mother sitting in the chair on the center aisle. Minerva fanned herself as the air grew warmer and warmer whilst the rest of the party guests filed in and took their seats, packing in closer than the room should have allowed. Despite Westerfeld's attempts to use status in London society as a tight control, the guest list had still been quite long. Minerva leaned her head toward Vivienne and spoke in hushed tones behind her fan. Vivienne merely nodded at whatever her mother said, her lips pressed tight together. Arabella had no doubt that the Irish issue was the topic of the one-sided conversation, and that the same conversation would occupy the Sortilege women for much of the next month leading up to the spring meeting of the Council of Witches.

Across the aisle, the influential Lords of Parliament and their ladies sat chatting with the two second-best alchemists in England and their ladies, but her father, Alexander Paul Leyden, Duke of Umbridge, was nowhere to be seen. By all accounts, he should have been there, considering he was the most talented alchemist in several generations and much more important than most of the men Arabella and her family shared the first row with. She found herself wishing that her father was here despite Mother's attendance, or that he had at least sent one of her brothers in his place. She sat back with a sigh and not for the first or last time wondered what had driven her parents apart. Alexander had known when he married Minerva that she would maintain her own name and titles, not take his, and that she would be much more independent than any mundane woman. He understood that any daughters produced by the marriage would be hers and hers alone, that he could not have any control over their upbringing. Any sons would be his, but not the daughters. And by all the whispered gossip Arabella was never supposed to hear, her parents had been madly and passionately in love. Minerva had been much younger than a witch normally was when they married, much to Grandmother's great consternation. And yet, not long after Arabella was born, there had been some sort of a rift and her mother and father would not be in the same room since.

Arabella shifted again, craning her neck to try and get a better look at the mundane people Westerfeld had invited. It wasn't often that Arabella got a chance to observe those not of the witch community. Minerva limited her daughter's outings and did as much as possible to ensure that the majority of them were restricted to witches and their families. Arabella noticed the women's skirts were belled out to a ridiculous circumference. Moria, the Housemistress for their London townhome, told Arabella that this preposterous skirt arrangement was all the rage among the women in mundane society. It took assistance from at least one, and sometimes more, maids to get a woman into them, and they were so stiff that any kind of freedom of movement was quickly stifled. Arabella was glad that witch society had their own views on fashion, and that independent movement and dressing was valued.

"Stop fidgeting, Arabella," Elizabeth sniped. "You're enough of an embarrassment already. The least you can do is comport yourself properly when we're in public."

"Lizzie," Rowena hissed from her other side. "The family must maintain solidarity in public at all times." Elizabeth flushed and pouted, training her eyes straight ahead and fanning herself. Arabella also locked her gaze straight ahead and endeavored to keep her emotions under control. She made every effort to focus on what was to come rather than all the people she was sure were staring at the back of her head with pity.

In the broad empty area in front of the seats hung thick, green velvet curtains obscuring whatever it was Westerfeld wanted to show them. It was an area large enough for a small play, but Arabella doubted that even the most stimulating theater production would be worthy of all the pomp and circumstance Westerfeld had poured into this event. Adopting a bland and socially acceptable countenance, Arabella stared off past the distance and let her mind wander over the possibilities of what those voluminous curtains concealed. Or at least she would have if she'd been able to concentrate. Her skin tingled all over and she felt a near overwhelming urge to get up and move. It took all of the self-control she'd managed to learn in her short life to keep from fidgeting so she could avoid another reprimand from Elizabeth, or worse, attention from her mother. Arabella wished that Rowena was sitting next to her. Perhaps then they might have some quiet conversation and that might distract her from the feeling that she could jump out of her skin.

At long last, the final guests took their seats in the rear of the room, and the servants shut the gilded doors. It hadn't seemed possible before, but the air grew even more stifling. Bartholomew Westerfeld paced up the narrow aisle from the rear of the room, rubbing his hands together. He tossed his head a bit to clear a thick lock of wavy chestnut hair from his eyes. The people in the audience who had never seen him before gasped. On the outside of his trousers a cage of shining brass encased each leg, with gears at his knees that allowed them to bend. His gait was slow and jerky, but he still smiled at anyone who would meet his eyes. Arabella had heard word of his disability before the party. According to rumors, he had suffered through some sort of a fever when he was a child that left his legs too weak to bear the weight of his body. Depending on which rumor you chose to believe, the healing witch who tended him had either worked a miracle for him to even survive and retain some control of his legs, or she had completely botched the spells and crippled a once healthy boy. Westerfeld stopped in front of the curtains and gazed at them for a moment with a proprietary gleam in his eye, then turned to his guests with a smile.

"Ladies and gentlemen, members of Parliament, and noble witches," he began, spreading his arms in an oratorical gesture. "Thank you for consenting to attend my humble little party." He chuckled at his own joke, well aware that this event had been one of the most sought after invitations of the season. "I do hope that you will consider your time well invested."

"For this very evening," he continued. "I shall show you a marvel for the ages, a spectacle such that you shall be proud to recount this evening to your children's children. So, without further ado..." The crowd murmured and chattered to each other as he turned and took two steps to the golden-tasseled ropes on the edge of the green curtains.

Westerfeld gave the golden rope a great yank and the curtains rose with surprising speed. Arabella gasped and barely resisted the urge to lean forward. A huge machine composed of gleaming copper, brass, and steel pipes, levers, and gears filled the whole of the dais behind the curtain. The broad rectangular shape captivated most of the audience, eliciting murmurs and cries of astonishment, and even a few small cheers from the more technophilic. Minerva Sortilege, however, appeared less than amused. Witchery and technology were uncomfortable neighbors at best, and more often could be considered bitter enemies locked in a cold truce. The mundane masses of the world desired the advances of technology to make their wretched lives less miserable, and perhaps slightly less dependent on the magical assistance and guidance provided by witches. The Council of Witches maintained that technology posed a danger to the natural world, the same world that they drew their power from. Parliament remained divided, usually right along the lines of families with close ties to witches, by blood or by marriage, and those without.

Bartholomew Westerfeld had to know that Lady Blackstone, and indeed all the witches in attendance, would be unhappy to have wasted an evening on some technological toy. Had they known that this monstrosity would be the wonder Westerfeld had promised, not a single witch would have accepted the invitation. Minerva frowned deeply and fanned herself harder, not quite willing to give such insult as to get up and walk out, but it was a near thing. Likely only the recent kerfuffle with the Irish witches kept her in her seat. There was a limit to how much rudeness would be tolerated in a single evening, even from the most powerful witch in the civilized world.

However, if Minerva had not been so absorbed in her own pique and her daughters had not been so focused on the harsh emotions seeping from the tight control of their mother's shield, they might have noticed Arabella and had more of a notion of what was to come. She sat

on the very edge her seat, back ramrod straight and hands clutched white-knuckled in her lap. Her mouth hung open and her breath came in short, small gasps, her wide eyes focused on the machinery in front of her.

To Arabella, the vision of metal and cogs and levers in front of her was the most divinely beautiful thing she'd ever seen. It didn't just gleam from the care of machinists with their oilcans and their burnishing cloths; it glowed with its own inner light. Arabella wanted to leap forward to stroke it and find out whether it would make her hands tingle like she thought it might.

"Ladies and gentlemen," cried Westerfeld over the din. "I give you the greatest advancement in technology thus far, the Distinction Engine. Now, I know some of you may say that this looks quite like Mr. Babbage's Difference Engine, but I assure you, that this fine piece of machinery is much more capable than that motley collection of bolts and cogs! Allow me to demonstrate..." He wobbled around on his better leg, giving a swirl of his coattails, and approached his machine. With a gentle hand he depressed one handle and a tray of closely packed, slender levers—each topped at the end with a flat disk—emerged from the machine with a hiss of steam. Most of the crowd gasped again. Arabella tried to contain her cry of delight over the shimmers of light that danced over the metal as it performed its task.

"From here," said Westerfeld. "I can enter some of the most complicated calculations dreamed of by man." His fingers danced over the levers, entering his promised complex formula. He stabbed one final lever with a great flourish. "And now this fabulous machine will complete its calculations in mere moments, with unparalleled accuracy, where talented mathematical scholars would take hours!" He gestured to the machine where it chugged and whirred, and occasionally let off a small puff of steam.

Arabella squirmed in her seat, watching the light as it travelled from left to right, each gear, each cog, each piston glowing brighter as the information danced upon it. All except for one place, a section of dull copper near the center of the machine where no light danced. Arabella almost wept as the light disappeared into the dense void, but then had to bite her lip to contain a cry of joy when it emerged again just a moment later. The light traveled to the far end of the machine where a stylus held by a slender, graceful arm of brass inscribed the machine's answer on a fresh sheet of paper. Westerfeld walked as fast as he dared, trying not to overbalance the delicate machinery that kept him upright. Arabella pressed her lips together hard to contain her gasp over the glow that shimmered around the gears at his knees. She had not noticed it earlier, and could only guess that something about the Distinction Engine had snatched a veil from her eyes. Westerfeld seized the paper and brandished it to his rapt audience. Several people applauded and the witches' frowns grew deeper.

"And even with all this wonder, there is yet more for me to share!" he cried. "Unlike the weak machines of Babbage and his compatriots, my machine is strong enough to withstand a room full of witches with no calculation interference. See how my machine bravely chugged along and produced the necessary answer despite all the magical interference in the room? My assistive leg braces struggle, but the Distinction Engine continues without any problems!" He waved the paper over his head again.

Minerva shot to her feet. "That will be quite enough, Mr. Westerfeld." Her voice rang out clipped and harsh.

"We are not amused to have been treated as props for your demonstration. We will take our leave now, and you might be wise to think twice before you insult witches again."

She turned on her heel and swept down the aisle to the doors where the footmen scrambled to open them for her. Her daughters followed, heads high and jaws clenched, all except for Arabella. She remained in her seat for a moment, her head whipping back and forth from the miraculous machine and her retreating family, nearly hyperventilating. It was Rowena who noticed her and stepped to the side to allow Elizabeth to pass while she turned back and hauled Arabella up by her arm.

"Now is not the time to act like a moonstruck owl, sister," Rowena whispered in her ear as she held her close and helped her to the aisle. "There's only so much I can do for you before Mother whips us both."

Arabella's knees wobbled and she stumbled just a little. She took that moment to look back behind her and caught one more glance at that marvelous machine before other witches with stormy faces cut off her view as they all marched out of the room in her mother's wake.

They gathered in the middle of the broader, airier ballroom outside the gilt doors to discuss the outrage in a cacophony not unlike a flock of crows. Westerfeld followed them and stood at the open door to the demonstration salon with his arms crossed across his chest and a smirk on his lips.

"Poor little witches," he mocked. "Finally getting a taste of what it's like not to be the most powerful people in the room and they don't like it."

Minerva turned to face him with a regal glare. "I fail to see how your little toy is any threat to our power, Mr. Westerfeld." Her voice was full of ice.

"Then that just shows what little vision you are capable of," Westerfeld guffawed. "This is just the beginning, Madame Sortilege. The minds of men will continue to advance these machines, they will become capable of greater and greater things, and you witches will be relegated to where you should have been all along, meekly at the sides of men just like all other women." His last words came out in a sneer.

The silence hung thick in the room as the Grande Dame favored Westerfeld with one last haughty glare and then turned her attention to her sister witches. Every witch in the room looked to their leader to see what she had to say.

"Sisters," she began. "We have been most grievously insulted this evening. To be treated as a prop in a parlor trick!" The witches nodded and grumbled in agreement. "We will take up the matter of this insult at the spring Council meeting, but until then Mr. Westerfeld and company are to be avoided at all costs. If he would use us in this way for simple amusement, who knows what else he is capable of." She took a moment to look each witch in the eye.

"Return to your homes, my Sisters, and I will see you in the spring."

"Call their carriages," Westerfeld gestured to his servants. "Get these witches out of my house!" He paused a moment before turning back to the demonstration parlor. "I am capable of quite a bit, Madame Sortilege, you should remember this before you try to push me." He started to stalk away, back to his other guests, while his staff scrambled to gather outerwear and call the coaches.

The second and third best alchemists in England, Mr. Yarrow and Mr. Fine, pushed past Westerfeld with their ladies on their arms, a few other attendees in tow behind them. Westerfeld almost lost his balance and had to grab the back of a chair to keep from toppling over.

"While we may not always be in complete accord with the Council," Mr. Yarrow said in a loud, booming voice as he yanked on his gloves.

"The Alchemist's Society still supports the Council of Witches and we cannot continue to be here when they have been so insulted."

"Fine," spat Westerfeld, his face an apoplectic red. "Betray your gender to those harpies, but you'll come begging when they fall and I will laugh in your faces!" He let out a maniacal cackle and turned back to Minerva. "You can have your Luddites and your witch lovers, but technology will still crush you and we will return you to your proper place." He creaked back into the demonstration parlor, and the room behind him became a swirl of noise and confusion from about half the party guests trying to leave at once.

Arabella yanked at Rowena's arm, pulling her to the edge of the flock of witches and leaning in to whisper in her ear.

"Did you see it? Did you see it?" She strained to keep her voice from rising up to the crystal chandeliers.

"See what?" Rowena whispered back.

"The machine! That wonderful machine!"

Rowena flushed red and pulled Arabella a little further from the knot of angry witches. "Hush, you. What are you, daft? You know how Mother feels about machines!"

"But it glowed, Ro. I saw it! I saw the light dancing through it while it was performing its calculations." Arabella clasped her sister's hands tight in her own. "Well, except for that little plate in the middle. That part didn't glow."

Rowena's flush turned pale as all the blood drained out of her face. "The plate was the only part that glowed for me, Ari. That glow is what magic looks like."

It was Arabella's turn to turn pale. "You mean…"

"Mother says the carriage is ready and we must leave immediately," Jessamine and Josephine said in unison, thrusting Arabella and Rowena's outer capes at them. They were already dressed to go out into the chill of the early April evening. The twins turned without waiting for a response. Rowena grabbed Arabella's hand and squeezed hard.

"Don't you dare breathe a word about that infernal machine and what you saw to Mother or anyone else… Mother barely tolerates you without magic; can you imagine what she'd do if she knew you had a sympathy for machines?" Rowena hissed in Arabella's ear.

Rowena yanked on Arabella's arm and they quickly followed the twins in silence. Even without any empathic talent, Arabella could see the rage seething off of her mother. This was most definitely not the time to disobey or make her cross.

The Sortilege carriage was waiting for them at the base of the Westerfeld estate's front marble staircase. Jeanette, their driver, already stood at the carriage door holding it open, ready to assist the Sortilege women in handling their dresses up into the carriage. She was a distant family relation from France, who had come to England for a job and to escape from a bad marriage to a wealthy man. She had mild magical abilities that seemed to focus on animals, horses in particular, and since she could receive a telepathic message, as long as it was spoken clearly and strongly enough, it made her the ideal carriage driver for a family of witches. The general populace might be scandalized by a woman in breeches but since she was a witch, and backed by the most powerful witch family in England, she could get away with it. Her telepathic receptiveness served them well that night, as she already had their carriage ready to go and at the head of a long line of carriages, thanks to Minerva's call before they'd even left the demonstration parlor.

The Sortilege carriage looked small from the outside, certainly not large enough to handle eight women and their voluminous evening wear, but on the inside it was four times as spacious as it appeared to be. This was just one of the spells Minerva Sortilege had perfected that guaranteed a steady stream of income for her family. The lists of people who desired this particular spell were long. Other witches wished to be tutored in the technique. There were even mundanes who wished to have a carriage like it for their very own. Although the first list was much smaller than the second. There were not many witches alive who could handle a spell so powerful.

The Sortilege ladies settled in for the long ride back to the family home in Boscastle, after a short stop at their London townhouse. Arabella's mother had already contacted Moria, the Housemistress, telepathically and the luggage they needed for travel would be ready for them. Tonight they would sleep in Oxford, 60 miles west. The horses tripped along lightly thanks to further enchantments on the carriage to make it lighter, and on their shoes to give an extra spring to their steps. They would be at their Boscastle home near the sea on Tuesday. The ladies in the carriage sat in silence, each wrapped in her own thoughts, which suited Arabella just fine. She took a seat next to the window and watched the city of London slide by. Everywhere she looked now she could see the glow — from the mechanisms embedded in the gas streetlamps, to the pocket watch a gentleman was checking on the corner, to a steam-powered riverboat on the Thames. As they slipped away from London proper and into the countryside, the glow and sparkles gradually diminished until they were gone. When she could only see dark countryside outside her window, she sat back with a sigh.

CHAPTER III

Where Dinner Proves Uncomfortable
and a Prophecy Is Revealed

DINNER AT BLACKSTONE MANOR WAS, AS IT USUALLY WAS FOR Arabella, an unpleasant affair. Almost everyone in the room had some sort of magical power, except for her and the men, of which there was only one at this point—Vivienne's husband, Nathaniel. Aside from her sisters, mother, and grandmother, even the servants had some sort of ability. Not every witch family could afford to staff their house with witch servants, but the Sortilege family could. Their cook was a talented hedgewitch with a touch of true earth magic who could bring the most succulent flavors from her herbs and vegetables. The maids, who cleaned the house and served the dinners, all had at least minor levitation skills, which came in very handy for dusting hard-to-reach places. And rather than come close to the table to serve food and drink, they stood at the walls and directed flying dishes about the room with consummate skill. The Blackstone Manor Housemistress had some small precognitive ability. More than once, Arabella had been about to sneak from her bedroom down to the kitchen to fix herself a cup of chamomile to help her sleep only to find Mrs. Holly standing at her door with a steaming cup.

A platter of roast beef hovered in front of Arabella and she helped herself to a small piece, replacing the meat fork and nodding when she was done. She snuck a look out of the corner of her eye, trying to determine if the look on young Ginny's face was mild disgust at having to serve a brown bud or just ennui. Rowena kept telling her that her lack of magic was not as much of a disaster as she thought, although what did Rowena know? She'd never had to overhear someone gossip about what an embarrassment *she* was to her family, nor had she ever endured Mother's punishments when, once again, she couldn't manage even the smallest magical task. Arabella sighed and pushed roasted carrots around her plate with her fork.

Down at the other end of the table, her mother, Vivienne, and her grandmother were deep in conversation over Westerfeld's insult and the Irish difficulty. Grandmother may have retired from active Council service, but she still kept abreast of the issues of the day and offered advice to her daughter and granddaughter. Amelia hung on their every word and nodded fiercely at everything Vivienne said, like she always did. Arabella wondered if she ever got tired of standing in Vivienne's shadow. Jessamine and Josephine ate quietly with their heads together, seeming to speak to each other without a sound. Nathaniel kept up light conversation with Rowena and Elizabeth, all the while keeping a weather eye on what his wife ate. As usual, Arabella was ignored. She sighed again and studied the wallpaper for the millionth time, letting her gaze drift over the servants.

Almost all the servants at Blackstone Manor were female, as was common for a witch household. They did keep a few men for heavy labor and tasks the witches did not want to waste their magical abilities upon. But the men were completely under the direction of the female members of the staff, and any man who could not stomach the arrangement was quickly replaced.

When Arabella first learned that this was not the common arrangement in every household across England it had puzzled her. Indeed, although she now knew that most of society regarded women as inferior to men, she still could not understand it. Witches were considered different from ordinary women, and therefore superior. The Council did much to encourage that posture. However, with her unique position of being utterly mundane inside of witch society, Arabella didn't think there was any difference between witches and ordinary women other than their magical power. She agreed with the budding Suffragist movement that all women should have at least some autonomy in their lives, not just witches.

"Arabella!" her mother's voice cracked through the air and snapped Arabella's wandering mind back to reality. "Your grandmother asked you a question." Elizabeth giggled.

Arabella blushed bright red right to the roots of her dark brown hair and stared down at her hands in her lap. "I'm sorry, Grandmother. I must have been wool-gathering. What did you say?"

"Look at me when you speak, child, and don't mumble." Her grandmother's voice was steady and firm.

"Yes, Grandmother," Arabella said, lifting her eyes to the grand matriarch at the other end of the table. Eleanor Minerva Sortilege, former Grande Dame of the English Council of Witches and dowager of Blackstone House, was a formidable woman. Even at ninety-eight, her eyes retained their bright intelligence and her back was straight and strong.

"I asked you if you've had any of the signs we've discussed." Grandmother lifted her wine glass to her lips.

Arabella flushed hard again and struggled not to look away from her grandmother's stony gray eyes. "No, ma'am, no sign of magic at all."

"Disappointing," she said, replacing her glass. She turned her gaze to her daughter. "I assume you've attempted the techniques I suggested?"

Mother drew herself up straighter and nodded sharply. "Yes, twice over."

"And you are sure you performed the techniques correctly?" Grandmother pursed her lips and raised an eyebrow. It was Mother's turn to flush.

Arabella sank a little deeper into her chair and groaned inwardly; dinner had just gone from unpleasant to dreadful.

"Yes, Mother," Arabella's mother said around a clenched jaw. "I am quite certain I performed all of your suggested techniques exactly as instructed, as well as attempting a few of my own."

Grandmother cut a delicate mouthful of beef, chewed slowly, then dabbed her lips with a napkin while all eyes at the table focused on her and conversation was suspended. "Perhaps Clytemnestra Kellar's daughter may have some suggestions for you. You know her, Minerva dear, that lovely young witch who almost took the position of Grande Dame from you when I stepped down, Cecilia I think her name was."

The blood drained from Mother's face and her fork clattered on her plate. Her mouth hung open for a moment, then she blew out her breath and snapped her jaw shut.

"Whatever you think would be prudent, Mother," she said, and she gulped down a hearty mouthful of wine. "I'm sure all of Thornfire House would enjoy hearing about the embarrassments and weaknesses of our house. Perhaps they can use what they've learned to prevent Vivienne from attaining Grande Dame when I step down. Yes, perhaps it would be nice if our family were to release the reins of power after holding them for nearly a hundred years. Fading into obscurity and having no control over our fate sounds quite lovely." Mother snatched up her cutlery again and began to saw at her meat.

"Oh, stop being so melodramatic, Minerva." Grandmother sighed and rolled her eyes. "It will take a lot more than a Brown Bud and a failed attempt to fulfill a prophecy to force our family from power. Your grandmother and I provided you with a very secure seat."

The two women glared at each other across the table. Mother's jaw clamped shut and her lips trembled, while Grandmother pursed her own and narrowed her eyes just a bit.

"Prophecy?" Chorused Jessamine and Josephine together, turning their disconcerting gazes toward their grandmother.

"Yes," she said, drawing out the word as she continued to hold her daughter's gaze. "I think it's time the girls heard about that prophecy, don't you, Minerva dear?"

"I can hardly see that it will serve any purpose, Mother."

"Oh, don't pout, girl. It will give you unsightly lines." Grandmother turned her eyes to her silent granddaughters down the table. "I do think it's time you all knew."

"Knew what, Grandmother?" asked Vivienne.

"The prophecy that your mother has been chasing since before you were born, child."

"Prophecies aren't all that uncommon, Grandmother," said Rowena. "We have many talented seers within our shores, and I seem to remember you had many accurate visions in your day. What makes this prophecy so special?"

Grandmother smiled indulgently. "I have made quite a specialty of the precognitive arts, Rowena, but this particular one was not one of mine. Before I was even born, the seers of House Cagliostro, the finest seers in Italy, and some would say the world, received a prophecy so strong that every witch in their House was overcome with it at the same time."

Amelia and Elizabeth gasped together. Jessamine and Josephine leaned forward and gripped the table in front of them. "Tell us," they cried together.

"Enough," Mother snapped. "Stop filling the girls' heads with fanciful notions. We need to focus on the issues of the here and now, not some wild stories from long-dead and far away witches."

"Just because you failed doesn't make the prophecy invalid, Minerva," Grandmother chided, and then she turned back to her granddaughters. "House Cagliostro saw that there would come a time of great change in the world and that in the midst of all that turmoil would come a great witch, the seventh daughter of a seventh daughter, and that she would hold power far greater than any had ever seen. This great witch would hold the key to balance in the world." She smiled at her daughter while Mother scowled back at her as she took a sip of wine.

"As you know, your mother was my seventh daughter," Grandmother continued. "And as she saw so much of the world changing, she decided to be the one to shape and mold the great and powerful witch of the prophecy."

"But, Arabella is mother's seventh," said Vivienne with a frown. All eyes turned to Arabella, and she squirmed in her seat, wishing again that she had the ability to disappear, or at least to cloak herself from all those eyes.

"Yes, I know," said Grandmother. "I always told your mother that chasing a prophecy would be useless. It will happen, or it won't. You cannot force such things." She turned the full force of her sharp gray eyes on her daughter as she said the last words.

Mother tossed her napkin onto the table and rose. "Suddenly, I have lost my appetite." And she stalked from the room.

Grandmother clucked her tongue and turned back to her meal. "Your mother never did like it when I corrected her in front of other people."

The sisters and Nathaniel looked from one to another with wide eyes.

"Grandmother Sortilege," Nathaniel cleared his throat. "If it would not be too bold of me to ask, I know I'm just a man and it's not possible for me to understand all the ways of the magical arts, but why did

Mother Sortilege's plan not work? If the prophecy was for a seventh daughter of a seventh daughter to gain great power in a time of change, shouldn't it have been Arabella?"

Grandmother tilted her head and she chewed thoughtfully before she answered. "You always were a forward one, weren't you, Nathaniel?" Nathaniel blushed and bowed his head, causing Grandmother to smile. "But yes, Arabella could have been the one the prophecy spoke of. She seemed to fit all of the criteria, but for whatever reason, she is not. That is the way of prophecy; it is never clear until after it has been fulfilled. And then usually in some way that you never expect."

"The prophecy is yet to be fulfilled," Jessamine and Josephine spoke together, their voices coming in harmony. Their eyes were focused into the far distance and their hands, Jessamine's right in Josephine's left, were on the table with their fingers intertwined. "She has yet to play her part and learn her art. Her time is yet to come."

The room was silent for a moment and then the twins seemed to come back to themselves. They shook their heads as a raven might to resettle her feathers then looked at each other and smiled.

"Yes," said Grandmother in a thoughtful voice as she focused on Arabella again with a sharp gaze. "It's possible that the fulfillment of the Cagliostro Prophecy is yet to come."

"But how, Grandmother?" said Elizabeth with a frown. "Arabella is obviously useless. If she was going to come into power she would have done it long before now."

"Elizabeth, speaking ill of a family member at the dinner table is behavior unbecoming of a well-bred witch." She waited until Elizabeth bowed her head and murmured an apology before she continued. "The prophecy said the seventh daughter of a seventh daughter was to be the powerful witch, and as Arabella is also a seventh daughter perhaps it is *her* daughter who will fulfill the prophecy."

With that startling proposal, Grandmother pushed away her dinner plate and clapped her hands. "The dessert if you please, Mrs. Holly."

CHAPTER IV

*Where Arabella Attempts to Satisfy Her Curiosity
at the Great Exhibition*

I T WAS LATE MAY IN LONDON, AND ARABELLA ITCHED FOR HER SISTERS
and her mother to be gone from their townhouse. She sat on the
window seat in the front parlor pretending to work on her embroidery, but really she watched as her family prepared to leave the
house. There was delay after delay—Amelia couldn't find the reticule
that matched the dress she wanted to wear that complemented the
embroidery of her new robe, Rowena's robe was far too wrinkled for
mother's taste and required pressing, and Jessamine and Josephine had
to be rousted out of the back corner of the garden where they had the
scrying bowl out for some odd reason. But the spring meeting of the
English Council of Witches wouldn't start without its Grande Dame, so
there was no fear of missing anything. The only Sortilege woman
feeling any urgency to get them out the door was Arabella.

Normally, she hated being dragged into London for the seasonal
Council meetings. Her mother wanted to keep her close, claiming that
it was important to keep the family together at all times, but with
Vivienne staying behind at Blackstone Manor to begin her confinement,
Arabella found confirmation of what she'd always believed. Her mother
wanted to keep her close just in case her talent manifested so that she
could begin her training the instant it did, that much was clear now. But

Mother could only keep Arabella so close when it came to Council meetings. Not having passed the admissions tests to the Sisterhood of Witches, Arabella was not even allowed into the Council building, and certainly not the Council Chamber itself, which one could only enter as a Council member or a petitioner.

The only non-witch petitioners allowed to enter the Council Chamber were young women there to take their admissions tests. Since magical talent could spontaneously manifest in any woman, even young women from mundane bloodlines could present themselves for testing. Those who did not pass the admissions tests did not survive. The Council was *very* closed mouthed as to why the young women did not leave the Council Chamber alive, but they hinted strongly that attempting magic was deadly for someone who was not actually a witch. If a young woman did not pass the tests, the Council always sent a letter of condolence to her family along with a one pound note to make up for any earnings that may have been lost. There were quite a number of poor London families who sent their daughters who had no hope of earning money elsewhere, because they were ugly, crippled, or stupid, to try the admissions tests. If the girl failed, they had one less mouth to feed and a fresh pound note to keep them for a while. If she passed, they had a witch in the family, and that had benefits of its own.

Arabella looked up from her embroidery again to see her mother and all of her sisters finally gathered in the front hall putting on hats and gloves.

"Arabella," Mother called.

Arabella jumped to answer her mother's summons and curtseyed to her in the hall. "Yes, Mother?" she said.

"I want *you* to clean up your sisters' mess in the garden, not the servants," she said. "And please try to remember to put the scrying bowl away properly this time. It should be *next* to the scrying mirror, not on top of it," she said with a sigh.

"Yes, ma'am," Arabella said as she bobbed another curtsey. Inwardly, she seethed at the delay, but there was no help for it.

Mother frowned. "I'll be looking for scratches."

"Yes, ma'am." Arabella kept her voice soft and meek through sheer force of will.

Her mother tilted her head and looked at her youngest just a moment longer, then sniffed. "Let's go, ladies. We should not make our sisters wait over much."

The Sortilege witches trooped out of the house and into their carriage without a backward glance. Arabella let her breath out hard as soon as the maid shut the door behind them.

"Will you be needing anything, miss?" Young Mary bobbed a curtsey to Arabella.

"No, nothing." Arabella clutched her hands in front of herself, trying to keep calm, but her heart felt like it was going to leap out of her chest. "After I put away the implements, I think I will retire for a while. I have a bit of a headache and I do not wish to be disturbed."

Mary curtseyed again and disappeared into the kitchen. As soon as she was out of sight, Arabella gathered up her skirts in both hands and ran for the garden. Jessamine and Josephine had left quite a mess. Arabella sighed with exasperation as she got down to work. She dumped the dew water, gathered by dawn light on the Solstice, at the base of the yew tree and murmured a hurried thanks for the gifts of the earth, just as she had been taught. She dried the inside of the scrying bowl with the hem of her skirt as she surveyed the rest of the debris strewn across the grass. The dried elder flowers had been thoroughly crushed and would have to be left where they lay. The white sage was still neatly bundled and unburned and so could be returned to herbal storage. She nearly missed the sparkle of the white quartz pendulum in the grass, and remembered that Jessamine and Josephine had tucked something into the pockets of their skirts when she came out to the garden to fetch them at Mother's request. What in the world had the twins been up to, Arabella wondered with a frown.

She shook her head, not that it mattered. The twins were always up to something strange and inscrutable. She tossed the sage into the scrying bowl on her hip and tucked the pendulum into her own pocket. She checked the sun's position in the sky and hurried back into the house, headed for the workroom next to the kitchen. She placed the bowl on the shelf — *next* to the mirror and *not* on top of it — the sage back in its proper drawer in the herbal cabinet, and hung the white quartz pendulum on the hook between the smoky quartz and obsidian pendulums when Moria, the Housemistress of the Sortilege townhouse, poked her head in.

"Mary said you weren't feeling well, dearie," she said. "Would you like me to make you a posset?"

"No, thank you, Moria," Arabella said with a smile. "I think I'll just lie down for a while. I should feel better in time for dinner with the family."

"You'll probably need your strength, child," Moria said with a wry smile of her own as she stepped aside to let Arabella out of the room. "Your mother always comes back from the Council in quite a temper."

Arabella stifled a chuckle with her fingers. Moria was one of the few that she didn't feel judged her for her lack of magic. Of course, Moria had been one of those plain girls from a poor London family who thought she wouldn't be worth more than a one-pound death benefit. She knew what it was to be considered a burden. Lucky enough for her she showed some talent for mindspeaking and a knack for organization, making her quite valuable as a Housemistress.

Arabella retreated up the stairs and waited by her window. It didn't take long. One by one the house servants slipped out the back entrance to enjoy an afternoon off. She knew the only servants left would be the cook and Moria, who would both be curled up by the kitchen fireside with a pot of tea and a few of the newest penny dreadfuls. A beef stew, or something else that would hold well for hours, would be simmering on the stove. Arabella's mother and sisters would not be back until well after sunset, perhaps even later given the topics listed for discussion in this session. But there was no predicting the exact time.

Smiling with real joy, Arabella gathered the hat, coat, gloves, and reticule she'd stashed in her bedroom the night before and crept down the back stairs and into the garden. In the other back corner of the garden from where Jessamine and Josephine had made their mess was an old gate that looked to be grown over with ivy. But it wasn't. In fact, the hinges were well oiled and never made a sound. She was fairly sure her mother was unaware of the gate. Arabella had discovered it by observing the comings and goings of their servants. Every common born witch in the house had used it for an assignation at some time or another.

Since witches were not required to marry and could live independently, and they had control over their daughters, many witches not born to a high house tried to better their lot by having a daughter with more magical power than themselves. Arabella knew that Mary was seeing a young alchemist's apprentice for just that reason. Alchemy was as close as men could come to real magic, and the gossips whispered that men with a talent for alchemy were more likely to amplify any natural talent inherited from the mother. Minerva did not dismiss girls who became pregnant by mysterious means, and — as long as they had daughters — they were allowed to remain employed after the birth. Goodwill from other witches, even minor ones, allowed Blackstone House to maintain its power over the whole of the Council and its territory. For now, Arabella had no plans for an assignation of her own, she was just grateful for a way to slip in and out of the house unseen.

Arabella looked up and down the alleyway and found it empty. She let the gate shut softly behind her. Looking back after a few steps she could see that the wooden gate dovetailed perfectly with the slats around it, looking like a solid wooden fence to anyone not in the know. She smiled and made her way to the street where she hailed a hansom cab and told the driver to take her to the Crystal Palace in Hyde Park. As she drew closer to her destination, Arabella could the growing glow in the distance from the Crystal Palace.

When she arrived at the home of the Great Exhibition, Arabella's mouth dropped open until she gaped like a country bumpkin. There was no one here to chide her for behavior unbecoming of the family. In fact, Arabella was pretty certain there would be no one there to carry tales to her mother. Witches as a group avoided the Great Exhibition because of the glut of technology in the exhibits. Prince Albert, who was the great patron of the Exhibition along with Henry Cole, was a great admirer of all things mechanical, like most men. And Queen Victoria, being indulgent, allowed him to have his head. She'd even hired some powerful weather witches, at no small expense, to make sure the opening day of the Great Exhibition was bright and sunny. The witches had not been fond of the reason for their task, but they had families to feed just like everyone else. Arabella had heard over dinner table conversation that the Council was not thrilled with their involvement, but they brought no censure. The older, more powerful Houses did not need the money as the smaller Houses did, but they did still need the votes of the smaller Houses on Council matters. So they looked the other way.

The massive Crystal Palace, constructed completely of glass panels set in a cast-iron frame, reared over the street, dwarfing the people, carriages, and trees. All of England, and indeed much of the civilized world, was atwitter over this architectural marvel and engineering triumph, except for the witches. Rowena shared council chamber gossip with Arabella that this Great Exhibition had initially been regarded by the Sisterhood with merely wary antipathy. Then after the fiasco with Westerfeld many witches came to regard it as flat-out dangerous. They feared that events like this would embolden men like Westerfeld and make life more difficult for witches. Another faction scoffed at the idea that witches could ever lose their position in society after all they'd done for humankind.

The glass panels glittered in the fresh spring sunlight, and out of every panel radiated the sparkling light Arabella had first seen at the demonstration of Westerfeld's Distinction Engine. Arabella finally noticed that she was not the only one gawking at the building with unabashedly childlike wonder. She laughed without thinking, but then put her gloved fingers to her mouth and blushed. A gentleman walking past her tipped his hat and smiled with a twinkle in his eye. The day felt full of bright promise and delightful possibilities.

The crowd shuffling through the lines for admission was claustrophobic, but Arabella didn't mind. She could not hide her enthusiasm. She paid her two guineas and let the crowd carry her forward on its surging tide. Once inside, the place seemed even more miraculous to Arabella. Full grown trees and beautiful, life-sized sculptures gathered underneath the soaring glass roof. The crowd was huge and many normal conversations came together into one roaring voice that bounced and tumbled off the roof creating a fearful din. Everywhere around her Arabella could see the glow, although some exhibits were stronger than others. Her skin tingled and her face felt hot. She was certain her cheeks gave away her excitement.

Arabella bit her lip and turned in a small circle. She could spend her whole afternoon here and not observe even a third of what interested her. She mentally calculated that there was enough left from her scrimped and saved allowance to come at least once more, perhaps twice. Time certainly was not an issue, as her mother and her sisters would be occupied with the Council for most of the next week, perhaps longer if there were many petitioners seeking to take the admissions tests. The servants certainly wouldn't care if she disappeared once or twice for most of the day; it meant less work for them. She turned in another circle, trying to decide where to start.

"Can I help you, miss?" asked a young man at her shoulder.

"Oh!" cried Arabella with a start.

"I'm sorry, miss." The young, sandy-haired man held out empty hands. "I didn't mean to scare you. You just looked a little lost."

Arabella blushed and looked down at the hem of her skirts. "It's quite alright, really. You just startled me a little."

She looked up to find the man smiling at her with a twinkle in his blue eyes. Arabella looked away, a bit scandalized that the gentleman had even approached her. She wondered if she was missing some nuance of mundane behavior unknown to her because of how much her mother kept her cloistered.

"Well, are you lost, miss?" he asked.

Arabella laughed and tried not to be rude. "Not lost so much as not sure where to start. This is the first time I've come to the Exhibition."

"Ah, yes, it can be quite overwhelming the first time," he said rocking back and forth from his heels to his toes. "But you are in luck, miss, as I have been here more than once and might be able to guide you." He extended his arm for her to take.

All at once Arabella was overwhelmed by nervous anxiety. She clutched her reticule to her chest, visions of handsome rakes with disreputable plans flitting through her head. She may not be an expert in mundane behavior, but she knew this was far beyond the pale.

"Oh, no, I couldn't possibly take up your time." She shook her head and backed up a step. The man opened his mouth to say something else, but Arabella turned and lost herself in the crowd hoping that he would not follow her.

She hurried down the path and then made a quick left as soon as she could. Only then did she dare a glance behind. She let out a heavy sigh of relief when she could not see the handsome stranger in the crowd at all. He might have been harmless, but all of her mother's warnings about the predatory nature of men, and her inability to protect herself because she could not perform magic, rang in her ears. Better safe than sorry.

Arabella took another deep breath to calm herself, willing her heart to stop hammering in her chest. She shook her head and told herself she'd been foolish, but that was no reason to let one chance encounter spoil the rest of her afternoon. She set off down the path with no particular direction in mind, letting her whims be her guide through the thick crowd.

It took her by surprise when she realized that she was following an intermittent clacking noise without being conscious of it. But once she grasped that her feet had found a plan, she followed them gladly. She had to know what that strange noise was. The sign at the exhibit that was the source of the sound proclaimed that it was an electric telegraph. Arabella watched with wide-eyed wonder as a gentleman pressed a metal arm. She saw a spark where metal contacted metal, and then the glow traveled down a wire to a receiving station with another man listening to the short and long tones. She looked at the people around her wanting to ask them if they too could see the sparks and light dancing, but she held her tongue. Rowena had been shocked when Arabella told her about the effect of Westerfeld's machine; there was no telling how an average person, unused to magic, would react to such an idea.

The crowd shifted and Arabella let herself be carried away from the telegraph. As she strolled on she wished she had a companion to share the experience with; Rowena would have been ideal. But with the Council in session it was absolutely impossible to pull her sister away. Arabella sighed and wondered if coming to the Exhibition was a mistake when a familiar voice caught her ear. Once again, she let the sound lead to her a new exhibit.

It was Bartholomew Westerfeld and his Distinction Engine. He stood in front of his great, gleaming machine with his thumbs hooked behind his lapels, beaming to the crowd around him. Arabella found a place to stand that afforded her a good view but kept her out of Westerfeld's line of sight. Everyone in the crowd was staring at the machine and its creator, so Arabella didn't feel out of place as she did so herself. The machine wasn't glowing yet, not like it had the night of the party when Westerfeld fed it the numbers. But there was a shimmering sheen to the metal and the air felt full and tense. Arabella twisted her fingers together in excitement.

Westerfeld started into his patter, much the same as the night of the party, except without any mention of witches. He turned to the keyboard with almost a dancer's twirl, his assistive braces obviously working better than they had in a room full of magical interference. The light from his braces spiraled hypnotically around the gear assembly at his knees. His fingers glided over the keys as he entered the equation. Arabella put her hand over her mouth to contain a gasp. Just as it had before, the light travelled from left to right, each gear, each cog, each piston glowing brighter as the information danced upon it. And, also as before, the dull plate near the center of the machine seemed to swallow the light for a moment until it emerged on the other side. Once again the light terminated at the stylus held by a slender, graceful arm of brass that delivered the machine's answer on a fresh sheet of paper. Westerfeld pulled the sheet from beneath the stylus and presented it with great ceremony to another man for verification. The crowd cheered when the apple-cheeked mathematician verified the machine's calculation.

Arabella felt giddy and lightheaded. She'd half-believed that the marvelous events at Westerfeld's demonstration had all been in her head, completely imagined. That all the sparkling and glowing she'd seen since had been some sort of a fever dream. But here it was, the experience repeating itself, and more, giving her hope that perhaps there might be something special about her after all. She wiped a bit of perspiration from her forehead with her handkerchief and hoped that she would not faint.

Westerfeld turned to the crowd and smiled again, showing all his strong white teeth. "But I'm sure you are all far too intelligent to be satisfied with a mere choreographed routine. Perhaps I can take some numbers from the crowd and I'll show you what this fine apparatus can do. Shall we start with some addition?"

Westerfeld returned to his keyboard and pointed to a man in a bowler hat. "You, sir," he said. "Give me a number, a large one."

"Four thousand, seven hundred, and thirty-two," the man in the bowler said.

"And you, madam," Westerfeld gestured to a woman in a smart gray tweed jacket and rose-colored walking skirt.

"Fifteen thousand, eight hundred, and ninety-three," she said with a blush.

And so it went that Westerfeld collected a dozen numbers from the crowd and fed them all into the machine while the mathematician scribbled furiously on a scrap of paper at the other end, trying to keep up with the excited yelps from the crowd. The machine whirred through its motions again, sounding like the sweetest symphony to Arabella, and it produced an answer out the other side again. Westerfeld had to wait several moments for the mathematician to finish, but once again he confirmed that the machine was correct. The crowd clapped and cheered, and Westerfeld bowed while they cried out for more. Westerfeld strutted back to the keyboard and started calling for numbers again, laughing and begging the volunteers to go slower because his fingers could not keep up.

This time Arabella focused solely on the machine. Every time Westerfeld pressed a key she could feel the pressure on her own body, as if he were tapping his finger on the top of her head and pressing down on her. As the information moved through the mechanical workings she felt it inside her own head, could feel each gear as it turned, each piston as it pumped, even if it were buried deep in the machine and she could not see it. When the light reached the dead zone of the plate, Arabella felt like two huge hands had clapped shut around her and cut her off from the world, crushing close and smothering her. She gasped and wobbled, her knees gone weak. But then the muffling hands were gone as quickly as they had come and her spirit zipped along the copper and steel, racing for the stylus. When the stylus wrote on the paper Arabella's right hand traced the same numbers on her left palm, and she knew the number before Westerfeld called it out to the crowd, and she knew it was correct before the mathematician's nod.

The crowd cheered again but they seemed to be coming from very far away to Arabella. Her world had dwindled down to her and the machine. If she could feel the machine within her, she wondered if she could make the machine feel her. Westerfeld moved toward the keyboard again as the crowd cried out for more, and he promised that this time they would try some more complex square roots.

But Arabella's mind was there before his fingers. She thought hard about some minor sums, the kind a housewife might be expected to use to keep track of the household accounts, and each key depressed in response to her thoughts. When she finished with her string of numbers, she sent the mental order to calculate and the light zipped through the machine, faster than it had before. This time when it came to the plate, Arabella was ready for the muffling sensation, which didn't make it any more pleasant, but at least she was able to retain her composure. The light exploded out of the middle of the machine and raced down to the stylus, and once again Arabella traced the numbers in her palm.

Westerfeld stood frozen, eyes wide with shock, halfway between the stylus and the keyboard, watching his machine move without any command from him. The crowd was silent as the stylus finished scratching out its answer. Westerfeld turned to the mathematician, bewildered. The mathematician grabbed the sheet and scanned the numbers.

"The Distinction Engine is correct," he announced and raised a fist over his head, as if hoping the crowd would not notice the machine's odd behavior and would cheer again as they had before.

"Of course it is," spat a dark-haired gentleman with a florid handlebar moustache at the front of the crowd. "Clockworks can be set to perform all kinds of tasks. This machine doesn't actually perform calculations; it's just an overgrown children's toy." He turned on his heel and marched away. The rest of the crowd flowed away after him, muttering darkly and casting narrow-eyed glances back at Westerfeld and his mathematician.

"You told me I was verifying real calculations, not something you programmed in to a clockwork!" cried the mathematician as he swatted Westerfeld's shoulders with the sheaf of paper from the machine. "Have you any idea what kind of damage this could do to my reputation?" He threw the papers at Westerfeld's feet and stalked off.

Westerfeld stood alone in front of his machine, his mouth opening and closing on words he couldn't speak. He spun back to his creation, arms held wide and helpless, then he ran his hands through his wavy chestnut hair and shook his head. "Not possible, not possible," he whispered to himself.

Arabella looked around. The word of the failed demonstration spread quickly on feather-light whispers, and the crowd started giving Mr. Westerfeld and his machine a wide berth. She took a deep breath and stepped closer.

"Mr. Westerfeld?" she said in a tentative voice. He seemed not to hear her; he kept muttering to himself and running his hands through his hair as he stared at his machine. Arabella tapped him on the shoulder. "Mr. Westerfeld?"

"What?" he roared as he spun around to face Arabella, panting.

Arabella took a step back and nearly lost her balance. "I just wanted to ask you some questions about your Distinction Engine." Her voice trembled.

"I suppose you want to ask me why I faked it, eh? You want to know why I would sully the name of Great Britain with my chicanery?" He sneered and leaned in to Arabella, his face growing red and his fists clutched at his sides.

"No," Arabella said, leaning back a little but not yielding another step. "I wanted to know how it works. It seems like a rather marvelous machine to me."

Westerfeld released his fists and stepped back as he let out his breath. Arabella heard the small squeaks of the gears and pulleys when he moved, now that she was close enough. "You believe me? You think it really works?"

Arabella nodded and bit her lip. Westerfeld tilted his head to the side and looked at her quizzically. "Have I seen you somewhere before? You look familiar."

Arabella blushed and shook her head. "I don't believe we've ever been formally introduced, but I have heard of your work and I find it fascinating."

"Really?" Westerfeld crossed his arms and smiled. "A woman who appreciates my work? I'm shocked that you can actually understand it."

"There's no reason to be rude, Mr. Westerfeld." Arabella's lips thinned.

Westerfeld guffawed. "My dear lady, I'm not being rude, just expressing my wonderment at how much you excel past the normal restrictions of your gender. Now, what is it you wish to know?"

"Everything," Arabella said. "I want to know exactly how it works, from start to finish. And where did you get your ideas? Who influenced you?" Arabella stepped closer to the machine, her hands clasped together as if in prayer, and looked up and down the gleaming metal with hungry eyes.

"You certainly are a curious little thing," Westerfeld's voice was soft in wonderment.

Arabella laughed and smiled over her shoulder at Westerfeld. "But what I'm really curious about is this part in the center," she said, stepping forward and laying her gloved hand on the mysterious plate. Cold so deep it nearly burned her made her snatch her hand away. She turned to Westerfeld as she rubbed her hand.

"The glow seems to disappear there, it just gets swallowed up," she said. "Is that a purposeful part of the design, or is it a flaw you just haven't overcome yet?"

"Glow?" Westerfeld choked on the word.

"Yes, the glow," Arabella suddenly felt unsure and wondered if approaching Westerfeld had been yet another mistake in an afternoon full of mistakes. "It happens when you put the numbers in, and then it travels along the length of the machine as it calculates. Don't you see it?"

"Witch!" The word hissed out from between Westerfeld's teeth. "Now I know where I've seen you before. You were with those damnable witches at my demonstration last month. You're here to sabotage me!"

Westerfeld grabbed Arabella by both arms and yanked her up so that her toes barely touched the floor and he shook her. "What did you do, witch? What did you do to my machine? Why are you trying to destroy me?" His voice rose to a roar and he shook Arabella hard again.

"Mr. Westerfeld, please, you're hurting me!" Arabella cried out. "I've done nothing to your machine, I swear. I only wanted to know how it works." Arabella began to sob.

Then a fierce voice came from behind her. "Sir, I think you need to put my sister down now, before I am forced to call the constables."

Westerfeld looked over Arabella's shoulder and growled, but he did let go of her and she dropped to the ground, falling into a puddle on the floor, shaking. A gloved hand moved into her line of sight to help her up. "Are you alright?"

It was her brother, John Ambrose Leyden, who was just two years her senior. He helped her to her feet and brushed the dirt from her skirts. "I didn't think I'd be rescuing you when I decided to come to the Exhibition today, Arabella."

"This creature is your sister?" Westerfeld's voice came out in a sneer.

"She's not a creature, she's a young woman," John said. "And yes, she is my sister. You would do well to remember that she is also the daughter of the Grande Dame of the English Council of Witches and of Alexander Paul Leyden, Duke of Umbridge." He turned to Arabella and took both of her hands in his. "Did he hurt you?"

Arabella took in a breath to respond but Westerfeld spoke over her. "I don't care who sired her, she's witch spawn and you had better keep her away from me and my machine."

"Let's just go, John," Arabella said. "I'll be fine, nothing that a quiet corner and nice cup of tea won't cure."

"Then I know the perfect place," John said, and he offered Arabella his arm. They walked away, leaving Westerfeld huffing and puffing with his fists balled up at his sides.

CHAPTER V

On Tea and Secrets

RABELLA ACCOMPANIED JOHN TO A TEA HOUSE HE KNEW AROUND THE corner from the Exhibition. As they waited for the server to bring their pot of Darjeeling and scones with clotted cream, Arabella squirmed under John's studied gaze and tried to look anywhere save at him.

"Does Mother know where you are?" he asked after a long silence.

"No," Arabella's voice came out in a whisper and she blushed. "And I'd be ever so obliged if you didn't tell her."

John tilted back his head and laughed long and hard, drawing stares from those dining around them. His blue eyes twinkled as he brushed his dark brown hair from his eyes. "Why should I tell her anything, Ari? I only wanted to know what I needed to avoid mentioning the next time I see her."

"She's your mother, John," Arabella frowned. "That hardly seems respectful."

"Arabella Helene Sortilege, I'm surprised to hear you lecturing *me* about respect when you've obviously snuck out of the house while Mother is occupied elsewhere," John said as he smiled at his sister and laughed more. Arabella's blush deepened.

"She's still your mother, John Ambrose Leyden, you at least owe her some respect for that." Arabella winced at how petulant her own voice sounded.

"Oh yes," said John. "I get so much mothering from her during the two weeks in midsummer I spend at Blackstone Manor that it fully makes up for the other fifty weeks of the year. Just like I'm sure you get a full year's worth of fathering from Father over two weeks in the early summer you spend with us. I'm really looking forward to seeing you soon for that, by the way. But frankly, I'd be surprised if the old girl was actually aware I was there last summer."

Any response from Arabella was forestalled by the arrival of the tea and scones. Both John and Arabella kept a tight lip on their family troubles until the waiter was well away.

"Can we not fight, John? I really don't have the strength for it today." Arabella sighed and poured the tea for them both.

"Who was fighting? I certainly wasn't." John sipped his tea. Arabella rolled her eyes and reached for a scone.

"So, what exactly were you doing sneaking out to the Exhibition today?" John asked. Arabella fumbled and dropped her scone onto her plate. John raised an eyebrow at the startled look on her face. She dropped her head and clutched her hands in her lap.

"You must promise me that you won't tell anyone," she said, her voice hardly a whisper.

"Who do I have to tell?" John shrugged. "It's one of the advantages of being the youngest son. No one really cares what you do or say, as long as you don't embarrass the family in the wrong circles. I could shout your secret from the rooftops, Ari, and no one would hear me."

"I'm sure that's not true..." Arabella started, but John interrupted her.

"It certainly is, Arabella, at least in our family. I'm just as good as invisible," he said as he slathered a scone with clotted cream. "How do you think I get away with having whole days free to stroll around the Exhibition and rescue my little sister, then take her to tea? As long as I don't over spend my allowance, Father doesn't care." He sank his teeth into the pastry with a decisive bite.

"I still would rather you didn't tell anyone," said Arabella as she righted her scone and dabbed on some cream.

"Fine," he said with a sigh and a small shake of his head. "You have my word I won't tell anyone why you were here today."

Arabella swirled the cream around on her scone for a moment while she thought before setting down the spoon. She then brushed non-existent wrinkles out of her skirt and folded her hands in her lap. Taking a deep breath, she turned to her brother with a serious face.

"I think there might be something worthwhile, something special, about me," she said.

John raised an eyebrow and frowned. "That's hardly news, Ari. I know Mother has you a bit beaten down, but that's no reason you're not worthwhile."

"No, no," she said with a frown of her own. "I don't mean worthwhile as a nice person, or an entertaining companion or anything. I mean worthwhile as in something Mother would accept as worthwhile."

"You have my attention." John leaned his elbows on the table, his face suddenly serious. Other diners sniffed as they watched his overly relaxed posture from the corners of their eyes.

Arabella rubbed her hands together and took another deep breath. "Do you know what magic looks like, John?"

"Of course not," John snorted. "I'm a man and therefore incapable of perceiving magic, as Mother and Elizabeth are so fond of reminding me."

"Neither did I," said Arabella. "Until about a month ago."

John choked on a mouthful of tea. "Excuse me?" he said.

"Do you remember Mr. Westerfeld's private Distinction Engine demonstration last month?"

"Yes," said John. "It disappointed me when Father didn't want to go and wouldn't allow me or Henry to use his invitation, but after I heard about what happened I was glad to have avoided the fiasco."

Arabella leaned forward and her words came out in a rush. "When he made the machine work, I saw it glow. I could see a light in the machine that no one else could see, and I could feel the information moving through the metal. And then riding home in the carriage, I saw it sparkling in the mechanisms to turn the valves of the gas streetlamps and in the workings of a gentleman's watch. I told Rowena about it right away, as soon as we were out of Mother's earshot. She told me that's what magic looks like, that that's what all the witches see that you and I never have."

John shut his jaw with an audible click and set his tea cup back on the table with a clatter.

"So, I came to the Exhibition today to see more machines, especially more complex ones," Arabella rushed on. "I had to see if it was some sort of a fever dream or if I was just going mad. I was so afraid I was going mad. But I saw it again. And not just in the Distinction Engine — everything mechanical looks magical to me, John, everything! And there's more!"

"More?" John said in a strangled voice.

"Yes, John, it was so marvelous." Arabella's cheeks flushed and her eyes glittered, her excitement and joy evident to anyone with eyes. "Not only do I see the magic in the machines, I can manipulate it too. Those last calculations that Mr. Westerfeld's machine made, that was me! I just thought the numbers to the machine and told it to calculate and it did. Although I do suppose I spoiled the demonstration a bit. I hope they won't hold that against Mr. Westerfeld, he really did build a wonderful machine. Well, except for that plate in the middle."

"The plate in the middle?" John's voice sounded lost and befuddled as he ran a hand through his dark hair and stared at his sister wide-eyed.

"Oh yes, John, the plate in the middle," Arabella said and then took a pause for a sip of tea. "There's this plate in the middle that covers something that doesn't have any mechanical magic at all that I can see, and when I let myself become part of the information flow I felt squashed and dead in that piece. But what's really odd is that Rowena said that that plate in the middle was the only piece that glowed for her. Don't you think that's odd, John?" She took another sip of tea.

"My dear sister," said John. "That may be the least odd thing you've told me yet. You can see magic in machines? Do you know what that means, Arabella?"

"That Mother may finally stop seeing me as an embarrassment? That I may finally be accepted to the Council of Witches?" Arabella laughed, a spot of color high on her cheeks. "Oh, John, I didn't know what was happening to me, but now that I've talked to you I can see what wonderful things could come of this."

"I think it's much more likely that Mother will disown you, Arabella," John said, frowning deeply. "You know how she feels about technology and machines. Dear God, girl, she's one of the biggest supporters of the Luddite Movement, in money and political clout. She'd see you as the snake in her bosom."

The color drained from Arabella's face. "Do you really think it would be that bad, John?"

"I think it could be worse," he said.

"Oh no, it couldn't possibly be that bad." Arabella waved her hand. "Mother has always wanted me to see magic, and now I do. She'll be overjoyed."

"She'll be furious is what she'll be." John's voice was flat and hard. "Haven't you heard a word I've said, Arabella? Mother will not consider anything associated with machines to be proper magic. She'll see you as some kind of freak, an abomination."

"Oh, John," Arabella gasped with tears welling up in her eyes. "What am I going to do?"

"First of all," he said, reaching across the table to grasp her hand. "You're going to keep your voice down and not make a scene. We're in public. Second of all, you're not going to breathe a word about this until I can talk to Father and see what ought to be done." He let her hand go and lifted his cup to his lips. He looked left and right without moving his head, trying to discern if the other diners were listening in on their conversation.

"Talk to Father?" gasped Arabella. "That might be worse than talking to Mother. You know how he feels about magic. He forbids our sisters to do even the most minor spells when we come to visit. And you promised me you wouldn't tell anyone why I was out today. You promised!"

"Well, it seems we're at an impasse," John pursed his lips together. "I think talking to Mother will be a disaster, and you think talking to Father will be a disaster. We certainly can't approach a stranger with such a private matter."

Arabella sighed and closed her eyes. "Just give me a little time to think about what to do, John. If I can't think of a better option than telling Father, then I'll tell him when we come for our early summer visit."

"Well, since I've already given my word," John said as he wiped his lips with a linen napkin. "I suppose I will have to be content with that. Would you like an escort home?"

"Yes, please," said Arabella, fairly wilting in on herself. "For an afternoon that started out so gay, it suddenly seems quite dreary."

John patted her hand. "We'll figure something out, Arabella, don't you worry."

They were quiet the whole way back to the Sortilege townhouse. Arabella slipped back through the garden gate and up the back stairs to her bedroom without incident. She stretched out on her bed and pulled the coverlet over her. Watching the late afternoon sun slant over the Oriental carpets and their rich blues and burgundies, Arabella wondered if she should have also told John about the prophecy Grandmother had told them about over dinner at the Boscastle house. She fell asleep with her fitful thoughts and had unsettling dreams.

CHAPTER VI

Wherein an Important Letter Is Delivered
While the Others Are at a Ball

T HE HOUSE WAS A SWIRL OF ACTIVITY. ARABELLA, ROWENA, AND Elizabeth leaned on the upstairs railing to the right of the stairs leading to the grand foyer below and watched the preparations with interest. Minerva, Amelia, Jessamine, and Josephine were preparing to go to the Thornfire House Spring Ball. Jessamine and Josephine were finally twenty-five, headed to their first ball. And after a week in session with the Council, with more business yet to be handled in the next, the older Sortilege women seemed eager to enjoy themselves.

"I still don't see why we can't go," Elizabeth pouted. "Mundane girls get presented at least by sixteen. I'm a whole two years behind."

Rowena shook her head. "If you want Mother to consider presenting you early you'd be better served improving your spell work rather than mooning over boys."

"You sound just like Vivienne and Mother, Ro." Elizabeth sighed and pouted.

"That's because I actually listen to what Vivienne and Mother have to say, Lizzie."

"Well," huffed Elizabeth. "I don't see you getting ready to go to the ball, Miss Know-It-All."

Rowena shrugged. It would be another three years until she, the oldest of the girls lining the railing, would be allowed to go. "Just because I listen and know what they say doesn't mean I actually follow their advice. Besides, what use is a husband anyway? We're witches; we don't need to be supported like ordinary women. And do you really want a house full of bawling brats?"

"You are utterly impossible, Rowena," groaned Elizabeth.

"No, Lizzie, I'm utterly practical."

Arabella snuck a peek at the frustrated pout on Elizabeth's face. She agreed with Rowena, but she didn't dare say anything and risk her sister's mercurial temper. Not all witch mothers were so controlling of their daughters, but Mother insisted that discipline and unity of household were the reasons Blackstone House remained in power.

Based on the conversation over tea earlier that day, Arabella knew her mother hoped to find suitable husbands for her three oldest unmarried daughters. Mother was quite discerning about whom she would allow to court her daughters. The gentlemen in question would have to come from well-bred, well-connected families. Aristocratic blood was not a necessity but would be considered a plus. They would have to be amenable to the independence a witch required, and Mother always looked up the family tree to see who might be more likely to sire daughters. Any young man who came from a family with witch blood would be a highly desirable candidate. Vivienne's husband, Nathaniel, was the oldest son of Madeline Thurston from Hazelrood House, and Mother was never one to pass up political advantage if she could manage it.

Amelia was quite amenable to the husband-hunting expedition, but Jessamine and Josephine were not cooperating. While not outright disobedient, they seemed to delight in confounding their mother by taking her instructions about dress and grooming in strange directions. When they finally appeared before her in the front hall in their fourth outfits, and they weren't strange enough to cause whispered gossip of madness, their mother declared victory with an exasperated sigh. Arabella, Rowena, and Elizabeth stifled giggles behind their hands. Their mother looked her three eldest up and down one last time after casting a quelling glare up at her youngest. She instructed Moria to bring their cloaks and called for Jeanette to bring the carriage around.

Mother spoke to the girls from where she stood in the open doorway, the starry night gleaming behind her. "You are to go to bed at a reasonable hour and get your rest, girls. Tomorrow we shall practice some shield and earth magic."

"Yes, Mother," the girls chorused, and they waited until the front door shut before they stuck out their tongues and crossed their eyes.

Arabella watched her sisters drift off toward their own bedrooms and Moria headed for the kitchen and the last of her evening tasks. She lingered by the stair railing, tracing the wood grain with her fingertip, and sighed. She wondered if Rowena might be amenable to company, or if she'd rather be alone with her latest novel. Arabella most definitely did not want to be alone with her own thoughts right now. She finally turned to head upstairs when there was a knock at the front door. Moria emerged from the back of the house while Rowena and Elizabeth joined Arabella by the railing again, all with startled looks on their faces. It was not long enough that the ball goers had gone, found the party dull, and returned. It was possible one of them had come back for a forgotten article. In either case, a member of the household would be recognized by the wards protecting the house and just come in. They all looked from one to another with wide eyes and mouths agape, wondering who would be knocking on the door at half past eight at night. The persistent second knock broke the shocked stillness.

Moria wiped her hands on her apron as she hurried to the door. When she opened the heavy oak door on the cool spring night, she found a young boy, perhaps seven or eight, standing on the doorstep.

"Evening, mum," he said as he touched his battered cap. "Is Miss Arabella Sortilege at home? I have a message for her."

"Let's have it then," Moria said and held out her hand.

"Oh, no, mum," the boy said. "I've been instructed to only hand it to Miss Arabella herself."

"Arabella?" Moria turned toward the stairs where the sisters were gathered. Rowena looked at Arabella with a cocked eyebrow and Elizabeth crossed her arms and frowned. Arabella shrugged and went down the stairs, her soft shoes shushed on the deep green carpeting of the landing. She scurried across the compass rose inlaid in muted shades of pink and beige marble that took up most of the foyer.

"I'm Arabella Sortilege," she said to the boy, who smiled and handed her a creamy ivory envelope closed with a raised seal in red wax.

"You can tell your friend that I'll carry a message for him any time, mum," the boy said with a laugh. "That's some easy money there." He touched his fingers to his cap again and scampered down the steps into the night. Arabella and Moria frowned after him.

Moria shut the door with a firm hand and turned to Arabella. "So, who is this friend who pays so well to have messages delivered at odd hours?"

Arabella flipped the envelope over to look at the writing on the opposite side from the seal. The script was formed of firm, dark strokes, biting deep into the paper. It was addressed to her, from Bartholomew Westerfeld. The blood drained from Arabella's face.

"No one," she said and put her hands behind her back with the letter. "No one at all."

Moria looked startled as Arabella turned and started to rush up the stairs. Elizabeth met her halfway down on the landing where the stairs turned with a wicked grin on her face.

"No one, Arabella?" She tried to snatch the envelope from Arabella's hand but Arabella stretched her arm a little further back so Elizabeth couldn't reach. "No one seems to have you awfully flustered."

She tried to reach again but Arabella just moved the letter to her other hand. Elizabeth grunted and stepped back, then narrowed her eyes and gathered her will, and flicked two fingers, sending the letter flying from Arabella's hand to her own. With a feral smile on her face, she held the letter over her head, far out of the reach of Arabella standing on the step below.

"Give it back!" Arabella cried. "You have no right to take it. Give it back!"

"I wonder who it is," Elizabeth crooned. "Perhaps a young man? Perhaps our little Arabella has been sneaking out while we're hard at work with the Council?" Arabella swallowed hard and felt her stomach drop. If Elizabeth read the name on the envelope, she was sunk. She hopped frantically, trying to reach the letter. Tears gathered in her eyes, blurring her vision.

Rowena, standing on the next step above, snatched the letter from Elizabeth's hand. "This kind of cruelty is beneath even you, Lizzie. Leave Arabella alone."

"I was only having a bit of fun," Elizabeth grumbled. She looked back down at the panting Arabella. "Fine. Keep your secret." She pushed past Rowena and started to stamp back to her bedroom. Then she turned with a nasty grimace on her face. "But wouldn't it be lovely for Mother to hear about your secret letter and punish you for it. You know how I love to chatter over dinner, and sometimes I forget things are supposed to be secret. Or perhaps I shall keep the secret of the letter so long as you please me."

Arabella blanched as she watched her sister turn on her heel and sweep down the hall. She turned back to Moria who was still standing in the front hall with a perplexed look on her face.

"Moria," Arabella said, twisting her fingers together. "Please don't tell Mother or Vivienne about this..."

Moria sighed and threw her hands up in the air. "What do I know? I'm just the housekeeper." She walked back to the kitchen shaking her head and muttering about the foolishness of girls.

"Thank you, Moria!" Arabella called after her. She then turned back to Rowena above her on the stairs. Rowena's arms were crossed and she tapped her foot. Her mouth was set in a hard line.

"Rowena, I can explain..." Arabella began.

"You had better be able to explain," Rowena said, letting her arms drop to the side. "How many times have I stepped in with Elizabeth, and even Mother, and now I find out you're keeping secrets from me? From *me*?" She emphasized the last with the letter in her grip.

"Rowena, can we please get off the stairs and find a little privacy? I promise I'll explain everything," she pleaded.

Rowena paused for a moment, but nodded and the girls adjourned to Arabella's bedroom. As soon as the door was closed, Arabella held out her hand.

"May I have my letter, please?" she said.

Rowena thrust it out to her. "This explanation had better be good," she said and then sank into one of the wingchairs in front of the fire. Arabella took the one opposite her.

"I don't know where to begin," Arabella said in a small voice as she stared down at the letter in her hands.

"The beginning is the usual place," Rowena said with a sigh.

Arabella closed her eyes and nodded, then took a deep breath and began. "Do you remember what I told you about what I saw when we went to the private demonstration at Mr. Westerfeld's?"

Rowena nodded and shifted in her seat with a frown on her face.

"Well," Arabella continued. "I couldn't get it out of my head so I decided to go to the Great Exhibition and see his machine again. I went last Tuesday."

Rowena gasped. "Mother would kill you if she knew you went out unchaperoned. And to see a machine!"

Arabella turned her head away. "I know, I know. But I had to know if I was going mad. I had to see if it happened again. And it did! Not just with the Distinction Engine either, Ro. Every machine I saw there glowed and sparkled."

Rowena shook her head and sighed. "So what does this have to do with the letter?"

"The letter is from Westerfeld," Arabella said and she held up the addressed side so her sister could read it.

"What does Westerfeld want with you?" Rowena asked.

"I don't know for sure," Arabella said. "But it might have something to do with how I spoiled his demonstration."

"You spoiled his demonstration? How did you manage that?"

"I could feel the machine working, Ro, and when the stylus wrote the numbers I knew what they were before Westerfeld read them off. And then when I thought about the numbers *I* wanted the machine to calculate, it did. The machine calculated the numbers I thought of and Westerfeld wasn't touching the machine, so the crowd thought he'd just put together a clockwork, not a real calculation machine." Arabella wilted in her seat.

"Wait a minute," Rowena leaned forward in her seat. "You *thought* numbers and told the machine to calculate them, and it *did*? Arabella, it sounds like you're saying you performed magic with machines."

"I know," whispered Arabella, tears gathering in the corners of her eyes.

"But that is just not possible, Ari, magic and machines don't work together. It makes no sense."

"I know, Rowena," Arabella wailed and put her head into her hands. "Don't you think the same thoughts haven't run through my head a million times? It's an impossible thing, but I know what I saw...what I *felt*."

The girls were silent for a long moment, then Rowena spoke up again. "But how would Westerfeld even know where to send a letter? Did he recognize you at the Exhibition? And how would he know what you did anyway?"

Arabella looked up and blushed. "I talked to him after the crowd left," she said. "I wanted to know how he built it and about the dead spot where the plate is. Then he recognized me from the private demonstration and started shaking me. He thought I was trying to sabotage him."

"Oh gracious," Rowena gasped and put her hand to her mouth. "How did you get away?"

"I got lucky," Arabella said. "John was there and he rescued me and took me to tea afterward. I told him everything too. He wanted to tell Father right away, but I convinced him to wait. If I can't think of something to do by the time we go for our summer visit, I promised I'd tell Father."

"Oh Ari," groaned Rowena as she collapsed back and slumped in her chair. "How did you get yourself into such a mess?"

"I don't know, Ro, I really don't," Arabella murmured and tears began to spill down her cheeks.

The girls were quiet again, watching the dancing flames. This time Rowena broke the silence. "I suppose we had better find out what the letter says."

"Yes," said Arabella as she dashed the tears off her cheeks with the back of her hand. "I suppose so." She tore open the wax seal and pulled out a small sheet of creamy ivory paper. It only took her a moment to read it, then she turned pale white and handed it over to Rowena with a trembling hand. Rowena read it out loud.

"Stop interfering, you foul creature. If I lay eyes on you again I can promise you will be sorry, and this time there won't be anyone to save you." Rowena turned pale herself and looked up at Arabella from the letter with her mouth agape. "Arabella! We have to tell Mother. This man means to harm you!"

"And tell Mother what?" Arabella said with a bitter twist of her lips. "That her embarrassment of a daughter has become a mortification, and one that draws danger to the household at that? Telling Mother anything about what I can see or do is completely out of the question, and that includes this business with Mr. Westerfeld."

"Arabella, I am your older sister and it's my job to look out for you. We have to tell Mother and that's final!"

"Rowena, please," Arabella tilted her head and let out a sour laugh. "You barely have five years on me, and you know just about as much of the mundane world and how its people act as I do considering the way Mother keeps us sequestered from anyone but witches. No, I'm not going to accept that you know any better than I do in this situation." She shook her head emphatically.

Rowena huffed and clenched her hands in her lap. "I think you are doing the absolute wrong thing, Arabella, but I won't tattle to Mother on you. However, if you don't keep your word to John and tell Father during the summer visit, I will tell him myself." She wagged the letter at Arabella.

Arabella snatched the letter back and let her breath out. "Thank you, Rowena."

"So what are you going to do about Westerfeld's threat between now and then?" Rowena asked with soft eyes and a tilt of her head.

Arabella shrugged. "I just won't go anywhere. He can't get into the house. Then, once the session is over, we'll return to the Manor and I'll be safely out of reach."

"I hope so, Ari, I sincerely hope so." Rowena squeezed her hand as she left the room. As soon as the door was shut, Arabella tossed the letter onto the fire. Both girls settled down to a long and restless night.

CHAPTER VII

*Wherein the Girls Practice Hard and Learn
Something More about Their Mother*

THE NEXT MORNING AT BREAKFAST, THE GIRLS WHO HAD BEEN LEFT AT home were greeted with the joyous news of the previous evening. A young gentleman had caught Amelia's eye. According to their mother's early inquiries at the party, he seemed to be a suitable candidate for a witch's husband. He was the only son of a first cousin of Cecilia Kellar, the Head of Thornfire House. He was handsome, docile and, based on the performance of other men in his bloodline, it seemed likely that he would father girls. He was also used to living with witches. Not all witch houses were exclusively female like the Sortilege household. Minerva was particularly pleased that the match had the potential to diffuse some of the residual tension from her ascension to the position of Grande Dame over Cecilia.

"His name is Harlan Gideon Zedock, and he's so handsome," burbled Amelia. "We danced every dance we could together. When Mother escorted us on a walk in the garden, he was so attentive; so interested in my studies and in what a young gentleman might do to help his lady love to polish her skills in charms and enchantments."

Rowena raised her eyebrow. "That certainly seems very sudden. You've only just met."

"Don't be such a killjoy, Rowena," Elizabeth said. She turned back to Amelia. "What color are his eyes?"

"Oh, they are a lovely grass green. His gaze is so gentle and intelligent," Amelia sighed. Rowena pursed her lips and kept her attention on her toast and marmalade while Mother smiled and patted Amelia's hand.

"Don't get your hopes up too high so early," she said. "We still need to look into his background a bit more before we can be sure he's suitable for you. We must make sure you have nothing but the best, my chickadee."

Amelia positively preened. "Yes, Mama," she said and applied herself to her eggs.

"So, girls," Mother looked down her nose at the three stay-at-homes. "Did anything exciting happen while we were out last night?"

Arabella swallowed hard and stared at her plate, pushing the last bits of bacon into her eggs.

"Absolutely nothing happened," Rowena said in a firm voice. "Just as usual," she finished with a smile.

Arabella stole a glance up through her lashes at Elizabeth, who was also pretending to be fascinated with her breakfast. Their mother looked back and forth between them with a frown. Arabella felt her shoulders relax just a little when their mother sighed and shook her head.

"We'll start with some basic shield exercises to limber up first, girls," Mother said after she blotted her lips with a napkin. "Then I believe we shall see who can perform a little advanced earth magic and force a sprout. As much as I don't want to, we may have to send one of you to look into the Irish problem."

Amelia and Elizabeth gasped, while Jessamine and Josephine merely looked at each other and smiled one of their odd, secret little smiles. Rowena and Arabella exchanged wide-eyed glances.

"But Mother, Aunt Leanore and Aunt Lorena died when they traveled to Ireland and tried to solve the famine issue," protested Elizabeth.

"I am *quite* aware of that, Elizabeth." Mother's tone was frosty. "But if we don't get a handle on matters in our own Council's domain, then we may have to deal with encroachment from Council witches in France or Germany or even Russia."

"But what about the Sisterhood? It's supposed to transcend nationality," asked Amelia.

"The Sisterhood is all well and good, as far as it goes," Mother began. "But seeing as none of the Councils of Witches actually have permanent standing in their home governments, including us, it's perfectly understandable to try to gain influence wherever you can, even outside your homeland. Why do you think I keep encouraging you to pay attention to international matters? It's certainly not for the gossip, Amelia."

"Yes, Mother," Amelia said and dipped her head as her cheeks flushed.

"Arabella, I want you to go gather the proper implements and lay them out by the garden pentacle," Mother said. "We'll need the hematite and opal for the shield work, and the usual salt, basins, wands, and candles."

Arabella shot up from the table and bobbed a quick curtsy. "Yes, Mother," she said and made for the door.

"And don't run off after you've laid everything out," Mother called after her. "We'll need you to fetch additional implements for the earth work."

Arabella had just finished laying out the last of the tools—a silver basin full of salt water next to clean white linen towels—when her mother and sisters came into the garden. Mother stepped up to the plain gray marble table set at the edge of the round granite terrace at the center of the garden. She looked over what Arabella had laid out, then nodded once and began to wash her hands in the salt water. One by one, each of her daughters, even Arabella, followed suit. The salt and the water cleansed them and made their hands ready to handle magic without taint or interference.

"Arabella," said Minerva. "Place the candle."

Arabella set a single thick, white candle in the center of the silver pentacle embedded in the round patio and backed away to the workbench. When she was done, Mother nodded toward the pentacle and Amelia, Jessamine, Josephine, Rowena, and Elizabeth each took up a place on the points of the star. Mother then nodded to Arabella who went around the circle clockwise and handed each of her sisters a pair of stones, opal for the left hand and hematite for the right.

"Jessamine, please light the candle," said Mother. Jessamine barely flicked a glance at the wick and it leapt up in flame. "Alright, girls, I want you to build a shield with each other and try to keep me out. I'm going to put out the candle. And it's not sporting to keep re-lighting the candle, Jessamine, shields only to defend it." Jessamine giggled and looked at her feet.

Mother clapped her hands twice. "Time to be serious, girls. Ready?"

"Yes, Mother," the five girls chorused together.

They lifted their hands waist high in unison, hands open and palms up, with the stones in the center. Their eyes were half closed as each one focused on building her shield and joining it to her sisters'. Rowena's face was serene, while Jessamine and Josephine frowned slightly. Amelia's brow furrowed and her jaw clenched. Elizabeth murmured under her breath and sweat beaded on her forehead, a deep crease developing between her brows. Mother's eyes slid over Arabella's sisters and settled on Elizabeth. She frowned and pushed her right palm out in front of her, following it with the force of her mind. Elizabeth yelped and stumbled back, landing on her bottom. With a contemptuous flick of her fingers, Mother put out the candle. The other girls let their arms drop to their sides, releasing their breath all together.

"Not fair!" cried Elizabeth and she slapped her palms on the granite. "I need more time to build my shield."

"What do you expect, Elizabeth?" Their mother's voice was as sharp as the edge of a well-honed knife. "Do you expect your opponents to wait patiently until you are fully ready, or do you expect that they will take every advantage they can? Don't be dense."

"But I'm still learning," Elizabeth whined as she clambered to her feet.

"Learn faster," Mother snapped. "No one will coddle or shelter you as I have. You need to be able to defend yourself when I am gone. Now, back to your positions."

Jessamine relit the candle and Elizabeth stepped back into place. The girls took a deep breath as one, raised their hands and began to build their mental defenses again. Once again, their mother raised her right hand and pushed Elizabeth. Elizabeth grunted and stumbled a bit, but she held firm. Mother smiled a little and began to pace around the circle widdershins. She drew even with Elizabeth and made a chopping motion with her left hand. Elizabeth cried out and fell to her knees, her opal and hematite flying out of her grip and into the ivy at the edge of the terrace. Amelia and Josephine extended their arms further and pushed out their mental shields to join and cover the hole Elizabeth had left. Mother whirled and shoved low with her right hand, catching Amelia in the gut and pushing her back three steps. This gave her just enough room in the shield, and she reached out with her fingers and made a twisting motion and the flame snuffed out.

"Better, but you still have more work to do. Back into position, girls," Mother said and motioned for Arabella to retrieve the stones that had flown from Elizabeth's hands. Amelia stepped back into the circle with a determined look on her face, but Elizabeth stayed on the ground panting, looking up at her mother with fire in her eyes.

"Why do we need to get better, Mother?" she asked, her jaw clenched. "We're already some of the strongest witches in Great Britain."

Mother whirled to face her sixth daughter. "And how do you propose we maintain that position, Elizabeth? Shall we grow soft and allow our skills to atrophy from disuse so that some other witch hungry for prestige and power can cast us out?"

"Fine," Elizabeth said as she regained her feet and wiped the dirt from her skirts. "We need to practice our skills. But why don't we spend more time on the useful things, like your carriage spells or levitation? These shield drills are useless."

"And why do you find these drills useless, Elizabeth?" Arabella heard the danger in Mother's voice, as did her sisters, and they desperately tried to get Elizabeth's attention for her to shut up.

"No one is going to attack us physically, Mother, not in the most civilized country in the world." Elizabeth rolled her eyes. "And besides, we're witches; the common people love and respect us. We might still need to win over some people in the higher strata of society, but it will come. As long as we are recognized for who we are, we're perfectly safe. And if by chance someone is silly enough to not recognize our superiority on first sight, we just have to perform a small trick and they will fall at our feet." Elizabeth put her fists on her hips with her chin lifted in defiance.

"You think we are universally safe and loved, do you?" Mother's voice came out in a hiss as she approached her daughter with her hands balled into fists at her side. "You think that there is no one who would wish us ill?" Elizabeth had turned pale and swallowed hard, but she nodded and let her hands drop to her side.

"The only reason you don't see danger is because I protect you from it, Elizabeth," Mother said. "I control who I allow around you, I control where you are allowed to go. You don't see the danger because I don't allow you to see it. The general public is afraid of us, the royals only tolerate us for what we can do for them, and Parliament is divided. Catholics want to see us dead, and the Anglicans see us as a necessary evil. Why do you think things are so bad in Ireland? When they think they can get away with it, they kill their witches." The girls all gasped and covered their mouths, including Arabella from where she crouched in the ivy still hunting for the hematite.

"Yes, that's right. Those barbarians still drag witches from their homes in the middle of the night and drown them or burn them because their Catholic doctrine says that we are evil. And unless the constabulary catches them in the act and is compelled to enforce the law against killing witches for simply being witches, they get away with it. Only your Aunt Leanore killed herself trying to defeat the blight. Lorena was too tired and too grieved over the death of our sister to fight them off when they came in the middle of the night. This is what I have shielded you from for years. I wanted my girls to have a gentler childhood than I did. But perhaps I have done you a disservice by letting you grow so soft."

Mother drew herself up tall and swept her daughters with a frosty look. "You will practice and you will not complain. You will continue to work on your skills until I am satisfied. Have I made myself clear?"

"Yes, Mother," Arabella and the other girls all chimed together, their voices shaking and cracking. Their hands trembled and their faces blanched. Even as the sun shone on their shoulders and a sparrow chirped cheerfully out in the garden, the world suddenly seemed darker.

Mother nodded to Arabella, who scampered forward to give Elizabeth back her stones. Without any further direction, the girls all resumed their positions and Jessamine relit the candle. They squared their shoulders and built their mental defenses as quickly and as strongly as they could manage.

Their mother was on them in an instant. In the space of three breaths, Elizabeth was on the ground again and Amelia had joined her. Josephine was on her knees, but still upright, wavering back and forth from the shock of the mental blow, but she still pushed out her shield even as sweat poured down her face. Jessamine looked to her twin and bit her lip. Mother took advantage of the hole afforded by the lapse in concentration and reached out to snuff the candle.

"Better, but still not good enough. You cannot allow yourselves to be distracted when others fall around you. Only when the danger has passed is it time to look to your sisters," Mother said. "Again." The pale-faced girls retook their positions without a word.

Mother allowed them a few moments to collect themselves and strengthen their shields. She circled the pentacle three times before she attacked. This time she went for Josephine first instead of Elizabeth. Josephine cried out in surprise and collapsed back to her knees, dropping her stones. Mother pinched out the candle with half a thought.

"Disgraceful." Her voice dripped with disdain. "What were you thinking?"

Josephine blushed deeply as she climbed to her feet and accepted her fallen stones from Arabella. "We thought you would go after Elizabeth first, like you did all the other times, and we shifted energy to her part of the shield."

"Indeed," Mother said, and quirked up an eyebrow. "Strategy is all well and good, girls, but never assume what your opponent is thinking, be prepared for all avenues of attack. And never divert so much energy to your weakest link that you cannot defend yourself. Again."

The girls sighed and reassembled themselves, getting ready for the next attack. Mother went for Rowena first this time, buffeting her with mental blows, but Rowena barely furrowed her brow and stood strong under her attack. Nodding as she moved on, Mother allowed a small smile and a murmured compliment. Jessamine was next in her contest of wills. She tried to pull her out of position, and while Jessamine rocked in place, she did not budge. Mother tried to shove harder and the shield colored with flames that even Arabella could see, but still she stayed firm in her position. Mother nodded and let up the assault on Jessamine, but with not even half a breath passed before she turned her attention to Elizabeth. Her mental blow threw Elizabeth six feet into the ivy, where she lay stunned and breathless. Mother whirled and executed the same maneuver on Amelia, who landed next to her sister, similarly breathless with tears streaming down her face. Rowena, Jessamine, and Josephine tightened up their circle and stepped into the pentacle to surround the candle, fingers nearly touching.

Mother prowled around them like a jungle beast, looking for an opening. She found it with Jessamine, who was still drained from her earlier efforts. Fire flared up again, but this time she lost against her mother and was blown back out of the circle, skidding across the patio to land at Arabella's feet. She stooped to cradle her sister against her, eyes glued to the final battle raging in front of her. Mother took Jessamine's fire and whipped it around to Josephine. Josephine pulled the moisture from the very air and managed to hold the fire at bay for a moment, but her barrier quickly vanished into steam, and Mother used her mental energy to shove her out of the circle, skidding along on her heels, still standing, right to the edge of the patio.

Rowena cast away the stones and stepped closer to the candle, cupping her hands directly above it and flooding her shield with as much energy as she dared. Sweat trickled down her temples and her breath was shallow and fast as Mother pummeled her shield with mental strikes. Rowena held fast but her shoulders hunched as their mother circled her, raining down blows relentless and fierce. Finally, Rowena's shield cracked and she cried out as Mother flung her into the ivy even farther than Elizabeth and Amelia. Mother then stepped up to the candle and extinguished it with a feral grin on her face.

The garden was silent except for the panting of the young witches. Josephine had collapsed to her knees, and all the other sisters remained where they had fallen, exhausted. Even Mother blotted away some sweat from her lip with a lace handkerchief. She surveyed them with a smile bordering on warm.

"Now that was an effort worthy of Blackstone House and the Sortilege line. Hopefully, you'll keep improving and soon you'll be able to do your shield work without focal stones, like Rowena did there at the end," Mother said. "I believe that will be all for today. We will have earth magic practice tomorrow." She swept out of the garden and into the house. The girls picked themselves up one by one and helped each other into the house where they tended to their bruises and scrapes, leaving Arabella alone in the garden to clean up the remains of the practice session.

CHAPTER VIII

In Which We Meet Amelia's One True Love

ARABELLA AND AMELIA PRESENTED THEMSELVES TO THEIR MOTHER IN the morning room the following Monday. Both wore smartly cut jackets and walking skirts in a light wool kerseymere, Amelia in a lovely robin's egg blue and Arabella in a much more sober hunter green. Mother looked up from the sheaf of papers in her hand and smiled.

"Eminently suitable for a walk in the gardens," Minerva pronounced. "You look especially lovely, Amelia, did Moria dress your hair?"

Amelia giggled and curtseyed, her fingers wandering up to the plaited loops that dropped gracefully from the elaborately braided bun on the back of her head. "No, Mama," she said. "The new girl you just brought in, Bridgette, dressed my hair."

"Ah yes," said Mother. "The young witch from Ireland. Perhaps I shall start using her to dress my hair as well." She ran her fingers over her own hair, with its severe center part and plain bun, and then patted the settee next to her. "Come sit, Amelia."

"Are you certain it's alright that I'm not attending the Council session today?" asked Amelia as she settled herself next to her mother. Arabella waited for a moment to be acknowledged but when her mother said nothing, she flounced down on the fainting couch opposite her sister and mother with a sigh. Neither one seemed to notice.

"I have a private meeting with the House Heads and there is a full docket of petitioners to join the Sisterhood today, chickadee," Mother said as she squeezed Amelia's hand. "But we've enough witches to administer the tests without you, and I'm certain a walk in the garden with your young man would be much more entertaining for you."

"Oh yes, Mama," Amelia gushed. "Thank you so much for letting me go."

"Think nothing of it." Mother smiled and stroked Amelia's hand. "I know I am hard on you girls, but it's only because I want the best for you. I want you to be comfortable and happy."

"Do you think Harlan will be the best for me?" Amelia asked.

"He's good enough at first glance," said Mother. "He has the right breeding and seems to be amenable to the way a witch must live. We will have to see if he continues to be such a fine prospect. Now, do you remember the rules, darling?"

"Yes, Mama," Amelia laughed and tilted her head to the side. "I'm not to allow him liberties; he can only hold my hand and nothing more. I'm not to try to get out of sight of Arabella. And we must be home in time for tea."

"Good girl." Their mother turned her attention to Arabella. "You do remember your rules, don't you, Arabella?"

"Yes, Mother," Arabella said as she drew herself tall in her seat. "I am to keep Amelia and Harlan in my sight at all times. If Harlan attempts anything beyond holding Amelia's hand, I am to interfere. We are to be home by tea, and I must tell you every detail about the excursion tonight when you return from Council."

Mother seemed about to say something, but was interrupted by a knock at the door. Amelia nearly squealed and she started to rise, but Mother pulled her back into her seat.

"Moria will answer the door," she said. "It wouldn't do to seem too eager, now would it?"

"No, Mama," Amelia said, but her eyes were glued on the doorway into the front hall.

The women waited in silence, listening to the murmur of voices in the front hall. Moria came into the morning room and dropped a curtsey to Mother.

"Master Zedock is here to see Miss Amelia," she said.

"Show him in, Moria," said Mother.

Arabella had to admit that Amelia's evaluation had been correct and Harlan Zedock was indeed a handsome young man. He was tall, but not freakishly so, and his golden red hair, a mark of the scions of Thornfire House, waved across his brow in an attractive manner. His grass green eyes sparkled as he caught sight of Amelia and smiled as soon as he entered the room and took off his black top hat. But he went to Mother first and bowed over her offered hand, touching his forehead to her knuckles in respect. He offered Amelia the same bow, but lingered just a little longer over her hand. He gave Arabella a small nod and stepped back to stand straight and tall in front of Mother and Amelia.

"Madame Sortilege," he said. "Thank you for receiving me."

"Indeed, Master Zedock, it is lovely to have you."

"Please, call me Harlan," he said. "If I may be so bold, I am quite smitten with your Amelia and I hope to one day be a member of your House. So perhaps we may abandon the early formal stages of this dance?"

Mother's eyebrows went up and her eyes widened as she drew in a shocked breath. "Well, you certainly are a forward one, aren't you?"

"Well, as I am being bold, Madame Sortilege," he began, staring down at the hat clutched in his hands. "I may as well make all my intentions plain, mayn't I?" He cleared his throat and shifted his feet, then began to speak again.

"Your daughter Amelia is one of the loveliest women I have ever met, both in her person and her personality. The night after we met I could not sleep for thinking of her and wondering what she might be doing at that very moment. If I were to look for a love match, I could do no better. And when you take into account the position of the Sortilege line and Blackstone House, I could do no better if I were looking simply for a political match. I see no reason why I should not pursue Amelia, the only question is whether or not you will allow it."

"Oh, Harlan," Amelia gasped. Mother held up her hand for silence.

"Indeed, that is the question, Master Zedock." Minerva held her expression in careful neutrality. "And if I may ask, what are you willing to offer my daughter and our family? And why should we believe this sudden ardent pursuit?"

"I do not have much to offer to such powerful women," he said, his face flaming. "All that I do have is my heart, which I would give freely and wholly. I would abide by whatever household rules you may set. I would work outside the home or not, as it pleases the family. And if we were to have sons, I would give them to the Sortilege line instead of keeping them to myself."

Arabella gasped, as did her mother and Amelia, stunned that he would offer over his sons so freely. Even the most docile of men who married witches usually held on to that last bit of control with an iron grip, since it was often the only dominion they had over their lives. Harlan hurried on with his speech.

"As for my sudden passion, I have no satisfactory explanation. I only know that when I met Amelia it was as if Cupid's arrow struck me to my very core, and there is no other woman to whom I could give my heart."

Amelia clutched her hands over her breast, her eyes full of unshed tears. Mother looked at her, then at the blushing young man before them. Arabella remained on the fainting couch, resolutely staring at her hands in her lap and blushing herself.

"And what do your own parents think of this sudden passion?" Mother asked.

"My father died of cholera years ago, and my mother approves of the match," he said. "Even Aunt Cecilia approves."

Mother nodded and rubbed her fingertips on her chin, looking at Harlan with narrowed eyes. "Is this submission to the will of witches of yours something you practice with all people? Since we are being frank, Master Zedock, I must tell you that we tolerate no weaklings here in Blackstone House. Witches are in charge, to be certain, but our men must be able to stand on their own feet."

"I do understand, Madame Sortilege," Harlan bobbed a nod. "While witches are positively superior creatures, mundane women are not and I would most certainly not bow to the will of a mundane woman. And as for mundane men, I feel I have a great advantage over them in both my breeding and my character. My mother and my aunts raised me well."

Mother nodded and allowed herself a small smile. "And what are your intentions with my daughter today?"

Harlan drew himself up and smiled broadly. "I had planned to take her to Kensington Gardens for a stroll, to show her the Round Pond and take in some of the wildlife. I understand there are quite a number of people who sail model boats on the water. I thought it could be an entertaining afternoon. I thought perhaps we might have some amiable conversation and get to know one another better."

"You will take the family carriage since Madame Thurston from Hazelrood House is sharing her carriage with us to Council today, you will be home by tea, and you will be accompanied by Amelia's sister Arabella as a chaperone," Mother said as she rose.

"Yes, ma'am," Harlan said, bobbing his head.

"I will be at Council for the day," she said as she began to leave the room. "You young people enjoy yourselves. And Harlan," she called over her shoulder from the doorway. "If you continue in this vein we shall be happy to welcome you into the family."

Harlan's face broke into a wide grin and he stammered his thanks to her retreating back. As soon as Mother was clear of the doorway, Amelia launched herself from the settee and wrapped her arms around Harlan's neck.

"Oh, Harlan, you are so romantic," she cooed with her face inches from his.

Arabella shot up from her seat. "Amelia! Stop that! You know what Mother said about liberties!"

Both Amelia and Harlan blushed and separated themselves, but they continued to hold hands. Arabella straightened the hem of her jacket, then ran her hands down the front of her skirt. Harlan and Amelia gazed into each other's eyes, fingers intertwined, and began to sway toward each other. Arabella put her hands between them and pushed their shoulders apart, causing them to stumble back and their hands to break apart.

"Please, control yourselves," Arabella said. "I don't want to be your chaperone any more than you want me to. But Mother gave me a job to do, and I will not suffer her wrath for not doing it. We will all have a much more pleasant day if the two of you can resist behaving like beasts. Have I made myself clear?"

"Ari…" Amelia began.

"Don't Ari me, Amelia," Arabella said. "I know that I am younger than you and I shouldn't be giving you any kind of instruction, but please do remember that you are not thinking clearly. Let me be your clearheaded guide before you slip and do something that will embarrass the family and yourself. Please?"

Amelia sighed and shook her head. "Arabella, it's not like we have to follow the same rules as mundane women. Even if the worst should happen and I am pregnant before Harlan and I may be handfasted, it's not the end of the world. I mean really, our own servants have children out of wedlock all the time."

"Our servants are not the ones trying to protect and benefit all of the British Empire with the skills and gifts of magic," Arabella said as she placed her hands on her hips. "You've heard Mother over dinner just as many times as I have, Amelia. As the daughters of the most powerful house in England, we must hold ourselves to a higher standard."

For this, neither Amelia nor Harlan had an answer. Chastened, the lovebirds nodded and followed Arabella from the room, surreptitiously touching fingertips behind her back.

CHAPTER IX

Wherein a Walk in the Garden Turns Sour

I T SO HAPPENED THAT HARLAN HAD CHOSEN A GLORIOUS DAY TO TAKE Amelia to Kensington Gardens. The sun was bright enough that Amelia and Arabella required their parasols, and the sky was a brilliant blue with just a few high, wispy clouds. He walked both ladies through the Black Lion Gate and they set off down the main avenue at a crisp pace, fast enough not to be slovenly but slow enough for conversation. Amelia threaded her left arm through his right while Arabella walked on the other side, holding only her parasol.

"I've studied these gardens a bit, Amelia," Harlan began. "Would you like to hear some of what I've learned?"

"Oh, of course, Harlan." Amelia squeezed his arm and leaned in as she smiled. "I enjoy improving myself ever so much."

Arabella groaned inwardly and hope the sugary sweetness of the two would not make her teeth ache by the end of the afternoon. She turned her attention to the well-dressed people strolling around them. There were nursemaids out with their charges, young women in their fashionable full skirts, and even men in their best suits, black coats and top hats gleaming while their vests popped with a riot of color. Everyone put on a show of chatting amiably while they watched each other with stolen glances.

"The Kensington Gardens were originally part of Hyde Park, until William and Mary moved into Kensington Palace and set aside these gardens for their use. They opened them to the public sometime in the 30s, I think. We should be able to spot the Palace on our right before we turn down the avenue to get to the Round Pond," Harlan said.

"Oh, how exciting," Amelia said. "Do you think any of the Royals will be at home? It would be so lovely to get a glimpse of them."

"I don't think they are staying at Kensington much, my sweet," Harlan said as he reached over and patted her hand on his arm with his other hand. "The word is that our Victoria and her family are quite taken with the Scottish people right now, and that they are spending a lot of time at Balmoral."

"How disappointing," Amelia sighed. "I should have liked to see them. But I do certainly understand a fascination with the people of Scotland. All the Scottish witches I've met have been so forthright and so strong, but without being vulgar."

"Have you met many of them?" Harlan asked.

"A few, when the Council is in session," said Amelia. "I've not had a chance to travel north yet to really meet them in their own environs."

"I've heard the country is quite wild up there, but breathtaking," said Harlan.

As Amelia and Harlan continued to chat about innocent things, like manners and fashion, Arabella privately wished she'd been able to stay behind with Jeanette and the carriage. She nearly groaned aloud when Harlan suggested that after they had had their fill of watching the boaters and waterfowl at the Round Pond, that they might continue East across the park. Then they could turn North up the Long Water, followed by the walk back to the Black Lion Gate and out onto Bayswater Road where the carriage was parked.

"Unless you would find that too taxing, my dear?" he said to Amelia.

"Oh no, Harlan," Amelia said. "Mother insists that we maintain our physical strength, some of our spells are quite strenuous. Such a walk should be no trouble."

"Of course," Harlan knocked the heel of his hand into his forehead. "I should have thought of that. It's just so surprising to find such hardiness in a delicate flower like yourself." He raised her gloved fingertips lightly to his lips.

"I think that's a little more than holding hands." Arabella's voice came out a little strangled. Amelia and Harlan laughed and blushed, but continued on to the water with hands clasped. Lagging behind, Arabella let the lovebirds get ahead by a few yards. She still had them in sight, so she was not breaking her promise to her mother, but at least she didn't have to listen to their syrupy sweet conversation.

The shore of the Round Pond was crowded. Young boys and gentlemen alike launched small sailing boats from the edge, sometimes guiding them with sticks from the perimeter and sometimes, in the case of a few plucky boys, kicking off their shoes and stockings and wading in up to the hems of their short pants. Further out on the water, swans and ducks glided by with a serene air, unbothered by the laughing and splashing on the shore. Nursemaids promenaded by with prams, exchanging gossip about their employers as they went, and young men and women exchanged smiles and covert glances under the watchful eyes of their chaperones.

Arabella sighed and twirled her parasol on her shoulder a bit. At least she was out of the house on a pleasant day, even if it meant following her sister and her suitor about and being the odd duck. Amelia and Harlan stopped right at the edge of the water and Harlan pointed out the various species of waterfowl, going on about how the female always had the duller plumage so that the male could use his brighter feathers to distract predators. Arabella looked out over the water to spot the birds Harlan was speaking about, but the sun flashed bright against the ripples. She raised a hand to shade her eyes, but the light was still too bright and she turned her face away.

That was when she saw him. Bartholomew Westerfeld stood not more than a half a dozen yards away from her, back in the direction toward the Palace, glowering. His dark eyes fixed on her and only her, his hands down at his sides clenching and unclenching. Arabella could see his shoulders rising and falling with heavy breathing from where she stood. The sun glinted off his leg braces. Her heart hammering in her chest, Arabella rushed to close the gap between herself and Amelia and Harlan.

"I've seen quite enough of ducks and noisy boys. Perhaps we should move on?" she said.

"The water is so relaxing, Arabella," Amelia said. "I thought we might take our time and stroll the shore for a while."

"But didn't you want to see the Long Water? We could stroll by the water there. Don't forget, we really mustn't be out too long or we'll be late for tea and Mother will be cross." The words all tumbled out of Arabella in a flood.

"Arabella," Amelia said with a frown. "Whatever is the matter with you? You're not being yourself."

Arabella dared a glance back over her shoulder. Westerfeld was still several yards distant, but he had followed and stood with his arms crossed as he scowled at Arabella.

"I say," said Harlan. "Who is that angry chap and why is he staring at us?"

"He's a man who doesn't like witches very much," said Arabella. "And I really would rather that we move on to somewhere that he isn't."

"Isn't that Mr. Westerfeld? From the Distinction Engine demonstration?" asked Amelia as she turned to stare at him directly. "Why would he be so interested in us?"

"Don't you remember, Amelia? He was so horrible and so angry at the demonstration after Mother and the rest of us left. For whatever reason, he hates us, and I really do think we should just move on before there's any kind of unpleasantness." Arabella walked away at a brisk pace. After half a dozen steps she stopped and turned. "Come on!"

Amelia and Harlan looked at each other and shrugged, then followed Arabella with swift footsteps. When they caught up, she turned sharply, her eyes focused on the ground, and resumed her brisk pace with determination. They walked in silence for a few moments before Arabella spoke.

"Is he still behind us?" she asked.

Harlan glanced back over his shoulder, trying to be casual. "Yes, and he's trying to catch up."

"Well," said Arabella. "We shall just have to walk faster." And with that she lengthened her stride and Amelia and Harlan rushed to keep up with her.

"Arabella!" Amelia puffed, nearly out of breath. "Would you mind telling me what is going on? Mr. Westerfeld may not like us very much, but we haven't done anything to him that would make him attack us in a public park."

"Just keep walking," Arabella panted.

Amelia stopped short and stamped her foot. "I'm not taking another step unless you explain what's going on right this instant."

Arabella was already several yards ahead and she stopped and whirled around. "We haven't the time for me to explain now! We need to go!"

Amelia set her jaw and crossed her arms over her chest, stamping her foot again with her eyes locked on Arabella. Harlan looked back and forth between the women and then back over his shoulder at Westerfeld shoving his way through the crowd.

"I don't know why you are trying to spoil my day, Arabella, but you had better stop acting like such a brat or Mother will be very cross with you." Amelia's chin tilted up.

"I'm not trying to spoil anything," Arabella said as she reached out with her arms imploringly. "Please, Amelia, let's just go."

"If Mr. Westerfeld tries anything unpleasant, I'm sure Harlan will defend us," said Amelia.

"Of course! That's not even a question," Harlan sputtered.

"Besides, the worst Mr. Westerfeld can manage in public is harsh words, Arabella," Amelia said.

"I can quite assure you that I can manage far worse than harsh words, you filthy witch," Westerfeld panted as he finally caught up with Amelia and Harlan. Arabella groaned and clutched the handle of her parasol.

"Now see here, my good man," Harlan said as he stepped in between Westerfeld and Amelia. "There's no need for that kind of language. The Gardens are big enough that we can all enjoy them without any kind of nasty goings-on."

Westerfeld's lip curled up as he looked Harlan up and down. "Traitor to your gender," he growled. "But as disgusting as you are, my business is not with you or your slut, my business is with *her*." He stabbed his finger at Arabella and began to stalk toward her. Harlan and Amelia both gasped and clutched at each other. Arabella looked about wildly for some kind of escape. Only there was nothing but open space filled with people to her right and water to her left and not a constable to be seen.

"What did I tell you about staying away from me?" Westerfeld roared, his face turning fiery red. Nearby garden visitors were starting to stare. Arabella froze just as a rabbit might when cornered by a stoat. She knew she needed to run, but could not convince her legs to move.

"I had no idea…" Arabella began to stammer.

"No idea," he sneered. "More like you are trying to taunt me, just like you are trying to destroy me. Typical for your kind!"

Westerfeld jerked to a stop and lost his balance, nearly falling as Harlan grabbed him by the elbow. "Sir," Harlan said in a firm voice. "I have no idea what you are going on about, but the young lady has done nothing to you, and I think it's time you left."

Westerfeld jerked his arm from Harlan's grip. "Open your eyes, boy! These harpies have you fooled and will suck the life out of you before you know it." He turned back to Arabella and began to advance again. By this time, every set of eyes were locked on the outrageous scene unfolding before them. Adults and children alike abandoned their diversions to openly stare.

Arabella backed up several steps, then her eye caught on a gleam that did not come from the sun on the water. She looked down at Westerfeld's braces with the spiraling glow coming from the gears around the knees, and then seized on a thought.

Arabella reached out with her mind and felt the teeth of the gears meshing together as they actuated the brass limbs. She pushed further and pinched her mind shut on the gears, stopping them cold without warning. Westerfeld's left leg froze midstride, his foot dangling in front of him. He lost his balance, windmilling his arms, but his effort was not enough and he fell onto the pea gravel path.

Harlan grabbed Amelia's hand, then skirted around where Westerfeld lay on the ground, rocking back forth, banging his bare hands on the braces trying to get them to move. The gears bit into his skin and bright red smears seeped out onto his fingers and palms. Arabella's stomach turned at the sight of blood. She stood stock still staring at Westerfeld, her mind locked on the gears to keep them frozen. Inside her mind, pity for the man thrashing on the ground warred with the fear of what he might do if she let go. She jumped when Harlan grabbed her hand. Amelia already clutched his other hand.

"I don't know what kind of divine providence has interfered," Harlan said. "But I think our excursion is at an end, ladies. Let's go."

They walked away as fast as they could, holding hands and looking back every few strides. Westerfeld still lay on the ground, his braces slowly grinding back to life now that Arabella no longer held them. The sun glinting off the tears of frustration that streamed down his cheeks.

Arabella hoped that she hadn't held them so hard that the gears were bent or damaged in any way.

Harlan, Amelia, and Arabella did not stop until they reached the carriage on Bayswater Road. Out of breath, they tumbled into the safety of the family carriage and ordered Jeanette to take them home with all haste.

Later that afternoon, Arabella paced the drawing room wringing her hands while Amelia and Harlan sat on the sofa and watched her try to wear a hole in the carpet. She dreaded having to give her mother the report about the afternoon before dinner. The tea that Moria had brought and Harlan had poured for her sat cold and unsipped on the side table.

"Arabella, please, sit down," Amelia said. "We're home and safe. There's nothing to worry about."

"Nothing to worry about?" Arabella said in a high, strained voice, pausing in her pacing. "How can you say that?"

Amelia sipped her tea. "We left that awful man behind, and I'm sure that once we tell Mother what happened she'll inform the appropriate authorities and we'll never have to worry about that unpleasantness again."

"Such composure with your beauty," said Harlan, and he reached to press Amelia's hand. She beamed up at him.

Arabella threw her hands up. "I don't see how you can be so calm, Amelia! That man nearly attacked me. Every time we see him, his behavior is worse. Next time he could do something truly awful." Arabella wrapped her arms around herself and shuddered.

"What man? Who attacked you?" Mother's voice cracked like a whip as she entered the drawing room taking off her gloves. Her bonnet was still perched on her head and her shawl was slipping off her shoulders. "I got a garbled message from Moria that there was some danger at home, so I came as quickly as I could. What happened?"

"Oh, Mama," said Amelia. "We had an unfortunate incident at the Gardens, but everything turned out alright. Moria exaggerates things."

"You only think she exaggerates things because you weren't the one almost attacked," Arabella shouted at her sister.

"Arabella, this is the second time I've heard you say a man nearly attacked you in less than a minute," Mother said. "You had better tell me what is going on, young lady, and you had better tell me now."

"We were at the Kensington Gardens," Arabella began with a shuddering breath, hugging herself. "It was a lovely day and we were having quite an agreeable time, when we got down to the Round Pond and Mr. Westerfeld was there."

"Mr. Westerfeld?" Mother said. "The man with that awful machine who gave that disaster of a demonstration?"

"Yes," Arabella sobbed and she sank onto a couch before her knees gave way. "He started yelling at us, and he called Harlan a traitor to his gender and he called Amelia a terrible name. Then he came at me like he was going to attack me." Arabella covered her face with her hands and sobbed again.

"Harlan was so brave, Mama..." Amelia began but Mother held up her hand for silence and went to Arabella on the couch.

"Did he touch you? Did he hurt you?" she asked in a fierce, hissing whisper.

Arabella shook her head and wiped away her tears with the heels of her hands. "His leg braces locked up before he could get to me and he fell over." Arabella sniffed as her mother gathered her in her arms and patted her back murmuring "there, there" as Arabella cried on her shoulder. Arabella felt the knot in her stomach ease as it became obvious that her mother believed her lie. Her secret would be safe at least a little while longer.

"Thank goodness that nasty technology failed on him, just another example of why you can't trust it as you can trust magic, too unreliable." Mother continued to rock her and comfort her.

"Amelia," she said. "Why did you not shield your sister, or use your telekinesis to shove that vile man out of the way? It's your responsibility to protect your little sister, especially since she cannot protect herself."

The blood drained from Amelia's face and she started to stammer. "I'm so sorry, Mother. I was just so shocked I couldn't think of anything to do, and I didn't have my focus stones for a shield or anything."

"And this is why I drill you girls like I do," Mother said in a harsh voice. "I know you think I am a monster for pushing you sometimes, but if you had worked harder on your skills this incident would have turned out very differently. You must learn to use your power without foci and in stressful situations if you are to be of any use, Amelia."

"Yes, Mother," Amelia said softly as she bowed her head and flushed.

"We must report this horrifying incident to the Council and other authorities tomorrow. We cannot let such appalling behavior stand. I'll need you to take a statement from Arabella in the morning, Amelia, after she's had a chance to recover from the shock, since she cannot come to Council with us." Mother paused and thought a moment. "You should write down a statement from Harlan as well, since you will be the only one who can testify in person."

When Arabella's sobs had slowed to fitful hiccups, Mother addressed Harlan. "Thank you, Harlan, for protecting my girls. My daughters are the most precious part of my life."

"It was my pleasure, Madame Sortilege," Harlan said. "There was no possible way my conscience would let me allow Amelia or her sister to come to harm while there is breath in my body."

Mother smiled at him over Arabella's head. "Would you care to join us for dinner, Harlan? I believe our cook has made a lovely eel pie for us this evening."

"I would be delighted," Harlan said as he beamed at Amelia and squeezed her hand while she smiled back at him wanly.

CHAPTER X

Wherein Arabella Recovers and
Discusses the Future Over Tea

ARABELLA'S MOTHER SHIELDED HER FROM THE CLAMOR SURROUNDING the Kensington Garden incident. She told Arabella that she need not worry, that Mother would take care of everything. Arabella stayed sequestered in her bedroom for the most part, only coming out for family meals and a stroll around the family garden in the evening for air, which Mother insisted on for her health. It was only from Rowena that Arabella learned anything about what was going on in the Council. The witches, of course, were outraged over Westerfeld's behavior. All the House Heads fawned over Mother, full of compassion over her fright for her endangered daughters. Amelia also gained much sympathy for having to endure the whole ordeal. The entire situation seemed to seal the alliance between Blackstone House and Thornfire House until the marriage of Amelia and Harlan was all but assured.

The witches argued for a full day as to whether or not they should just take care of the matter themselves and have Mr. Westerfeld suffer some mysterious fate, or if they should take the matter to the Parliament and ask them to sort the man out. In the end, the witches who wanted to take things through proper channels won out, and work began to get a hearing before Parliament. Rowena confided in Arabella that the witches who wished to handle Mr. Westerfeld themselves were only temporarily at bay. The general feeling was that if Parliament did not act swiftly enough, that they would take matters in their own hands. It shocked Arabella that the entire witch community stood up for her so quickly, considering what an embarrassment they'd always considered her.

"But you're still one of us, Ari," Rowena said one evening after dinner when Arabella shared her feelings. "We can argue and fight all we want among ourselves, but if an outsider threatens us we close ranks."

Arabella laughed bitterly. "All it took was a threat of bodily harm to make me one with the Sisterhood. I should have tried this sooner."

"Please don't be sulky, Ari," Rowena asked. "We may not be the best family in the world but we are still family."

"Ah, the sweet familial embrace!" Arabella proclaimed and then laughed, this time with real humor. Rowena laughed along with her.

"Oh! I almost forgot to tell you," Rowena said. "The Kensington Garden incident has been all over the papers for the last three days. They might not have pursued it at all, but Westerfeld has been saying the most awful things and ranting about the influence of witches on society. They seem to think it's the most delicious scandal. Moria has had to chase off several reporters who wanted to ask you questions, and sketch artists who wanted to draw your likeness."

"What does the public think?" Arabella asked, twisting her fingers together.

"For the most part they are rallying behind you," Rowena said. "The part of the public that is pro-witch is, of course, calling for Mr. Westerfeld's head. And even the people who don't normally support us think that Mr. Westerfeld far overstepped the bounds of proper behavior."

"Do you think anything will come of this?" asked Arabella. "Or do you think there'll be a lot of noise and in the end nothing will be different?"

"I don't really know, Ari," Rowena sighed.

The girls sat quiet for a moment, each lost in her own thoughts as they stared into the flames of Arabella's bedroom fire.

"I've been meaning to ask you something," Rowena said, breaking the silence.

"Yes, go on," said Arabella in a distracted voice, her eyes still on the hypnotic flames.

"Mr. Westerfeld's mechanical leg braces didn't just fail on their own, did they?"

Arabella startled up and blushed. "No, no, they didn't," she murmured.

"How did you do it?" Rowena leaned in with a conspiratorial whisper.

"I just reached out with my mind, pinched the gears and made them stop. It wasn't all that difficult, really." Arabella shrugged.

"That's amazing, Ari," Rowena said. "No other witch can make metal respond like that. Oh sure, there are a few dowsing witches with an affinity for metal, the mining companies love them. Sometimes very strong telekinetic witches can bend metal, but no one else can make a machine respond like that." She shook her head.

"I'm just very pleased that I was able to do something to protect myself," said Arabella. "I don't want to think about what would have happened if he hadn't had mechanical leg braces for me to stop." Rowena murmured her assent and squeezed Arabella's hand.

The next morning Moria brought a note from John up to Arabella. She had to squint a little to make out her brother's rushed script, but she gathered that he was asking to visit that afternoon. With a little smile, she made a mental note to tease him about not taking care with his penmanship despite all the lessons Father paid for.

"Shall I tell the messenger there will be a reply?" Moria asked.

"Yes," said Arabella as she added her own note, in a much fairer hand, under John's and slid the creamy paper back into the envelope. "I told John to come around for tea at three. We shall take it in the back garden. It should please Mother that I'm getting more air."

"That will be lovely," Moria said as she bobbed a curtsey and left the room with the note.

John shocked Arabella and Moria by arriving right on time. Arabella was just coming down the stairs thinking that she would have time to enjoy a few poems in the lovely spring breeze before her brother arrived.

"John!" Arabella cried as she threw her arms around his neck. "It's so good to see you."

John embraced her hard. "I'm glad to see you too, little sister."

"Are you sure you're feeling well," Arabella teased and laid the back of her hand on his forehead as if to check for fever. "I don't think I've ever seen you on time before."

"I told myself tea was at two o'clock instead of three," he smiled and rocked back on his heels, hooking his thumbs behind his lapels. "So, you see, I'm really right on my usual schedule."

Arabella tilted back her head and laughed, then held out her hand to John and they headed out to the garden arm in arm. They strolled a bit and John admired the rose bushes that were Vivienne's pride and joy while they waited for Moria to set out the tea and scones under the arbor. Arabella served tea and inquired after their father's health.

"Father is deeply involved with some new avenues for old transmutations," John said as he sipped his tea.

"Oh?" Arabella said as she selected a scone. "Which transmutation is he after again? Lead into gold?"

John shook his head. "No, Father thinks he's on the right track for a nickel to silver transmutation, but our dear brother Henry disagrees. *He* is convinced zinc into silver is the key. They've rather made a contest of it to see who will be the first to achieve the transmutation. I hardly see them at all these days they spend so much time in the lab."

"So they've given up on gold completely?" Arabella sipped her tea.

John shrugged. "Who knows? I'm sure they'll become obsessed with it again at some point in the future."

"When do you think they'll finally drag you into the family business, brother dear?" Arabella smiled.

"Oh, I think not." John barked with laughter. "I haven't the patience, the talent, or even the slightest inclination to follow our father or Henry into the alchemical arts."

Arabella fiddled with her tea cup. "Don't you ever feel bored or left out when you can't participate with the household obsession?"

John raised his eyebrow and regarded his sister with a sharp eye. "Are we talking about you or me, Ari?"

Arabella blushed.

"Ari," said John. "There is more to the world than magic and alchemy, despite what Mother or Father would have you think. There's a whole wide world to explore that doesn't involve spells, incantations, or esoteric knowledge of any kind."

"Maybe for you," Arabella pouted. "But the options for an unmarried brown bud are not as abundant."

"That's part of why I came to see you today," John said. "I wanted to talk to you about your future, Arabella."

"What about my future?" Arabella frowned.

"It's not safe for you to stay with Mother, Ari," John started. "This recent incident at Kensington Gardens just proves it."

"What do you mean I'm not safe staying with Mother?" Arabella spluttered. "What a perfectly horrible thing to say!"

"Arabella, Mother is just not as interested in protecting you as she is our sisters because you can't contribute to the prestige of Blackstone House. And after Mother finally passes, who will take care of you then? Vivienne? Amelia?"

"You certainly seem convinced that I'll become a wretched old maid. Who's to say I might not meet a lovely gentleman and get married and have a family?"

"Be realistic, Arabella." John's voice took on a harsh tone. "No family in the Houses will want you because they're afraid your children will be just like you — avatic, not a drop of magic in them. And it's unlikely you'd find a husband in normal society; you come from a witch house and they would fear any children would carry on the trait. Besides, how would you meet them anyway? Mother keeps you sequestered, unless it suits her to trot you out."

Arabella stood abruptly, her face flaming and her hands balled up at her sides. "If I had known you were going to spend the afternoon insulting me, I would have never invited you to tea."

"Arabella, please..." John reached up toward her with imploring hands. "Ari, please, sit down. I'm not trying to be cruel; I'm just trying to get you to think."

"Get me to think about what?" Arabella crossed her arms over her chest.

"Your future, Arabella, and how you haven't got much of one if you stay here," John said. He gestured to her bench. "Please, sit down."

Arabella paused for a moment, staring at John with narrowed eyes, and then she sat. "I still don't know what you're driving at, John."

John sighed. "Have you thought about what we discussed after the Exhibition? About telling Father?"

Arabella shook her head. "No, no. It's just impossible. It would drive even more of a wedge between Mother and Father if I told him and not her, and I can't tell her. What would Father be able to do anyway?"

"Drive more of wedge between them?" John scoffed. "I hardly think that's possible. They haven't spoken in seventeen years, Ari, not since the day you were born. As for what Father can do, he can take you away from all this." John swung his arm around, gesturing to the garden and the house.

"Take me away?" Arabella's jaw dropped wide open. "What do you mean, take me away?"

"I mean, you leave this house and come live with us, me and Father and Henry," John said. "Father can protect you, and he can even introduce you to some proper people in normal society. You might actually get married, Arabella. You could have a normal life."

"A normal life, John?" Arabella spat out a sour laugh. "You mean be some man's property and never be able to call anything my own without his permission, don't you? My life may not be ideal here, but it's certainly better than being some man's chattel."

The corner of John's mouth quirked up. "So you'd rather be Mother's chattel?"

"I am not chattel to Mother!" Arabella huffed.

"Oh, I think you certainly are, Arabella," John sipped his tea. "Mother just hasn't decided how to spend you yet. Haven't you watched what she's done with Vivienne and Amelia? Each match is for the greatest gain to Blackstone House."

"Tosh," Arabella said, waving away his words. "Vivienne married for love, and Amelia is absolutely over the moon for Harlan."

"I see," said John as set down his cup. "It's just an interesting coincidence that both matches are so politically advantageous for Blackstone House."

Arabella tightened her jaw and focused her fierce attention on the crumbling pieces of her scone.

"Ari," John sighed and rubbed the bridge of his nose. "I know I sound harsh and my words are hard to swallow, but I'm really looking out for your best interests. I wouldn't be suggesting any of this unless I really cared for you."

"Have you said anything about this to Father?" Arabella's voice was tight and hot.

"No," John said. "I promised that I wouldn't say anything until the summer visits. I've kept my promise, and I have no intention of breaking it."

Arabella nodded sharply with her eyes focused on the elegant shapes of the far garden. "I think it's time for you to go, John. I'm sure you can show yourself out."

John closed his eyes for a moment and gave her a weary nod. "Please, Arabella, think about what I said. It comes from a place of love, truly."

Arabella said nothing, made no movement. She simply stared off into the distance. John sighed and saw himself out of the house. Arabella listened to his footsteps receding, and when she was sure he could not hear her, she put her face in her hands and sobbed.

CHAPTER XI

Wherein Croquet Is Played and a Watch Stops

I REALLY WISH YOU'D TELL ME WHAT HAPPENED WITH JOHN, ARABELLA," Rowena said as they strolled arm in arm toward the broad swath of lawn past the formal gardens of Blackstone Manor, lagging behind their sisters. The day was bright and sparkling, with the refreshing sea breeze keeping the unseasonable early June heat from becoming unbearable. "Moria told me he came for a visit but left in a hurry without a proper good-bye, and now you won't say a word about it. What happened?"

"Nothing worth mentioning," Arabella said as she mashed her lips into a hard line.

"I don't believe it for a minute, Ari," Rowena stopped and looked at her sister. "You'll talk about inconsequential things; it's the important things that keep you silent."

Arabella sighed and closed her eyes. "He said some hurtful things, Ro, and I'd rather just forget about it."

"I know John can be a little caustic sometimes," Rowena said with a frown. "But it's hard to believe he would say something to hurt you on purpose."

"Oh, don't you start with that," Arabella yanked her arm out of Rowena's and her face colored. "He said the same thing, that he was saying it out of love, and I just can't believe that someone would say something so hurtful to someone they love."

Rowena shut her jaw with a click. "You do realize that now I'm absolutely on fire with curiosity over what he said?"

"Please don't make me..." Arabella turned her face away from her sister.

"Ari, whatever it was obviously hurt you. I just want to help. Will you talk to me, please?" She put her hand on Arabella's shoulder.

Arabella lifted her face to the bright sky and blinked several times to clear unshed tears from her eyes. Then she took a deep breath and clasped her hands in front of her.

"John thinks I should leave Mother's house and come live with Father," she said, turning toward Rowena.

"What? Why?" Rowena's eyes widened, startled. "What purpose would that serve?"

"That's just what I said," said Arabella with a shake of her head, throwing up her hands. "John thinks that I will never marry so long as I live with Mother. He thinks that no one in the witch community will want to marry me for fear of avatic children, and that no one in the normal community will want me because I have the taint of witches. Once Mother is dead, I'll become a burden on one of you, the maiden aunt. He seems to think Vivienne or Amelia is the most likely candidate for my keeper."

"But..." Rowena started.

"That's not all," Arabella said, her words coming out in a rush now that the dam was broken. "He thinks I'm unsafe in Mother's house because I'm a brown bud and therefore not worth protecting, and he thinks the Kensington Garden incident just proves it. John thinks I can have a better life in their home because Father might be able to use his influence to get me a husband and I could have a normal life."

"That's just absolutely ridiculous," Rowena said. "Mother may play favorites sometimes, but she would never let you be in danger. And how would being married to some mundane man be better than your life in the witch community? That's just preposterous!"

Arabella shook her head. "But there is some truth in what he said, Ro. Why would anyone be interested in marrying me? Anyone from the Houses will fear that I will bear more brown buds and anyone not of the Houses will fear that my children will have magic. I'm not a witch with any marketable skills either. He's probably right that I'm going to be a sour old spinster living off the generosity of one of my sisters."

"Arabella, have you thought about, well, you know..." Rowena said as she twisted her fingers together and furrowed her brow. "Those new things you've been seeing and doing?"

Arabella let out a short bark of a laugh. "Let Mother or anyone else know that I have some sort of affinity for machines? Rowena, you're not thinking straight. Mother would disown me and then I'd *have* to go live with Father. Everyone knows that all magic comes from natural sources. I have no idea what is going on with me, Ro, but it can't be magic."

Rowena caught Arabella's hand in both of her own. "Ari, I don't know what the future holds, after all, I didn't get Grandmother's talent for prophecy, but you can't just give up. Besides, even if you don't find a husband, you can always live with me. You wouldn't be a burden at all, you're my best friend."

The girls hugged each other close and Arabella tried to force back tears. They broke apart when Elizabeth called to them from the lawn.

"Come on, you two," she called, motioning them closer. "Stop lollygagging!"

"We're coming!" Rowena called. She grabbed Arabella's hand and squeezed it hard. They continued down to the lawn hand in hand to join their sisters. Jessamine and Josephine watched their arrival with gimlet eyes. Jessamine leaned in to whisper something in her sister's ear, but Josephine shook her head sharply. Jessamine looked confused and bit her lip.

Nathaniel and Harlan were already on the lawn waiting for the Sortilege sisters. They had installed wire hoops in the grass and stood next to a collection of brightly colored balls and long wooden mallets with broad grins on their faces. The servants had set up tables and chairs with glasses and pitchers of lemonade off to the side so that they could have a comfortable place to observe whatever entertainment the young men had planned for them.

"So, what is this game you've got all set up for us?" said Vivienne as she stroked her hand over her five-month belly. She wore one of her mother's old high-waisted maternity gowns, fluttering in the breeze. The cornflower blue complimented her glowing complexion and Nathaniel gazed at her with adoring eyes. Harlan flushed a bit at Vivienne's condition, but since Blackstone House and Thornfire House had formally agreed to his betrothal to Amelia, they were quite nearly related. In the witching world it was nothing to see your sister heavy with child at the family home.

"It's a new game called croquet," said Harlan, bouncing from his heels to his toes to hide his unease. "Although, it's apparently very similar to a game in France called Pell Mell, at least according to your Jeanette."

"It isn't physically taxing, is it?" Elizabeth said as she scanned the broad lawn with hooded eyes and the generous space between the wickets as she pursed her lips.

"Oh no," said Nathaniel. "It's a gentle enough sport that even Vivienne can play in her delicate condition." He reached out and caught her hand, bringing it up for a gentle kiss. Vivienne rewarded him with an indulgent smile.

"We can't all play at once," Harlan said. "It's played in two teams of two, so we'll have to take turns."

"Who gets to play first?" asked Amelia.

Harlan favored her with a wide grin. "Nathaniel and I thought perhaps the couples could play, you and me, and he and Vivienne, and the rest of the ladies can watch to learn the rules. Then the winner of our round can play the next team."

"That sounds delightful," Amelia laughed and clapped her hands together.

The rest of the ladies murmured their approval of the plan, and Arabella, Rowena, and Elizabeth retired to the table while Nathaniel and Harlan launched into the complexities of how to hold a mallet and where to try to hit the ball with Vivienne and Amelia. Jessamine and Josephine flopped into the grass at the edge of the croquet field, in front of the table, and began to pluck blades of grass and weave them into knots.

"I do hope this won't be a dull afternoon," Elizabeth said.

Rowena sighed and shook her head. "You can't even let the entertainment start before you complain about it being dull, can you?"

"I only said I hoped it wouldn't be dull," Elizabeth pouted. "I didn't say it was dull already."

Rowena chuckled and shared a glance with Arabella, who smiled back. At the other end of the croquet field Amelia squealed with delight over whacking the ball solidly for the first time. Nathaniel and Vivienne giggled behind their hands because she'd hit the wrong ball, and in the wrong direction. Harlan trotted off with a laugh and a smile to rescue it as it rolled past the boundary of play.

Jessamine's head jerked up and she gasped. She looked at Arabella first, and then at Josephine. "Should I tell them now?" she asked.

"Not yet, darling," Josephine said as she patted her hand.

"When?" Jessamine asked with a frown.

"They'll find out on their own like they are supposed to, just finish your weaving."

Jessamine cocked her head to the side and regarded her sister with narrowed eyes. Then she shrugged and turned back to the grass in her hands, humming tunelessly.

"Who will find out what, Jo?" Elizabeth asked.

Josephine turned to the girls at the table and smiled, then put her finger to her lips. She said not a word and turned back to the knotted grass in her hands with a giggle. Jessamine began to giggle too, and the twins put their heads together in mirth.

"Lunatics," Elizabeth muttered. "Sometimes I wonder whether or not Mother should just have them put away."

"What an awful thing to say!" Rowena said. "Just because they are eccentric there's no reason to lock them away."

"Eccentric is just the nice way of saying crazy," Elizabeth said as she stuck out her tongue at Rowena.

A bright red ball bounced past Jessamine and Josephine's feet with Nathaniel quick after it, laughing as he went. The players at the other end of the field were also laughing over Vivienne's wild stroke. Nathaniel plucked the ball from underneath a holly bush that marked the edge of the formal garden and waved it over his head as he turned around, calling to the others that he had found it. As he jogged back to the playing field, he stopped at the table for a generous swig of lemonade after he tucked the ball under his elbow. He reached into his waistcoat to pull out his silver pocket watch, clicking open the engraved cover to reveal its ornate face. He frowned for a moment, then chuckled.

"You've killed another one, my love," he called to Vivienne as he held it out at arm's length dangling it on its chain, twirling and sparkling in the sun.

Vivienne's laughter carried over the field. "Then I suppose I know what your anniversary present is… Again!"

Nathaniel tossed the stopped watch on the table without a backward glance. "Maybe I can have one of those filigreed brass ones this time?" he said as he trotted back across the grass to the rest of the players.

The pocket watch slid across the table and stopped mere inches from Arabella's fingertips. She looked away and bit her lip, carefully tucking her hands in her lap. She focused first on the sea birds circling overhead, then tried to keep her attention on the game, but her eyes kept wandering back to the watch.

The glow was vanishing, the silvery sheen swiftly fading to a dull pewter. Arabella clutched her hands tight in her lap because they itched with the urge to reach out and touch the watch. She glanced around at her sisters—Rowena watched the game with polite interest while Elizabeth examined her nails, then fidgeted with one of her curls. Jessamine and Josephine sat where they had been, but their eyes were now fixed on Arabella. Their hands lay still in their laps, grass weaving forgotten. Jessamine's eyes were wide and she nodded encouragement to Arabella.

Arabella closed her eyes tight and shook her head as if to clear it, clutching her hands even tighter in her lap until her knuckles turned white. When she opened her eyes, the glow was almost gone and she could no longer help herself. She snatched the watch off the table and tucked it into her lap. She looked around at her sisters again. Rowena and Elizabeth hadn't noticed at all, and Josephine had turned back to her grass weaving. Only Jessamine acknowledged Arabella in any way. She smiled and nodded once, sharply, before she turned back to her own grass weaving.

The watch she clutched felt hot, like it was fevered. Arabella glanced down, parting her hands just enough to see the timepiece. The glow had stabilized, and Arabella couldn't be sure but she thought it might be the slightest bit brighter. She closed her hands tight over it again, and once again surveyed her surroundings. No one was looking at her. No one seemed to notice her flush or quickened breathing. She took a deep breath and tried to steady herself.

Arabella closed her eyes and reached down into the pocket watch with her consciousness. She almost whimpered at the poor little gears seized together and the springs wound tight with nowhere to move. The mechanics fairly screamed to be let loose to do their job, to tick and tock and count off the minutes and hours and days and serve their purpose with pride. Arabella huddled in closer to the watch, her brow furrowing as she dug deeper to discover what the matter was. She probed with her mind until she found it, streamers of black energy wrapped tight around each gear, nearly smothering the main spring. As if she were picking loose wool caught on the low branches of bushes, Arabella teased out each thread and let it flap in an unseen psychic breeze. For every piece she released, the watch felt less fevered and she imagined that if she had opened her eyes she would see the glow getting brighter and brighter. She finally fished out the last stubborn streamer of black energy, and she felt the little watch tick again. Each release of the gears, each push of the springs, pulsed in her hands and Arabella let out a loud sigh of relief, her shoulders dropping from tension she hadn't realized she'd been holding.

"What are you doing?" Elizabeth's voice came sharp and hot. Arabella's eyes flew open and she blinked hard against the sudden brightness. Elizabeth was staring at her with a thunderous look on her face, and even Rowena was looking at her quizzically.

"Nothing," Arabella said. Her voice didn't sound convincing to her own ears.

"Nothing has you all hunched over and breathing like you've run a race, then sighing like a lovesick schoolgirl?" Elizabeth raised an eyebrow. "Somehow, I'm having trouble believing you, sister dear."

Arabella felt her stomach drop at the note of menace in Elizabeth's voice. She threw Rowena a stricken look.

"Elizabeth," Rowena said. "Don't be uncharitable. Arabella probably just isn't feeling well. The sun is a bit much for you, isn't it, sweetheart?"

"Yes," said Arabella, licking her lips. "Yes, it must be the sun. I'm suddenly feeling very light headed."

"Well then," Rowena said as she stood. "I'll just walk you up to the house and you can have a nice lie down."

"That would be lovely," Arabella said as she stood herself. She still clutched the watch in her hands in front of her. She had nowhere to hide it.

"What are you hiding there?" Elizabeth hissed.

Arabella shook her head slowly from side to side, jaw working but unable to speak. Trembling, she stepped back a pace. Elizabeth shot forward out of her seat and snatched the pocket watch from Arabella's numb fingers.

Elizabeth turned the watch over in her hands and frowned. "Why would you want to steal Nathaniel's broken pocket watch?" The minute hand ticked forward again and Elizabeth started. She looked from the watch, to Arabella, to Nathaniel and back to the watch again with her mouth agape.

"Nathaniel," she shouted, holding the timepiece aloft, fingers curled tight around the body and the chain swirling around her upraised arm. "Your watch is still working, come see!"

Nathaniel looked up from his interrupted croquet stroke with a frown on his face. "But I'm sure it was stopped," he called. He passed the mallet to Harlan and walked over to Elizabeth, who handed him the watch with a smirk on her face and a sidelong look at Arabella. Arabella put her hands over her mouth, still shaking her head, and took another step back.

"Arabella was trying to steal it," Elizabeth said in a voice loud enough so that even the players still on the field could hear her clearly.

"Elizabeth!" Rowena's voice was full of shock and she put an arm around Arabella's shoulders. Jessamine and Josephine scrambled to their feet and stood close together holding each other's hands. Vivienne, Amelia, and Harlan exchanged glances and shocked exclamations, then came to join the group around the table.

"What do you mean Arabella was trying to steal it, Elizabeth?" Vivienne said as she stepped up to her husband's side.

"Nathaniel left his watch on the table, then Arabella took it and tried to hide it. She was making some silly excuse about not feeling well so she could take it up to the house, to hide it, no doubt."

"But what would Arabella want with a stopped pocket watch?" Vivienne tilted her head to the side and looked at Nathaniel with confusion. Nathaniel shrugged with a similar look of confusion on his face.

"But it's not stopped!" Elizabeth exclaimed. "Just look at it! I saw the minute hand move myself."

Nathaniel popped open the cover again and looked down at the watch in his hand. "The time is different than when I left it on the table." He waited a moment. "Ah, the minute hand did move, but it's a bit sluggish." He handed the watch to Vivienne.

"It's completely stopped for me. It was probably on its last legs and moving slowly before," Vivienne said after she examined the face herself, then handed it back to Nathaniel with a shrug. "Elizabeth, it is completely unacceptable to accuse your own sister of improper behavior and we shall have to bring this to Mother's attention. But Arabella, it is not polite to take something that isn't yours, even if it is broken. You should have asked Nathaniel if you could have it if you wanted it, though I'm not sure what you would want it for."

"Oh, I don't mind at all. You can have it if you want it, Arabella," Nathaniel said as he stepped forward already holding out the watch.

Arabella stepped back and tucked her hands under her elbows. "Oh, no, thank you. I was just looking at it before. I didn't really want it."

"Liar!" Elizabeth knotted her fists at her sides and stamped her foot. "You took it on purpose! You wanted it for something!"

"Elizabeth," Vivienne reproved her sister. "That is hardly behavior becoming of a lady, especially one of the Sortilege line. Mother will hear about this."

"Mother should hear about what she was doing," Elizabeth said as she stabbed her finger at Arabella. "She was doing something that made the watch work again. I saw her with her eyes closed and breathing hard, just like any of us do when we are working a difficult spell for the first time."

"A spell with a pocket watch? Why, that's just preposterous," Vivienne tilted back her head and laughed with Amelia joining in quickly. "You need to go back to your earliest lessons, Elizabeth. Magic is of nature, not of mechanics."

"Elizabeth, you've been surly all afternoon," Rowena said. "Perhaps you ought to go up to the house for a lie down yourself."

"But I saw it! I did!" Elizabeth protested. "Make her do it again. You said the watch is stopped for certain this time. I don't know what she did, but she can do it again and the watch will work."

Vivienne rubbed her temples and sighed. "Arabella, will you please take the watch from Nathaniel so that we can prove to Elizabeth that there is nothing going on before she passes out from apoplexy?"

Arabella backed up again and looked to Rowena. "There's nothing... I couldn't..."

"Arabella," Vivienne put her hands on her hips. "Just do it so we don't have the whole day spoiled."

Rowena shook her head and held up helpless hands, while Jessamine chanted *do it, do it, do it* in a whisper. Arabella's shoulders drooped in defeat and she held out her hand to Nathaniel. He placed the open watch on her palm. Arabella stood that way for several moments, her face turned away from everyone and her arm outstretched. She ignored the pressure in her head to pull the black streamers from the innards of the watch, planted there by Elizabeth and her sudden wash of emotion, so that it could work freely again.

"Well?" said Vivienne finally.

Nathaniel stared at the watch where it lay in the flat of Arabella's palm for a long minute before he shrugged and said, "It's still not working."

Vivienne took in a breath and began to turn to Elizabeth, but Elizabeth interrupted her. "That's not the way she did it before! She has to close her hands over it and hold it close. She has to close her eyes." Elizabeth thrust out her chin in defiance.

Vivienne sighed and pinched the bridge of her nose. "Arabella? If you please?" she asked.

Arabella let out her breath and brought the watch over her heart, clasping both hands over it and closing her eyes. The pressure to reach out and release the gears and springs from their bondage was too much. She stifled a sob and ripped the black streamers away from the springs and gears. The work went faster, it was easier this time. In two breaths, the watch ticked merrily along in her clasped hands. Arabella allowed herself another slow breath to enjoy it before she unclasped her hands and presented them, open, with the watch cover open for all to see. She kept her eyes squinched shut and waited for the blow she was sure would come.

"It's working!" she heard Nathaniel cry as if from as distance. She was sure she was going to pass out any moment.

"I told you!" crowed Elizabeth. Then there was silence. Arabella did not move or open her eyes. She heard footsteps and could feel the body heat of someone standing in front of her, close.

"Arabella," Vivienne's voice was as soft as a feather, but it carried threads of steel. "What is going on?"

Arabella opened her eyes and the tears that had been trapped there tumbled down her cheeks and she sobbed. "I don't know."

"How long has this been going on?" Vivienne asked, her voice still soft and slow.

"Since Mr. Westerfeld's demonstration of the Distinction Engine." Arabella let her hands drop, but held on to the watch and wiped her nose with the back of her right hand.

Vivienne grabbed her right wrist and began to drag her up the lawn to the house. "Mother needs to know about this."

The rest of the group followed her in silence, their game and refreshments lying out in the sun, forgotten.

CHAPTER XII

Wherein an Uncomfortable Revelation Is Made

ARABELLA STRUGGLED TO KEEP UP AS VIVIENNE DRAGGED HER INTO Blackstone Manor by her wrist. She felt like a felon being led to the gallows, her eyes already swollen from weeping. Around her the family displayed a gamut of emotions. Nathaniel and Harlan looked confused while Vivienne and Amelia looked determined. Elizabeth looked triumphant, and Jessamine and Josephine were grinning wildly and skipping. Rowena followed right behind looking like she was about to burst into tears. They all stopped in front of their mother's desk and waited for permission to speak.

Minerva Sortilege looked up from the paperwork covering her desk and sighed at the sight of all seven of her daughters, along with her son-in-law and future son-in-law, waiting expectantly for her to speak.

"This had better not just be some playroom argument. At least you are all not arguing at the top of your lungs this time," she said, peering over the top of her half-moon glasses. "What seems to be the trouble, *children*?" She emphasized the last word with a frown.

"It's Arabella…" Elizabeth began with her voice full of glee.

Vivienne silenced her with a glare. "It seems, Mother, that our Arabella may have developed some unusual new abilities."

Mother gasped and dropped the fountain pen she had been holding. She stood and clapped her hands together. "At last! At last!"

She cried and sprang from behind the desk to pull Arabella into a tight embrace, pulling her wrist out of Vivienne's hand.

"I'd despaired that you would ever come to your true birthright, but Mother Earth has finally seen fit to bless us." She held Arabella out at arm's length by her shoulders, tears in her eyes. "I'm so proud."

"That's not what I meant, Mother," Vivienne said. Arabella felt as though she were on the verge of weeping again.

Mother frowned. "What do you mean? You said she's developed her abilities, didn't you?" She turned to Arabella and smiled with real warmth. "What is it, chickadee? Are you levitating things? Perhaps you dowsed for water?" Arabella started to sob and shut her eyes, her head wobbling back and forth in negative. She couldn't bear to meet her mother's gaze.

"Oh, you poor thing," she said as she pulled Arabella close to her and stroked her hair. "Magic is rather overwhelming the first time it courses through your veins. Why you should have heard Vivienne wail the first time she levitated her doll." Arabella froze in her mother's embrace, torn between fearing what her mother would do when she heard the truth and wanting to finally be able to bask in her mother's affection and pride.

Vivienne blushed bright red. "Mother, I don't think you understand me. Arabella is doing something, but it's not magic. It's downright unnatural."

"Not magic?" Mother furrowed her brow and tried to look at Arabella's face where it was tucked into her shoulder. "Arabella, what have you done?" Arabella began to sob harder.

Mother squared her jaw and guided Arabella into her desk chair, where she slumped forward and wept into her hands. She turned and swept her daughters with a fearsome glare.

"Someone had better start explaining what is going on this instant," she said in the same tone of voice the girls had grown used to hearing whenever their childhood arguments had grown too large and involved magic and breaking things or each other. Nathaniel and Harlan fairly wilted under her gaze. Elizabeth took a breath to begin speaking, but Mother held up her hand for silence.

"But first, perhaps the gentlemen should occupy themselves elsewhere, since this seems to be a private matter."

Harlan and Nathaniel immediately started bobbing their heads and backing out of the room. "I think that's a lovely idea, Mother

Sortilege. We should go clean up the croquet equipment, shouldn't we, Harlan?"

"Absolutely, Nathaniel," said Harlan in a tremulous voice. And with that, the men were gone and it was just the women. Arabella's sobs had slowed to fitful sniffs, but she still sat with her head bowed, staring down at her fingers laced tight together around the pocket watch in her lap.

"Now," Mother focused on Vivienne. "Tell me what is going on."

"I think it might be easier to show you," Vivienne said. "Arabella, do you still have the pocket watch?" Arabella nodded without raising her head.

"Give it here," said Vivienne as she extended her hand. Arabella held out her own trembling hand with the watch, again with her head still bowed. Vivienne sighed with exasperation and stepped forward to snatch it from her shuddering fingers. She popped open the cover and showed it to her mother.

"You see the watch working?" she said.

"Of course, I do, Vivienne. It's Nathaniel's watch and it seems to be working just fine. You might want to see that watchmaker again when this one eventually fails. It's lasted quite a while for a witch household."

"It already failed today, Mother. It stopped while we were playing croquet." When her mother frowned, crossing her arms over her chest, Vivienne said, "Observe."

Vivienne cupped her hands around the silver timepiece and shut her eyes. She reached out with her mind and pumped magic into it until the gears ground to a halt. It only took a moment. In her seat, Arabella whimpered and clutched the armrests with white knuckles, but still she didn't raise her head.

Vivienne held out the watch to her mother again and said, "What do you see?"

"The watch stopped," said Mother with a shrug. "But that's nothing unusual. Magic and technology don't work well together."

Vivienne thrust the watch out to Arabella and said, "Arabella, fix it."

Arabella whimpered again. "Please don't make me." Her voice came out in a strangled whisper.

"Fix it, now," Vivienne demanded and she shook the watch at Arabella.

Arabella lifted her tear-streaked face and took the watch from Vivienne. She looked around at her sisters and settled on her mother, and said, "I'm sorry."

She cupped the watch in her hands and closed her eyes to see the thick web of cottony black streamers wrapped around the gears and springs where Vivienne had put them. It was even easier to get rid of them than the last time. It was as if she exhaled and all the darkness disappeared on a psychic wind. Between one breath and the next, the watch sprang to life again and Arabella felt like each tick echoed off the walls around her. She held the watch out to Vivienne, her eyes screwed shut on her tears.

Vivienne took the watch and held it out to her mother. "See?"

Mother glanced at the watch with half-lidded eyes, but when the minute hand moved smoothly from the five to the six, her eyes flew open and her brows shot up. Her jaw dropped and she grabbed the watch from Vivienne to look closer, holding it up to her ear to hear the ticking.

"You see what I mean?" Vivienne said as she crossed her arms and stared at Arabella with a pensive face. "What are we going to do about this? She said it started at the Distinction Engine demonstration at Mr. Westerfeld's."

Mother traced a finger around the edge of the watch face, and with hardly a thought she dumped enough magic into it to stop it cold. Then she clicked the cover shut and placed it on her desk. "Ladies," she said. "I think Arabella and I need to have a private discussion. If you please…?" She gestured toward the door.

They all exchanged startled looks but it was Vivienne who spoke up. "But, Mother, this is a family matter and I think we should all be present for the discussion."

"I decide what is a family matter and what is not, Vivienne," Mother's voice was full of steel. "You may decide what family matters are when you are the head of the household, but not until then."

"Yes, Mother," Vivienne said as she blushed and meekly hung her head. She straightened and nodded to the other girls. They all curtseyed to their mother and trooped out of her library without another word. Once the door was shut behind them, she turned to Arabella with her hands on her hips.

"What is the meaning of all this?" Arabella winced at her mother's soft tone holding the hidden menace of a snake in the tall grass.

"I don't know, Mother," Arabella hiccupped as she wiped the half-dried tears from her cheeks. "I started seeing glows around machines at Mr. Westerfeld's demonstration and ever since I've been able to make machines do things with my mind. I'd hoped it would go away, but if anything, it's been getting stronger." She sniffed and looked up at her mother with worried eyes.

Mother began to pace back and forth and tapped her chin with her fingertips. "It's entirely possible that you're manifesting some sort of metallurgical magic talent. It's not a common talent, especially in our line, but it is possible." She whirled to face her daughter. "Have you been able to access any other talents since this started? Telepathy? Telekinesis? Dowsing?"

Arabella shook her head and bit her lip. Her mother resumed pacing and tapping.

"It would be rare indeed for your power to be so focused on one thing. Most witches can access at least two of the talents, and with training can unlock more. You would think with all of the talent coming down our line that you would be able to do at least as much as the weakest of witches." She whirled again to face Arabella. "Have you even tried to access any other talents?"

Arabella shook her head again. Her mother hauled her out of the chair and pulled her across the room to the more practical end of her study. Her personal workbench, laid out neat and orderly with some of the finest accoutrements available for magical practice, faced a broad bay window looking out on the rose bush area of the formal gardens. Arabella felt her stomach clench at the sight. Throughout her childhood and adolescence this very spot had been the site of many torturous afternoons as her mother tried to unlock the magic she insisted was within her. Once more, Mother laid out the common magic test necessities—a small dish of clear water, an unlit white candle, a peacock feather in a narrow silver bud vase, a potted lily with several unopened buds, and a deck of tarot cards. Arabella twisted her fingers together to try to keep them from shaking.

"We'll start with some simple telekinesis, like so." Mother said. She barely glanced at the peacock feather before mentally lifting it up out of the vase, turning it around, and returning it neatly, quill down. She gestured to Arabella and said, "Now, you try."

Arabella squared her shoulders and stilled her mind as her mother had always told her to do. She focused her gaze on the feather, first thinking about how the heft of it would feel in her fingers, then imagining it lifting into the air. Nothing happened. She shook her head like a wet dog and settled her stance a little wider. Clutching her hands in fists at her side, she shut her eyes and tried again, focusing on the feather and only the feather. In her mind's eye she saw exactly what she wanted it to do. But when she opened her physical eyes the feather remained ensconced in the vase. Arabella let out her breath in a *whoosh* and shook her hands out.

"So telekinesis is still not your talent," Mother said. Arabella pressed her lips together and nodded.

"Let's try the candle exercise then, like so," Mother said. She passed one hand over the candle and the wick jumped to life in flame; she passed it back over the candle and the flame disappeared. She nodded to Arabella.

Arabella repeated her mother's actions. Nothing. She tried again. Still nothing. Grimacing, she lifted her hand for a third try, but Mother said, "Enough. Move on to air manipulation."

In the still air of the room, from across the workbench, Mother flexed her right index finger and the peacock feather twirled around in the bud vase. Arabella took a deep breath and shook out her shoulders, then imitated the gesture. The feather didn't twitch. She raised her whole hand and made a pushing motion to mimic the force she tried to produce with her mind, but the feather remained still. Arabella grimaced.

Mother shook her head. "Water," she said as she twirled her index finger over the dish of water, creating a tiny whirlpool, which she then flattened out with the palm of her hand held eight inches above the dish. She nodded to Arabella. Once again, Arabella followed her mother's example, used all of the mental tricks her mother and sisters had previously suggested to unleash the power of her mind, but the water remained flat and still as glass. Mother frowned deeply and an intense furrow appeared between her eyes.

"Let's see if you've developed any talent for earth magic," she said with a sigh. "As you seem to be controlling metals, that may be where your talents lie."

"But we've never practiced anything with earth magic, you and I," Arabella said, twisting her fingers together again.

"Then it's about time we started, isn't it?" Mother said as she walked down the length of the worktable to the potted lily. "Perhaps that was my mistake before, thinking that earth magic would be too advanced for you because you couldn't manage the simpler tasks."

Arabella blushed and bit her lip. "What do I have to do?"

"It's very simple and quite complex all at once," Mother said as she contemplated the lily. "You simply encourage the plant to bloom, but getting it to hear you in the first place requires some finesse. Like so." Mother stroked her forefinger down one of the unopened buds. The moment her finger left the waxy surface, the petals peeled back and the flower opened in full bloom, filling the work area with its heady scent. Mother then took a step back and gestured for Arabella to step up to the plant.

"But a lily is so different from a pocket watch," Arabella protested as she stepped up to the plant.

"Don't whine," Mother said. "You said you saw the glow, the mark of magic, and that you've made machines do your bidding. Simply access the same part of your mind and tell the lily to bloom."

Arabella nodded and then closed her eyes, thinking about how things had felt when she made the pocket watch run again. She reached out with her mind in the direction of the plant, searching for the glow or any feeling at all. There was nothing. Arabella frowned and drew on the same power she'd used on the watch anyway, and reached out with a blind hand until her finger tips touched a waxy bud. She kept her eyes shut and poured in the same energy she had with the watch. When she heard her mother gasp, her eyes flew open. Not only was the lily bud still stubbornly closed, it had browned where she touched and had begun to droop.

"Moving on to telepathy," Mother said in a clipped, harsh voice as she went around the table to retrieve the tarot cards. Without shuffling them she drew the top card and held it so she could see it but Arabella could not. "I'm thinking very hard of the card I'm looking at, what do I see?" she asked with her eyes boring deep into Arabella.

"Nine of Wands?" Arabella's voice came out in a squeak.

"No." Mother tossed the Empress face up on the workbench and drew another card. "Again."

Arabella swallowed hard and thought for a moment. "The Hanged Man?"

"No!" Mother tossed down the Three of Cups and drew another card. "Again!"

"Five of Pentacles?" Arabella blurted in a trembling voice.

"No!" she shouted as she slapped down The Lovers. "Are you even trying?"

"Yes, Mother, I am trying. I'm trying very hard," Arabella said as she clenched her jaw and felt the anger and frustration of a lifetime's aggravation well up inside her.

"Collect yourself, Arabella, and we'll try a prophecy exercise," Mother said. She waited for Arabella to take a few deep breaths, blinking and looking up at the ceiling. After a few moments she said, "Ready?" and Arabella nodded.

"What is the next card I will draw?" Mother asked.

Arabella shut her eyes and clasped her hands in front of herself. "The Emperor."

Mother laid down the Six of Wands. "And the next?" she said.

"The Two of Pentacles," Arabella said.

Mother laid down The Hierophant. "And the next?"

Arabella was silent for a long moment, tracing her bottom lip with her tongue. "The Fool?"

She laid out the Ace of Pentacles with a sigh and pinched the bridge of her nose.

Arabella opened her eyes and asked, "How did I do?"

"You couldn't even guess a card in the correct Arcana, Arabella. You got nothing right." Mother's voice was weary. She threw down the rest of the cards and they scattered across the work bench. "What is wrong with you, Arabella? I've given you everything, the finest blood line, the best education, and still you can't manage a bloody thing." She turned to Arabella with her jaw clenched and her fists curled at her sides.

"But what about this?" Arabella said as she scampered over to her mother's desk and retrieved the pocket watch. This time she didn't even have to close her eyes, she just pulled out the dark streamers of magic like a bit of cotton stuffing and cast them away on the psychic wind. She held out the ticking watch to her mother.

"I don't want useless parlor tricks from you," her mother cried as she snatched up the watch and hurled it at an oak bookcase, where it shattered into pieces and scattered all over the floor. "I want you to fulfill the destiny I meant for you!"

"Well, I can't do that," Arabella shouted as she gestured to the workbench with her right hand. "But I can do that." She pointed to the smashed watch with her left.

"Fine," Mother growled. "If you want to impress me with that mechanical rubbish, I have something you can do."

She grabbed Arabella's wrist, dragging her out of her work room past her sisters still gathered outside the door, arguing in low voices. Arabella stumbled along behind her mother down the stairs and into the front hall, where they stopped in front of the enormous grandfather clock. It was as wide as two people standing shoulder to shoulder and soared nearly to the height of the vaulted ceiling. For as long as Arabella could remember, it had been silent and stuck at fifty-nine minutes past eleven. Her mother clutched her shoulders from behind and thrust her toward the clock. Arabella's sisters stood on the stairs, wide-eyed with their mouths agape.

"Your father built this clock as a gift to me when we first married, and he built it so sturdily that it continued to work in a household of witches for over fifteen years. It stopped the moment you were born." Mother leaned into Arabella's ear and hissed. "This is why we thought you were the chosen one, the powerful witch of the prophecy. We thought you stopped the clock. If you wish to impress me, make these clockworks move."

Arabella looked back at her mother, then at the clock. She took two slow steps forward, letting her fingers trace over the shape of the ivy circling up Doric columns carved into burnished red wood making up the sides of the clock. She'd never really given the clock much thought, it had just always been there. No one ever talked about it, and questions were strongly discouraged. An intricate compass rose took up the glass inset in the door to the massive compartment that showed the bright brass pendulum. Arabella let her fingertips drift along the grooves in the glass as her eyes traced upward to the clock face. Now that she knew her father had built it, the mix of alchemical and magical symbols on the face made sense. The wood around the face was carved with all manner of corvids—ravens, crows, rooks, and the like. The most impressive were the two ravens perched right above twelve, facing each other, with a scrolled banner proclaiming the names Huginn and Muninn. A wreath of oak leaves crowned the top, with fist-sized acorns for finials at the corners. Carved down the sides of the cabinet was a mix of dryads, satyrs, and the greatest alchemical minds from Rome of the far past, all sitting on branches and thick vines, hidden amongst leaves of oak and ivy. There was not a single uncarved surface anywhere on the grandfather clock. Even the narrow edges of the wooden

frame of the compass-rose door were carved with tiny, twisting knotwork.

Arabella opened her senses and touched the clock with her mind as she did with her hand. The grandfather clock was swathed with more magic than she'd thought would be possible, even for being in a house full of witches. Thick layers spiraled around every mechanism and stuck out in clumps at odd angles. With hardly any effort at all she began to tear great handfuls off and toss them away behind her. She heard her sisters gasp, but she paid them no mind. However, the grandfather clock did not behave as the pocket watch had. She'd pulled away huge hunks of magic, but she couldn't feel the clockworks straining to be free as she had before. Something else held them still.

Arabella frowned and shut her eyes. She laid her hands on both sides of the pendulum case and leaned her forehead onto the glass. The clockworks remained still but full of expectation, like standing outside alone in the gloaming waiting for the first star to appear so you could make a wish. Something *other* lay beneath the thick blankets of magic holding the clockworks still. Arabella burrowed down, yanking off the black streamers and tufts with furious speed. Yet she still could not see what held the clockworks in abeyance.

Without opening her eyes, she popped the catch on the pendulum case door and swung it open. She dropped to her knees and leaned forward. Reaching out for the grand pendulum, which seemed big enough to be a shield for an errant knight of old, she grasped the edges of the pendulum in both hands. Her body stiffened as shockwaves of power, pure golden power, coursed through her veins and every nerve ending. She could see now what held the clockworks so still.

Seven golden bands of power wrapped in a star pattern around the clockworks. Each one had a word emblazoned on it. The first read "bravery" and when Arabella touched it with her mind it fell away. For the first time she could feel the clockworks begin to strain against their bonds, ready to go to work again counting off the minutes and hours and days. The second band read "compassion" and it also fell away when Arabella touched it. The third band, stretched horizontal across the clockworks, said "sisterhood." Arabella cast it away and looked at the next band in confusion. Rather than letters it was etched with pictograms, whatever it said was a mystery to Arabella. When she touched it, it didn't fall away as the others had. She ran her mental fingertips down the pictograms, memorizing their shape. Then she wrapped her mental hand around the band and pulled as hard as she could. It resisted her for a moment, and then it too fell away.

Panting, Arabella felt her physical body sag forward until the cool brass of the pendulum pressed against her forehead. Her body screamed at her to stop, every muscle in her body trembled with exhaustion, but Arabella pressed on. She had to make the clockworks move and prove to her mother she was worth something.

The next band was emblazoned with the word "war," and red flames licking up and down its surface. It burned her as she cast it away and Arabella could hear her own voice cry out as if from very far away. The sixth band said "evolution" and Arabella had barely a moment to reflect on what *that* meant before it melted away under her touch and revealed the final band. It was the largest and thickest one yet. Under it, Arabella could feel the clockworks straining to move, nearly begging her to release them and let them do their job. She let her consciousness stroke across the surface. It didn't burn her, but stayed implacably resistant to her touch. It read "balance."

Arabella dug her fingers in. For a moment the band resisted her, but then her fingers began to sink in, like a hot knife into cold butter. She tensed her hands and checked her grip. Underneath she could feel something swirling that was not the straining clockworks, something that tickled at the edges of her thoughts. Taking a deep breath, Arabella exerted all her might to pry off the final band. She could feel her physical back straining so hard it formed a rigid crescent. The band held. Arabella thought she would burst apart from all the power hammering against her veins. Then the final band shattered. The rush of power and light over her psyche dwarfed the golden rush that had come when she grasped the pendulum for the first time. What she saw in her mind's eye made no sense. There were swirls of dark and light, and keys, many, many keys of every size and shape. It all rushed past her in deafening waves. At the last she heard her own voice as a child whisper in her ear, "Be ready."

Arabella's eyes flew open and her hands dropped from the pendulum, giving it a soft push as she let go. She toppled to the side and laid upon the floor in front of the grandfather clock, trembling and covered in sweat. Her heart hammered against her chest and her breath scraped ragged and shallow in her throat. Her hands—locked in stiff claws before her, as if still clutching the pendulum—vibrated, while her head felt light and disconnected. The cool floor soothed and comforted her fevered cheek.

Above her, the pendulum swung and the clockworks turned. The minute hand ticked up, and for the first time in seventeen years, the clock rang twelve. The complex carillon rang out all through the house.

A sense of darkness smothered Arabella. She just wanted to sleep. Waves of hot and cold washed over her body. Then she felt hands on her shoulders and arms lifting her up.

"Stay with me," she heard Rowena's voice in her ear, though it seemed so very far away. "Please stay with me, darling."

Heat radiated from Rowena's hands and Arabella wanted to bat them away, but she couldn't make her own hands respond. Then her breathing became easier and her heart slowed just a bit. She tried to reach out and push Rowena and her hot hands away, but other hands caught hers and she heard Amelia say, "Not yet."

Arabella groaned as feeling rushed back into her deadened limbs and her heart slowed to a normal pace. She sucked a ragged breath into her hungry lungs, and then another.

"I think she'll be alright now, Rowena," she heard Vivienne say. "You should stop before you hurt yourself."

Arabella felt the hot hands withdraw as she sank down into a deep, dreamless sleep.

CHAPTER XIII

Wherein Arabella Begins Her Recovery

ARABELLA WOKE IN HER OWN BED WITH THE COVERLET TUCKED UP TO her chin. Late afternoon sun slanted across the carpet. The room was quiet. Her head ached and her entire body felt as if she'd spent a week at hard labor. Her stomach growled and let her know it would not be ignored for much longer. Struggling up onto her elbows, she rubbed the sleep from her eyes and tried to remember how she got there.

"Oh, thank goodness!" cried Rowena as she let the book she was reading fall from her lap and clasped her hands to her breast. "I despaired that we might have to work some additional healing spells you'd been under so long."

It all came rushing back to Arabella—the croquet game and the pocket watch, her mother's tests and the grandfather clock, the seven shining gold bands and the last whisper in her ear. *Be ready.* A shiver rippled through Arabella. "How long have I been asleep?" she asked.

"A full day and then some," Rowena said as she bustled to Arabella's bed and felt her forehead with the back of her hand before smoothing Arabella's hair back. She gathered pillows and fluffed them so that she could sit up comfortably. "Just sit back, darling. I'll see about getting some tea and broth from Mrs. Holly so you can start to regain your strength."

Rowena's eyes took on a momentary faraway cast as she as she contacted Mrs. Holly. Arabella waited until Rowena's eyes refocused before she spoke.

"Tea and broth?" she said. "I'm absolutely starving! I want more than tea and broth."

"If the tea and broth stay down, then you may have plain toast," said Rowena. "And if the toast stays down, we'll move on to some scrambled egg."

"What am I, some sort of sickling? I'm starved, Rowena! At least let me have a bit of chicken or cold mutton."

"Arabella," Rowena put her hands on her hips and frowned. "You've never been through recovering from straining too hard on a spell. You'll just have to trust me that this is for the best. The more you cooperate the faster you will recover."

"Spell strain? How can I have spell strain? I'm no witch."

Rowena bit her lip. "Whatever you did, it's like nothing we've ever seen before. But your body reacted exactly like a witch stretching her limits too far. There's obviously something magical about it. Mother, Vivienne, and Amelia have been combing through every text we have in the library to try to account for your unusual power."

As if summoned by their names, their mother and eldest sisters trooped into Arabella's bedroom. They wore the same clothes from two days before and had deep circles under their eyes. Arabella wondered if they'd slept at all since she'd awakened the grandfather clock. Mother nodded to Rowena and joined her at the edge of Arabella's bed, where she laid the back of her hand on Arabella's forehead, and then picked up her wrist and checked her pulse.

"I've already requested tea and broth from Mrs. Holly," Rowena said. "I called you the moment she woke up." Mother nodded again and patted Rowena on the shoulder, then made an indifferent come hither motion that brought a chair sliding across the carpet to right behind her. She settled in and smoothed her skirts before she spoke.

"Well, Arabella," she began. "It seems that we have a lot to talk about. We need to decide what is happening with you and what we are going to do about it. I understand that you are still recovering, but please try to focus your attention as much as you can."

Arabella tilted her head to the side. "Mother, I don't understand."

Mother heaved a great sigh and leaned heavily, clearly exhausted, on the right arm of her chair. "Something has happened to you, Arabella, and we are not quite sure what. We've combed the library and its not inconsiderable resources," she gestured over her shoulder to Vivienne and Amelia. "But we can find no mention of any talent remotely like the power you have exhibited. And yet, everything you've done and the way your body reacts is exactly as any witch would manipulate her talents. The only conclusion I can draw is that we are dealing with some kind of new magical talent."

Behind her Vivienne and Amelia nodded wearily, and Rowena put her hand over her mouth.

"There have been no reports of undiscovered types of magical talents since we pulled humanity out of the Dark Ages and saved them, or as many as we could, from the Black Death," Mother continued. "Five hundred years without a change to our magical landscape, and now *this*." She gestured to Arabella.

"But isn't *this* a good thing, Mother?" Rowena blurted. "I mean, if Arabella is breaking new magical territory, doesn't it mean that she really *could* be the fulfillment of the Cagliostro prophecy?"

"Yes," Mother said as she pinched the bridge of her nose and sighed again. "That is one interpretation. But there may be just as many who think Arabella is an abomination who cannot be allowed to live."

Arabella felt the blood drain from her face. "What?" she squawked. "What do you mean by abomination and not being allowed to live?"

"Arabella, witches have been fighting machines and technology ever since common man started to build them. We've always seen them as unnatural, as dangers to the earth that supports us, and now you come along manipulating machines just like the rest of us might work with air, fire, water, or earth. It's unnatural, and I can be sure that there are those who will see you as a danger and who will want you dead."

Clutching the coverlet in white-knuckled fists, Arabella swallowed hard. "And how do you feel about this, Mother?"

Mother regarded her in silence for a long moment. "I have not made up my mind yet, Arabella. You could be dangerous, or you could be a new adaptation for our kind. After all, we adapted to living openly after the Plague even though we'd hidden for millennia. And in any case, I will do everything I can to protect you. You are my daughter, of Blackstone House and the Sortilege line. Do as I say and I can protect you; if you defy me you could bind my hands in such a way that I cannot."

"Mother," Rowena said after she cleared her throat. "There's something that might help convince the skeptics that Arabella is not a danger and could, in fact, be a benefit to witch society."

Mother looked down her nose at her fifth daughter. "You haven't been hiding anything from me, have you, Rowena? There's been quite enough of that going on."

Rowena and Arabella exchanged guilty glances, but Rowena went on before their mother could question them. "When Arabella fixed the clock, she threw off all that energy."

"I did what?" Arabella said, looking around at her sisters and mother with a confused look on her face.

"You threw off energy, Ari," Rowena said. "As you were doing whatever it was you were doing with the grandfather clock, you threw off these great streamers of energy."

"Yes," said Mother with a nod. "I remember. What was it that you were doing, Arabella? How did you produce that energy?"

"I don't think that I produced it so much as I pulled it out of the clock, Mother," Arabella said. "To my mind's eye it looked like black roving wrapped all around everything. I just pulled it out and threw it behind me."

"There, you see, Mother, that's how Arabella could use her talent. I was able to draw the energy in. That's the only reason I could give her so much when I performed the healing after she collapsed," Rowena said. "Maybe if we frame her power in terms of her being able to provide energy..."

Mother held up her hand to stop the rush of words. "I will not have my daughter treated like some kind of well. Until we are certain of Arabella's position in the Council, no one must speak of this aspect of her power, am I understood?" She looked each of her daughters in the eye and held their gazes until they nodded and agreed to the restriction. Vivienne was the last. "And Vivienne, we will need to watch your child closely to see if she manifests anything like this. Now that we know it's in our line, we must remain vigilant." Vivienne paled, but she nodded again as she clasped protective hands around her belly.

A maid came into the room bearing a tray with a covered bowl and a small pot of tea with a cozy wrapped around it, which she set before Arabella. She stepped back and withdrew a square of creamy white paper from her apron pocket and presented it to Mother.

"This came yesterday afternoon after Miss Arabella collapsed," the maid said. "Mrs. Holly only just remembered it what with all the ruckus and said I ought to bring it up to you."

"Thank you, Edith," said Mother as she took the note. "You may go now." Edith bobbed a curtsey and left.

Mother yanked open the green wax seal and scanned the contents quickly. She grunted and refolded the message before tucking it into her pocket.

"Cecilia Kellar says that Parliament has granted us an audience over the Kensington Garden incident a week from Monday." She frowned and rubbed her chin as she looked at Arabella, all pale and wan in her bed. "What day is it, Vivienne?"

"It's Sunday, Mother," Vivienne said.

"Well, Rowena," she said as she stood. "You have until Friday morning to get Arabella well enough to travel. I want to have her testify at the Parliament hearing, and we'll need to demonstrate her power to some of the House Heads before we take her to the full Council. I'll need Vivienne and Amelia to help me prepare our arguments, so if you need help, Elizabeth and the twins will have to do. I trust you won't disappoint me?"

"No, Mother," Rowena said as she dropped a quick curtsey.

Mother turned her attention to Arabella, her face softening a bit around the eyes. "Your responsibility is to get well. No straining, and follow your sister's instructions."

"Yes, Mother," Arabella said as she gave her mother a shy smile.

Mother gave the girls a sharp nod, and then swept out of the room with Vivienne and Amelia in her wake. The door had barely latched when Arabella burst into tears. Rowena sat on the edge of the bed next to her and pulled her close, patting her back and murmuring "there, there."

"What am I going to do, Ro?" Arabella sobbed. "You heard Mother, the Council might want me dead."

Rowena gripped her by the shoulders, holding her out and shaking her just a bit. "And they also might see you as a witch messiah. We don't know what they are going to say until they say it. I know I don't have the power of prophecy, and unless you've been hiding something from me, neither do you." She gathered Arabella close again. "Besides, Mother, Vivienne, and Amelia are working on what to say to make the Council love you. Everything will be fine, just you wait and see."

Arabella sniffed and peeked up from her sister's shoulder. "You really think so? You really think everything will be fine?"

"Absolutely!" Rowena said, giving Arabella a tight hug.

"Now," Rowena said as she released her. "You need to eat your broth and drink your tea. Remember, Mother said I'm in charge." She smiled as she stood and removed the cloche from the soup bowl.

Golden broth steamed in the broad, shallow bowl. Rowena poured one cup of tea for Arabella and one for herself before she settled into the chair their mother had vacated. "Go on, eat up," she said as she blew on her tea.

"Chicken broth? If I have to suffer through broth, can't it at least be beef?" Arabella whined.

"Trust me," Rowena said with a smirk as she sipped her tea again. "Chicken broth is exactly what you want right now."

Arabella sighed and glared at her sister sideways, but she tucked into her broth without another word. Three spoonfuls in the truth of what Rowena had said became apparent. Her stomach clutched and knotted over the simple broth. Arabella moaned and grabbed her abdomen. Rowena calmly set her tea down.

"Do you need the chamber pot?" she asked in a matter of fact voice.

Arabella took a few deep breaths with her eyes closed, and shook her head when she felt her gorge finally begin to subside.

"Eat slowly," Rowena advised. "It's much easier that way."

Arabella nodded and carefully sipped another spoonful, then set down the spoon to wait for her body to accept the nourishment without a temper tantrum. After the nausea passed she asked, "Is it always this bad when you push yourself?"

"No, not always," said Rowena. "It all depends on how hard you push. I've gotten sick like that a few times, but never this bad. Mostly I just get a bad headache for a day or two. You have to learn your limits, Ari. You pushed yourself way too hard, you could have killed yourself."

"Well, how am I supposed to know?" Arabella said with a frown as she sipped another spoonful of broth. "I've never practiced magic at all. How should I know when too much is too much?"

"You learn by practicing," said Rowena.

Arabella sighed and took another sip of broth. "Are you practicing to be like Mother?"

Rowena stuck out her tongue, then leaned over the side of the chair to gather her fallen book. Arabella snorted and shook her head with a small smile before sipping her broth again. The sustenance began to rest easier on her stomach.

"What are you reading?" asked Arabella.

"The old Arthurian legends with Merlynne and Morgaine," Rowena said with a sigh and a smile as she traced her finger down the spine.

"It's been forever since I've read those," Arabella said with a dreamy smile of her own. "Will you read to me?"

"Finish your broth like a good girl and I will." Rowena wagged her finger at Arabella.

Arabella tilted the bowl so Rowena could see it. "Almost done, just a bit more to go. See?"

"Good girl," Rowena said with a wink. "So, where did you want me to start? When the brave witch sisters Merlynne and Morgaine venture out into the wide world from their safe enclave at Avalon? Or perhaps you'd like me to skip to the juicy bit when their mutual attraction to young King Arthur causes the jealous rift between them?" Rowena's eyes sparkled with mischief.

"I know it's the sad part," Arabella said as she scraped her spoon against the bowl to gather the last bits of broth. "But I've always liked where Morgaine sacrifices herself for her sister. When she puts Merlynne and Arthur into the deep sleep to heal their wounds so they can rise up to defend England in her hour of darkest need. Then poor Morgaine goes back to Avalon to take up the heavy burden of Lady of the Lake all alone." Arabella sighed and let her spoon clatter down into the empty bowl.

Rowena stood and took the tray away, then climbed into bed next to her sister with the book in her hand. "Sentimental featherhead," she murmured and kissed Arabella on the forehead.

"Am not," Arabella said as she tucked her head onto Rowena's shoulder and yawned.

"Of course you are," Rowena said.

"Do you really think the Lady of the Lake exists, and that Merlynne and her beloved Arthur will rise again one day to save us all?" Arabella asked as Rowena opened the book and sorted through the pages.

"It's certainly a lovely thought, isn't it? I suppose anything is possible," Rowena answered as she stopped flipping pages at the spot

Arabella had requested. She tried to stay awake to hear her favorite part of the story, but soon faded into her own healing sleep well before Morgaine put Merlynne and Arthur into slumber.

CHAPTER XIV

A Midnight Visit and Vision from Grandmother

ILVERY MOONLIGHT STREAMED IN PAST THE HEAVY CURTAINS ROWENA had left open when she crept out of Arabella's bedroom. The moon was almost, but not quite, full, the room lit almost as bright as day. Arabella shifted in her nest of blankets, prodding her muzzy mind to see what had wakened her. Then she heard the rustle of fabric again, followed by a plaintive *merowr*. She felt a rush of adrenaline and pushed herself up in the bed, knuckling the sleep out of her eyes.

It was only Grandmother Sortilege laying out small, stoppered earthen jars, a mortar and pestle, and a flowered tea cup with curls of steam rising from it on the bedside table. Her four cats gathered in the shadows around her feet watching her with upturned faces and big moon eyes.

"Good, you're awake," her grandmother said. "It will make it easier to give you your tisane." She held up one bottle in the moonlight to read the label and clucked her tongue, then set it down to pick up and examine another.

"Grandmother, what are you doing here?" Arabella asked as she tried to stifle a yawn.

"Helping you get better, what else would I be doing?" she said with a shrug. She found the bottle she wanted and gave a little exclamation of "ah, yes!" Then she worked out the stopper and measured out two pinches into the mortar. Arabella could tell it was Calamus by its sweet and spicy scent.

"Why did you have to come in the middle of the night?" Arabella asked. "I was sleeping."

"Don't whine, child," her grandmother said. "This particular spell works best by moonlight. It will be over before you know it and you'll be back to sleep." She shook a generous sprinkle from another jar into the mortar. The heady scent of Adder's Tongue wafted toward Arabella, and she rubbed her nose to stop a sneeze. Grandmother Sortilege must indeed be invested in her return to health if she was using so much of such a rare flower. It mostly grew in North America, and very few witches in the Isles had managed to coax it to grow.

"Yes, ma'am," Arabella said with a sigh.

Grandmother added one last dash of Tear Grass grains and began to grind it all with the pestle. The sweet, heady, spicy, and musky smells all mixed together in an unpleasant aroma.

Arabella wrinkled her nose. "It doesn't smell very appetizing."

Her grandmother poured the crushed herb mixture into the steaming water and gave her granddaughter a quelling look with one raised eyebrow. Arabella dropped her eyes. Grandmother murmured a few words over the cup and twisted her fingers in arcane ways. The water below her fingertips shifted and tumbled, swirling like a tiny maelstrom in the china cup. With one last sharp word of power, she flattened her hand and the steaming water calmed to glass perfection. She picked up the cup and turned to Arabella with a smile.

"It's going to taste horrid," she said in a cheerful voice. "But it will help you recover, so you must drink all of it."

Grandmother Sortilege then said "hup" and gestured from the cats to the bed. The four felines, all named after characters from Shakespeare's plays, jumped up onto Arabella's bed with such ease she would have thought they knew how to levitate as well as any witch. The cats all looked to Arabella's grandmother, and she made a circle with her index finger three times. The cats marched in line around Arabella thrice, even climbing on the mountain of pillows behind her head. Then each one settled down around her. The orange tabby tom, Puck, draped himself across her feet; the sable male, Othello, curled himself by her right hip; and the tortoiseshell female, Desdemona, took a spot on her left. Titania, the slender dilute tortie female made herself comfortable by Arabella's head. The four started to purr in unison as they looked to Grandmother Sortilege once more.

"I'm surprised you're using animals to focus yourself, Grandmother," Arabella said as she let her fingertips drift through Othello's sable fur. He rewarded her with a blink of his large yellow eyes and redoubled purring.

"Your mother is the one with a bias against using outer foci in magical workings," said Grandmother. "I, for one, think it's silly to pass up any advantage you can, especially when it's an important working."

"It's not the crutch of a weak witch?"

She snorted. "Of course not. It's wise not to become dependent on them, that is true, but to use them at all is not a sign of weakness."

Her grandmother raised the tea cup before her in both hands to head height and let her eyes droop halfway shut. She sucked in her breath through her teeth, and on the exhale she muttered a string of Latin so crushed together that Arabella couldn't tell where one word ended and another began. She knew her sisters delivered their chants in perfectly understandable English, but Grandmother had been raised in the old way and she clung to it.

The cats' purring hard against her skin, Arabella struggled to keep her mind focused on the scene in front of her. But she kept feeling like her mind was drifting upward out of her skull. She shut her eyes and took a deep breath to try and center herself, and nearly yelped when her grandmother clamped her hand down on her forehead.

"It's not going to do much good if you let your spirit go traipsing about instead of focusing on healing," she said.

Arabella felt suddenly quite present in the light of the moon, the smell of the tisane, and the rumble of the purrs around her. "What happened, Grandmother?" she said in a wary voice.

"It looks like you were about to astral project for the first time, sweeting." She blew on the tisane and then dipped a pinky finger in it. Satisfied, she extended the cup to Arabella

Arabella sputtered and took the cup without thinking about it.

"Oh, you'll be fine," her grandmother said with a flap of her hands. "A little night roaming never hurt anyone, so long as she knows what she's doing. But you *don't* know what you're doing yet, so you need to stay put." She wagged her finger at Arabella then turned back to her herb bottles, packing them in their carrying case.

"But how?" Arabella asked as she sniffed the steaming liquid and wrinkled her nose again.

"I suppose it's because this little potion tends to help you with visions. I've found this particular combination helpful to waken new abilities." She tucked the last bottle in the case and snapped it shut.

Arabella paused with the cup at her lips. "Are you mad? Mother and Rowena say I'm spell sick and you want to give me something that's good for dragging more magic out of me?"

Her grandmother turned and cocked her head to the side. "Well, of course I'm mad. All of us who look into the future get to be a little mad. You would be too if you saw some of the things we see. That's why most of us have handlers to help us navigate this reality." A fond smile touched her lips and her eyes took on a far off look. "Your grandfather was a lovely handler, always there when I needed him, always gentle with his guidance." She sighed and pulled a lace handkerchief from her sleeve cuff to dab the corner of her eye.

"But this?" Arabella said and held up the cup.

"Drink it, drink it all," her grandmother said. "It does help with visions and powers, but it's primarily for healing so it's what you need. And I saw you drink it in my vision. Won't you drink it?" She twisted her hands together and her brow furrowed as her voice took on a plaintive tone.

"Of course, I'll drink it," Arabella said with a sigh. She took an experimental sip and nearly gagged. It was hard not to spit out what was in her mouth, but she forced herself to swallow. The drink was sweet, spicy, and musty all at once, and it had a thick, viscous quality like tea with far too much sugar.

"By the Holly King, that's positively wretched!" She coughed on some of the flavor lodged on the back of her tongue. "It's truly vile."

"I told you it would be horrid," her grandmother said as she laughed with glee and clapped her hands. "Now, you must drink it all." She sank to her knees on the floor and began to sway back and forth humming tunelessly with a glazed look in her eyes.

Arabella pinched her nose and took a huge gulp, then shook her head like a wet dog. She looked into the cup to see how much was left and had to stifle a groan, still a little more than half. Cradling the cup in her lap, she decided to give her stomach a moment to settle before she tried to drink again.

"Grandmother," she said. "Are you alright?"

"Fine, just fine," she intoned in a sing-song voice. "There's so many pretty things to see."

Arabella felt a prickle run up and down her spine. "What is it that you see, Grandmother?"

"The same thing I've seen ever since you were born, sweeting, sparkling machines dancing at your command." Her grandmother let loose a high-pitched giggle. "It never made sense before, but now that the now has caught up with the then it does."

Arabella swallowed hard and swirled the tisane in her cup. She forced herself to take another healthy swig, making a bitter face.

Her grandmother's brow furrowed and her voice took on a high, keening note. "But there is so much strife to come before the bright days, sweeting. You'll be strong enough, even if you don't believe it. Don't let them shackle you, but trust the yew and the birch."

Arabella tossed back the last of the cup and said, "What do you mean by the yew and the birch?"

"I have no idea what you're talking about, Arabella," her grandmother grunted as she climbed to her feet. "You should be trying to get some sleep and not asking me silly questions." She took the empty teacup from Arabella and tucked it and the herbal case into the carpetbag on the floor.

"But you said..." Arabella began.

"There are a lot of things I say that I don't remember, child," her grandmother said in exasperation with her hands on her hips. "That's why we seers have handlers. Someone needs to remember what we say." She shook her head and clucked her tongue against her teeth.

Grandmother collected her bag and headed for the door with a wave over her shoulder at Arabella. She weaved a bit, as if she'd taken one too many sips of sherry.

"Sleep well, sweet dreams. Get better and all that," she called from the doorway. Then she let out the perfect imitation of a trilling meow and all four cats sprang from the bed and followed her out.

Arabella sat alone in the silent room trying to puzzle out the meaning of what had just happened. Had it been safe to drink what her grandmother had given her? Would she wake up feeling better or worse, or even at all, in the morning? And what did birch and yew have to do with her future? How did you trust trees? She tried to stay awake to sort through it all, but the weakness from the spell sickness and whatever else had been in the tisane conspired against her. Before long she was sound asleep.

Arabella did wake in the morning, and when she did she felt almost well. Rowena was shocked when she asked to sit in the garden and managed cold sliced chicken and toast without a single protest from her stomach. By Wednesday, Arabella felt nearly normal and walked in the garden instead of just sitting. When Mother saw her enjoying the day, she gave the order to leave on Thursday, so that Arabella would have more time to recover from the journey once they reached London.

As she climbed into the carriage, Arabella looked back on Blackstone Manor and could not shake an ominous feeling that clutched at her heart. As she settled down in her seat she heard Elizabeth mutter, "It couldn't have been that hard if she recovered so fast."

"Shut up," Rowena hissed, and Mother gave her sixth daughter a harsh glare before settling back and mentally giving Jeanette the instruction to go. Arabella leaned out the window and waved to Vivienne and her grandmother where they stood on the front steps to see everyone off. She watched the Manor get smaller and smaller, not sitting back until she couldn't make Vivienne and Grandmother out at all. She sighed and clasped her hands tight in her lap, wondering again at the anxiety that clutched her throat.

CHAPTER XV

On Parlor Tricks and Political Alliances

THE GATHERING IN THE FRONT PARLOR OF THE SORTILEGE LONDON townhouse could have passed for any other gathering of well-heeled women across the city, were it not for its size. Minerva had invited the Head of each of the Thirteen Houses of England, plus a visiting House Head from Scotland because it would have been impolite to exclude her. Refined ladies typically gathered in groups of half a dozen or less. The parlor was near overfull with eleven other women besides the family, and there was one yet to come.

Eudora Goodwin of Ashblaen House chatted amiably with Katherine Wardlow of Rowanbry House and Mildred Bowen of Oakhurst House on the sofa. Emma Tibbet of Aberdean House sat with her head together with Beatrice Paskin of Fossdrum House on the settee. They spoke in whispers, stealing glances at Minerva, sitting with the other two most powerful House Heads, Cecilia Kellar of Thornfire House and Madeline Thurston of Hazelrood House.

"We're going to have to keep an eye on those two," Madeline murmured as she pretended to sip her tea, her eyes flicking to Emma and Beatrice on the settee.

"Quite the social climbers, they are," Cecilia said, hiding a wry smile with her teacup.

"I don't think we have anything to worry about, ladies," Minerva said and she sipped her tea for real. "They may want to be at the top of the mountain but they haven't the strength to climb." The three chuckled amongst themselves while still surveying the room with studied casualness, noting alliances and covert glances, filing the information away for later through force of long habit.

"Those are the ones really interesting me," Minerva said with a barely perceptible nod to the corner to her left.

Theodosia Boscoe of Crawmere House, the oldest House in England, held court with Charlotte Anwell of Mynydd House and Lilly Ferguson of Dunleah House, the visiting witch from Scotland. Theodosia was also the oldest witch still in active service on the Council. At a hundred and four many thought it was time for her to step down but Minerva quelled those requests whenever they came to her as the Head of the Council. Theodosia still had much wisdom to share, as Charlotte and Lilly were obviously aware as they hung on her every word.

"Indeed," said Cecilia. "Charlotte may try to pass herself off as a simple witch from Wales, but she's much shrewder than most give her credit for. And with advice from Theodosia, she just may become a force to be reckoned with."

"Oh come now," said Madeline. "She's a dowsing witch, and with an affinity for metal to boot. She hasn't got much power at all."

"She may not have much of what we would typically consider strong power," said Minerva. "But she's made quite a nice little fortune for herself working with miners, blacksmiths, and those gentlemen who want to build the railroads. Perhaps it's time we started thinking in less traditional ways." She sipped her tea.

Cecilia and Madeline both looked at her with raised eyebrows but said nothing and drank their tea. Minerva let her eyes roam across the room to where Margaret Lodwick of Elmswell House, the youngest and newest of all the House Heads, sat with Selina Mortimer of Yewlin House. Selina winked at her over the rim of her teacup, her eyes dancing with mischief.

"I'm never quite sure how to take Selina," Minerva said with a sigh. "She never seems to be serious."

Madeline snorted. "I'm not sure she knows how to be serious."

"I don't know," Cecilia snuck a glance at Selina out of the corner of her eye. "It's like she knows something we don't, and yet she shows no talent for prophecy."

"That we know of," said Madeline. "You know those Yewlin House witches are notorious for keeping secrets."

The servants might be preparing the pots of tea and other refreshments in the kitchen, but Minerva's daughters wove through the parlor serving the House Heads as a sign of respect for their elders. Amelia carried a tray of petite sandwiches with the crusts cut off, cucumber, watercress, and smoked salmon. Rowena and Arabella split the duties for tea. Rowena with a pot of Yunnan and Arabella with a pot of Darjeeling, to suit guests with either a taste for traditional Chinese tea or for the newer tea coming from India. Elizabeth wore a pout as she flounced about the room with a tray of tiny cakes and pastries to satisfy the sweet tooth. Minerva frowned as Elizabeth passed by. She would have to take that girl to task later.

"How long are we going to wait for Philomena?" Cecilia asked Minerva with a sigh.

Minerva glanced at the new clock on the mantelpiece. "She's only ten minutes late so far, and you know Philomena. We have to give her at least twenty."

Cecilia frowned. "I can't abide when she's late like this. It's so disrespectful."

"Are you sure you won't give us some kind of clue about your fabulous revelation, Minerva?" Madeline asked, giving a mischievous grin. "We are your best friends after all."

"I really think it would be best if you just saw it with your own eyes," Minerva said with a secretive smile.

"How impish of you," Madeline said with a chuckle. "Oh, and how is Vivienne doing with her condition, by the way?"

Minerva's smile grew to one of real joy. "She's doing fantastically. So far the midwife is very pleased with her progress. And all the early scrying is pointing to a girl."

"You have such a lucky family, so many girls," Madeline said with an envious sigh. "I mean, we do have enough witches to support the House, obviously, but we have so many boys to marry off. Are you sure I can't interest either one of you in another son-in-law?"

Minerva tilted back her head and laughed. "Nathaniel has been lovely for Vivienne, but I'm afraid Amelia is quite taken with Cecilia's

Harlan. Do you have any sons in your House that would be willing to take on my twins?"

"That's a lot to ask of anyone," Madeline said as she wagged her finger at Minerva, but her eyes twinkled with merriment.

All conversation stopped at the sound of a loud, and frantic, knock at the front door. Moria had been informed that at least one more guest would be arriving, so it wasn't but a moment before Philomena Beedlebaugh of Birchwold House fluttered into the room. Her round face was flushed bright red and she fanned herself with her hands. She first went to sit down in the only empty seat in the room, but bounced right back out of the chair with a startled "oh!" and scampered over to Minerva. She bobbed a wobbly curtsey.

"I am so sorry I'm late, Minerva, so very sorry." Her words bubbled out of her in a breathless rush.

"That's quite alright, Philomena," Minerva said as she waved the witch back to her seat before setting down her own teacup to stand. "We've been having a lovely chat, but now that you're here we can get started."

"Oh, Minerva, I think everyone is going to want to hear what I have to say first," Philomena said in a breathy voice as she settled into her seat. "Do you think I could have a cuppa, dear?" She called to Rowena and waved her over.

The room was silent as Rowena poured Philomena a cup of tea and offered her sugar. Philomena helped herself to two heaping spoonfuls and took a deep draught from her cup, then sighed with contentment.

"Philomena?" Minerva asked as she crossed her arms over her chest. "Your news so that we can get to the business at hand?"

"Oh, oh yes!" Philomena startled and looked around for a place to set her cup. The end tables on either side of her seat were so crowded with bric-a-brac that she had to settle for holding it. She heaved a great sigh as she looked around at all the witches in the room. "Parliament has already settled the Kensington Garden Incident, and I don't think any of you will be pleased with how it sorted out."

The room exploded into a gabble of shocked voices before Minerva held up her hands and called for silence.

"That makes no sense, Philomena," she said. "We're supposed to testify before Parliament tomorrow about the incident."

Philomena shook her head. "They moved up the hearing because they said the summer was getting too warm too early and they wanted to call for the summer break and send everyone out to the country before it got too hot."

"Wait a minute, Philomena," said Cecilia. "How did you come by this news if even Minerva doesn't know, and she was supposed to testify?"

Philomena blushed. "I know all of you get upset with me for my obsession with mundane people, but in this case it's served us well! It really has!" She again looked unsuccessfully for a place to put her cup. "I was reading last evening's newspaper over my luncheon today, and there it was on page nine, right below the fold. *Humph.* Perhaps now you'll reconsider insulting me when I keep track of ordinary things. Think of how embarrassing it would have been to show up tomorrow to testify and find Parliament all locked up for the summer."

Minerva sighed and pinched the bridge of her nose. "I will never again tease you, not even a little bit, about your obsession with the mundane, Philomena. Now, please, just tell me what the newspaper said."

"Oh yes!" Philomena drew herself up. "The article said that Bartholomew Westerfeld was found guilty of conduct unbecoming of a gentleman and was ordered to give one hundred pounds, fifty for each witch he insulted, to the Witch Support Fund." She blinked owlishly and looked at Minerva.

"Money? They think a few pounds will make up for his outrageous behavior? And then leave us unconsulted and uninformed, treating us like their own vapid wives?" Minerva said through clenched teeth. She exchanged glances with Cecilia and Madeline. Both of them had clenched jaws and stony faces, just like she did.

The room exploded again in shock and outrage that they, the witches, the saviors of England in its darkest hour against the ravages of the Black Plague, could be treated so shabbily. Once again Minerva called for silence. She drew in her breath to speak, but a quiet voice from the corner of the room stopped her.

"It would seem," said Theodosia. "That the gentlemen who rule our island need to be reminded of precisely how much they owe us. There is not a man sitting on those benches who does not either issue from a line our foremothers saved from extinction or partake of the wonders we provide to make their lives more comfortable. I dare say that most of them would satisfy both requirements."

"Indeed, Theodosia," said Minerva. "I was just about to say much the same thing myself. We must come up with a plan to bring them back in line." There were murmurs of assent all around the room.

"It is true that we cannot allow the insult to stand, Minerva. But I hardly think that this is something we will solve in one afternoon over tea. Perhaps we should call an emergency session of the Council in a week's time to give us an opportunity to think of what the appropriate response would be. However, I cannot presume to speak for you. You are, after all, the Grande Dame," said Theodosia.

Minerva lifted her chin and narrowed her eyes slightly. She had no idea what game Theodosia was playing, but she would play along for now. Minerva inclined her head and smiled.

"Your wisdom sees clearly, as always, my dear Theodosia," she said. "I will indeed call an emergency Council session in a week's time that we may all think about this situation with clear heads."

"Very good." Theodosia's wrinkled face broke into a broad gap-toothed grin. "Now, let us turn to what you brought us here for, my dear. I don't know about everyone else, but I am on fire with curiosity." Around the room there were chuckles and nods as all the ladies agreed that they were most curious about what Minerva had planned.

"Girls," Minerva said and clapped her hands together twice. "If you will collect the dishes and fetch the demonstration pieces."

Amelia, Rowena, Elizabeth, and Arabella collected up all the plates and cups and handed them off to the servants waiting at the parlor door. At the same time, they took boxes of pocket watches from them. Amelia gave Minerva the nod that they were ready, and Minerva began to speak.

"My dear ladies," she began. "It has been quite some time since our way of life, our way of using magic, has changed. But it would seem new days are now upon us. It is time for us to consider how we will move forward into the future."

"But I thought we stopped discussing the Parliament issue," Philomena said with a frown.

"We have, Philomena. It just so happens that what I brought you all here for today is also, quite possibly, a fundamental change in the way we live." Minerva gestured to her daughters and they began circulating through the room handing a pocket watch to each witch present.

"These are certainly a lovely party favor, Minerva, but I don't understand what these have to do with magic," said Katharine.

"I think it would be better if you saw it with your own eyes," Minerva said. "Everyone, please, I want you to stop your watches with your magic."

All the ladies exchanged confused glances, but shrugged and did as they were asked. For the more powerful witches it took only the barest whisper of their strength to stop the watches in their hands cold. Emma and Beatrice had to work a bit harder, staring at the watches in their hands for a full minute with fine beads of sweat popping out along their hairlines. When each witch was done and the watch in her hand was well and truly dead, Minerva beckoned Arabella to her.

"Are you ready?" She asked Arabella when she came to stand next to her. Arabella nodded. "You're sure you're strong enough?" Arabella nodded again. Minerva turned back to the House Heads.

"Ladies, my daughter, Arabella, is about to show you something, well, quite different. Please hold your comments until she has finished so everyone can have an unspoiled view." Minerva gave Arabella a little push in Theodosia's direction.

Arabella smiled and curtseyed to Theodosia, then took the pocket watch from her and held it close to her chest for a moment with her eyes closed. When she handed it back to Theodosia, the aged witch's eyes widened but she did not utter a word. Arabella repeated the process with Charlotte and Lilly. Charlotte frowned thoughtfully over her pocket watch, but Lilly could not suppress a gasp of surprise over what she saw.

Arabella went to her mother's best friends next, Cecilia and Madeline. When they received their watches back they both looked back and forth from the watch to Arabella with their jaws hanging open. Tilting her head to the side and smiling sheepishly, Arabella curtseyed to them. She moved on to the sofa where Eudora, Katharine, and Mildred sat. Their reaction was much the same as that of Cecilia and Madeline. Emma and Beatrice were next, followed by Margaret and Selina. All of them seemed shocked, except for Selina, who gave Arabella a dimpled smile and a wink as she accepted the watch back. Arabella went to Philomena last and when she handed the watch back to her, the tardy witch exclaimed sharply. Arabella returned to her mother's side and stood with her hands clasped in front of her, head bowed. She was breathing just a little faster than when she'd started.

"You should all now have working pocket watches in your hands, despite the fact that you stopped them yourselves," Minerva announced, looking around the room at the wide eyes and shocked expressions. "It would seem, ladies, that for the first time in five hundred years, there is a new power in the witch's magical arsenal. It is possible to manipulate mechanical things with magic. Does anyone have any questions?"

"Yes, Minerva, I do," Charlotte said. "How does this work? Will this be something that we will all eventually be able to tap into?"

"We don't know quite yet..." Minerva began, but Emma interrupted her.

"Oh for the love of Demeter, don't encourage her, Charlotte!" Emma exploded. She stood and faced Minerva. "You just can't stand that there is a flaw in your family. You can't stand that you didn't birth the Chosen One like you bragged you had right after Arabella was born. I don't know how you've accomplished this sleight of hand, but it's certainly not magic."

Minerva's chin went up a notch and her nostrils flared. Arabella stared at the floor harder and turned bright red.

"How can it be?" Beatrice said from where she still sat. "There's no such thing as mechanical magic, all magic comes from the earth. Even a child knows that."

"Indeed," said Emma as she tossed the watch on the cushion behind her. "Minerva, I am going to write this insanity off to the stress you've been under since the attack, but unless you start making sense we may have to look into finding a new Grande Dame."

Emma swept from the room and Beatrice scrambled to follow. Margaret also stood and said, "I'm afraid to say I agree with Emma, Minerva. What you're asking us to believe is quite mad." She shook her head as she left the room.

"Ladies," Minerva began, her voice trembling ever so slightly. "I can assure you that I am not mad and I am not trying to pass my daughter off as something she is not. The talent she has shown you today is quite real."

"I don't know, Minerva," said Eudora. "What you are suggesting violates everything that we were taught from the time we were girls, from the time our mothers and grandmothers were girls, even."

Mildred nodded in agreement. "We can't just throw out everything we've known for our entire lives in less than five minutes, just because you say we ought to."

Eudora and Mildred stood and started toward the door. When Katharine did not follow, Eudora turned and said, "Are you coming?"

Katharine bit her lip and looked down at the watch in her hand, and then joined the other two with a sigh. "I'm sorry, Minerva," she said. "I'm willing to consider what you've presented to us, but I need some time to compose my thoughts. Would you like to come around for tea this coming Thursday?"

"That would be lovely," Minerva said.

"Perhaps you two young witches wouldn't mind an old crone joining you for tea?" Theodosia asked as she levered herself out of her seat with a grunt. "I'd also like some time to meditate on this issue before I pass judgment."

"I'd be honored, Theodosia," said Katharine as she offered the elder witch her arm to steady her as they followed Eudora and Mildred from the room. The color rose in Minerva's face as she watched them go and looked over the dwindling number of guests in her parlor.

"Oh, Minerva," said Philomena, fiddling with the watch chain in her hands as she bit her bottom lip. "I just don't know. You've never steered me wrong before but this just sounds so fantastic. I'm sorry." She also left her pocket watch on her chair and withdrew from the parlor.

Minerva clutched her hands in front of her and swiveled her head around looking at the five women left from the thirteen House Heads. Charlotte and Lilly had their heads together in intense conversation. Selina saluted her with the pocket watch as if she were toasting with a glass of sherry, and rose to come to meet her. Minerva turned to Cecilia and Madeline where they sat behind her, and her friends looked at her with pity.

"But I'm telling the truth!" she protested.

Cecilia stood and put her hand on Minerva's shoulder. "I'm sure you think you are, dear."

"I know I'm telling the truth." Minerva pitched her voice low to keep it steady and shrugged off Cecilia's hand.

"Think of what you're asking us to believe, Minerva," Madeline said, standing herself. "You're asking us to turn our world completely upside down."

"I understand it's difficult," said Minerva. "I didn't want to believe it myself at first, but you know I would never lie to another witch, especially not the two of you." Minerva hugged her elbows to herself and glanced over at Arabella, who hugged herself as well, looking as if she wished she could melt away into the carpet.

"Minerva," scolded Cecilia. "If Arabella were already a full-fledged witch, if she'd shown any inkling of power as we understand it, this would be easier to swallow. But as it is…" She shrugged.

"We trust you." Madeline emphasized the first word. "And if we are having trouble believing this, think of how the rest of the Council must feel."

Minerva pursed her lips and muttered. "I think I have a fair idea of what the Council will think after today."

"Madeline," said Selina. "Since when did you speak for all of the Council? Did I miss an edict?"

Madeline narrowed her eyes at the slender little blonde woman. "I'm simply stating that if we, Minerva's best friends and true confidants, find the concept of mechanical magic to be difficult to believe, then the rest of the Council, who are not so emotionally attached to Minerva, would find it even more so."

"I see," said Selina as she looked down at the watch in her hands. "Well, Minerva, I may not be your proclaimed 'best friend,' but I believe you. I'm willing to believe my own senses rather than centuries-old teachings that have been proven wrong before."

"Well, I never!" Madeline reared her head back and stomped from the parlor in a huff.

"I'll call on you later," Cecilia said as she patted Minerva on the shoulder and followed Madeline out. Amelia, Rowena, and Elizabeth watched them go, and then made their way through the crowd of furniture to where their mother and sister stood.

Minerva blew out her breath and put a hand on a chair back to steady herself. She turned and looked at Selina with a wan smile. "Thank you."

"Just remember who believed in you when the war comes," Selina said with a serious face.

"War? What war?" Minerva's eyes grew wide, but Selina merely smiled her dimpled smile and winked.

Minerva jumped and turned when Charlotte tapped her on the shoulder, putting her hand to her throat.

"I'm sorry, I didn't mean to startle you," Charlotte said.

Minerva pulled a face and said, "I suppose you'll tell me that I'm mad and that this is utterly unbelievable and take your leave as well."

"Actually," said Charlotte. "Lilly and I were talking and we've both come to the conclusion that we support you."

"Really?" Minerva trembled and sank into the sofa behind her. Charlotte sat next to her and took her hands, while Lilly took the seat next to her.

"Really. You know my House has an affinity for rock and metal, and that we tend more toward dowsing. Because of our focus and our work with the men in the mechanical industries, Mynydd House does not have as much antipathy toward technology as the other twelve Houses. I'm just hoping that Arabella may be able to teach us how she does it." Charlotte offered a warm smile to Arabella where she stood with her jaw hanging open. It took Arabella a moment to close her mouth and offer Charlotte her own weak smile.

"And this strikes to the heart of the matter of why I've come to speak to the Council," said Lilly in her lilting brogue. "We're not so united in the Highlands because those of us who are younger see the value of mechanical things, the value of integrating them into our lives, while our crones and wise women are much like your Emma and Beatrice, maybe even worse. I came in the hopes that the more cosmopolitan witches of London might be able to speak some sense into them."

"Have any of your young witches exhibited mechanical magic like my Arabella?" Minerva's voice quivered.

"I'm afraid not," said Lilly. "Or at least not that I know of. But their mothers may not be as accepting as you are, and the girls may be scared to show what they can do. I'll make some discrete inquiries when I get home."

Minerva nodded and sat back with a sigh, closing her eyes. Arabella twisted her hands and bit her lip while Rowena put her arm around her and squeezed a little.

"What are we going to do, Mother?" Amelia asked in a soft voice.

"I don't know yet, Amelia," Minvera said with a shake of her head, and then she focused her eyes on Arabella. "If only you had exhibited true magical talent first, any kind of talent, we wouldn't have to worry."

"We'll just have to think of something else to change their minds, Mother," said Rowena. "It's not like we can force talent out of Arabella, can we?"

Minerva paused before she shook her head, but there was something thoughtful in her eyes. The same thing that echoed in Elizabeth's eyes.

CHAPTER XVI

A Nightmare in the Cellar

ARABELLA WAS READING A BOOK OF POETRY IN THE GARDEN WHEN Elizabeth found her the next afternoon.

"Mother asked me to fetch you for some herbal work in the cellar," she said.

Blinking in the bright sunshine, Arabella looked up at Elizabeth and frowned over the broad grin on her sister's face.

"I thought Mother wanted to focus on the issues with the Council," she said.

"Don't get snippy with me, Arabella," Elizabeth huffed and put her fists on her hips.

"I'm not getting snippy," Arabella said as she closed her book and stood. "I was just curious why she's choosing now for her herbal work. It's not even the right time of year."

Elizabeth shrugged. "She said it helps her relax, and you know how stressed Mother is right now."

Arabella shrugged as well and followed Elizabeth into the house. As they bypassed the still room Arabella asked, "And why the cellar? Shouldn't we be doing herbal work in the still room?"

Elizabeth let out a theatrical sigh. "You seem to know an awful lot about real magic for someone who doesn't have any true talent. Don't you think Mother knows what she's doing?" She gestured for Arabella to precede her through the cellar door.

"Well, of course she does," Arabella said as she started down the cellar stairs with Elizabeth following behind with an oil lamp. "She's the most powerful witch in the Isles, but I think I have learned a few things while I've helped the rest of you over the years."

The last word ended in a shriek as a shadowy someone put a burlap sack over Arabella's head. Arms wrapped around her and dragged her deeper into the cellar even as she thrashed and fought like a freshly hooked trout. Roughly shoved into a seat, her feet were bound to the legs and her left arm was twisted behind her back and lashed to the slats of the chair back. For some reason her right arm was left free.

The sack was yanked off her head. Before her in the golden light of the oil lamp was her mother and Elizabeth. There was a worktable off to the right with all the magic-testing supplies she was used to seeing, as well as a large wooden tub just past them with a block-and-tackle rig dangling above it.

"Mother?" Arabella gasped. "What's going on?"

"It is apparent, Arabella, that your abilities as they stand are a danger to your family," Mother said. "We must somehow get you to manifest some sort of acceptable talents before the next meeting of the Council. Perhaps my previous methods to coax out your power were too gentle. It's time we tried something a bit more extreme."

"What do you mean my power is a danger to the family?" Arabella asked.

"Neptune's beard! Are you really that dull?" Elizabeth spat. Mother held up her hand for silence.

"Arabella, you were there yesterday. You heard members of the Council threaten to have me replaced. What do you think would happen to this family, to all of Blackstone House, if I were forced from my position as Grande Dame in shame?"

"I don't..." Arabella started but her mother interrupted her.

"Our family and our entire House would fall into disgrace, Arabella. And who do you think will buy charms and spells from disgraced witches? No one, that's who. We're fighting enough fear and jealousy over our power as it is! Without the protection of the Council, the mundane people will fall on us like hungry wolves. Do you want to be responsible for your family being ripped to shreds, Arabella?" Mother's voice rose into a strident shriek. Her face was flushed red and panted lightly.

"Of course not, Mother!" she protested. "But surely it can't be that bad?"

Mother grabbed Arabella's chin hard and put her face down so close to her that Arabella could not breathe without sucking in her mother's hot breath. "I will tell you how bad it is. It is not just bad, it is devastating. And I have other children to think of than just *you*." Mother's voice came out in a hiss. She let go of Arabella's chin and patted her on the cheek. "Just remember that I am doing all of this for the good of us all, including you."

She stepped away, shutting her eyes and blowing out her breath to compose herself. Elizabeth giggled. Mother's eyes popped open and she frowned. "Control yourself, Elizabeth. This is important work, not some frivolous lark."

"Yes, Mother," Elizabeth said as she bowed her head and bobbed a curtsey, but Arabella could see Elizabeth's mouth turning up at the corners ever so slightly, hidden in a menacing shadow.

Arabella sawed her left arm back and forth testing the rope and she found the knots were good and tight. She reached behind the chair with her right arm to see if she could pick one of the knots apart. Elizabeth leapt forward with a savage hiss and yanked her arm forward. Arabella cried out from the pain that lanced through her shoulder.

Her mother *tsk*ed at her and wagged her finger back and forth. "Oh no, my little chickadee," her voice dripped with cold malice. "There will be none of that. If you wish to be released from that chair you must perform some feat of true magic. Anything will do." Mother gestured to the table of implements.

"Levitate that knife to you so that you can cut your bonds. Light the candle or create a tempest in the water and I will cut the bonds myself. Just tell me you wish to be released by speaking into my mind and it will be so. Why, we've even left your hand free so you can make the appropriate gestures or trace whatever sigil you like. All you have to do is *do* it."

"But, Mother," Arabella protested. "I've never been able to do any of this before, what makes you think I can start now?" Cold fear swirled in her belly as her mind raced through the possibilities of what could happen to her, none of them good.

"Stress has been known to bring about the most recalcitrant power in even the weakest witch. You obviously have not been stressed enough to bring your real power out of hiding," Mother said.

"I don't even know if she can do it, Mother," Elizabeth said as she crossed her arms and smirked. "She's such a weakling."

"Yes, mock her," Mother said with a sly smile. "Arouse her anger, her frustration, any high emotion that will bring the power out of her."

Arabella strained against her bonds and fought to keep the tears collecting in her eyes from spilling down her cheeks. "Mother, this is mad! You have to let me go!"

Mother tilted her head back and laughed. "Don't be naïve, Arabella. I don't have to do anything. You are my unmarried daughter and I can do whatever I like with you." She reached out and pinched her cheek.

Arabella yelped, then sobbed. Elizabeth sniffed and said, "Just as I thought, such a weakling." She began to chant "weakling, weakling" over and over in a singsong voice.

Arabella sagged against her bonds, shaking her bowed head back and forth, feeling the anger bubble up inside her. She threw her head up and screamed, "Shut UP!" Her screamed echoed off the walls of the cellar and both Mother and Elizabeth fell silent. Arabella stared at her mother and sister and could feel her face ablaze with bright emotion, her breath coming shallow and fast.

"Good," Mother purred. "Now we're getting somewhere."

Arabella strained against the ropes and let out an inarticulate howl of impotent rage.

"Yes, good," said Mother. "That's it, get angry. Channel that anger into a spell."

Arabella looked up with narrowed eyes and her mouth set in a grim line. She lifted her right arm and traced a fire sigil in the air in sharp strokes with her finger and then stretched her hand out toward the candle. It remained stubbornly unlit. She screamed in frustration and did the same thing again with the very same result. She dropped her arm, panting, sweat rolling down her forehead.

Mother sniffed. "Fire still eludes you, I see. Perhaps water or wind will be easier." She paced around Arabella and leaned in close from behind and whispered in her ear. "Just one little spell, one little push, and all will be right with the world."

Arabella closed her eyes and dug deep down inside her, looking for the power she tapped when she re-started the clockworks. In her mind's eye, it was like there was a glow deep inside her and she grabbed two fistfuls and threw them at the table of magical implements. Nothing shifted on the table of traditional magical implements. But above their heads the brand new grandmother clock her mother had purchased for the entrance hall before Westerfeld's fateful demonstration chimed all the hours at once. Then there was a great thundering crash.

Mother looked at Elizabeth and jerked her head toward the stairs. "Go find out what happened, and make sure no one gets curious about what is going on in the cellar."

"Yes, Mother," Elizabeth said as she bobbed a curtsey and then scampered up the stairs.

Mother continued to circle around Arabella. "It's good to see that you are making some sort of effort, Arabella, but you must try harder. Our family will be destroyed unless you manifest true power." She leaned down and hissed into her ear, "Try again."

Arabella whimpered, but she gathered herself and tried to think of what to do. She fumbled through her memories of all the lessons her mother had given her and tried to think of one that might have felt different, one that might have been a true magical talent about to bloom but not quite getting there. Nothing came to her. She reached out her hand again and spoke the word of power for wind and twirled her index finger in a circle as she'd seen her mother do so many times. The peacock feather in the silver budvase remained unmoved in the still air of the cellar.

Her mother slapped her hard across the cheek. "Don't you dare give up! Don't you dare doom us all!"

Both of them whipped their heads around at the sound of the cellar door opening and closing, followed by footsteps on the stairs. It was Elizabeth.

"The grandmother clock is in pieces all over the floor, like it exploded or something," she said. "It seems that Arabella did let some energy go, but it went to the wrong place."

Mother frowned and asked Elizabeth, "That can't have gone unnoticed. What did you tell everyone?"

"Oh my, yes, everyone noticed. I was barely the first one to make it into the hall," said Elizabeth. "I told everyone that I was trying to access the new powers that Arabella has but that the clock just came apart. Amelia and Rowena are very cross with me, but Jessamine and Josephine gave me the oddest looks before they went out to the garden. I told Moria to clean it up and left."

Mother patted Elizabeth on the shoulder as she let out a relieved breath. "Good girl," she said and then turned back to Arabella. "Try to keep your power contained to the cellar, Arabella. Destroying every clock in the house won't get you out of that chair any sooner."

"I wasn't trying to destroy the clock," Arabella said. "I just thought if I threw enough power at the implements that something would happen. It was like it had a mind of its own and went straight to the clock."

"Typical novice mistake." Mother sniffed. "Raw power is not very useful unless it can be controlled. A witch with less power but better control can best a more powerful witch who cannot focus her power."

"Yes, Arabella," said Elizabeth. "Listen to Mother, this is one of the most important lessons you can learn."

"Don't be a sycophant, Elizabeth," said Mother as she drifted over to the table of testing implements.

"I'm not..." Elizabeth started to protest but she was immediately silenced by an icy glare from her mother.

"I might actually believe you if I'd seen you taking this lesson to heart yourself," Mother said. "But I've yet to see you demonstrate an understanding of the importance of focusing your power." Elizabeth blushed and looked away.

"Since the elements don't seem to be responding to you, Arabella, then perhaps we should try some prophecy or telepathy." Mother picked up the deck of well-worn tarot cards. "I will hold up a card facing me and picture it in my mind, then you tell me what I see. If you get ten in a row correct, I'll let you out of the chair."

"But you only ever asked me to do three in a row before!"

"Three could be blind luck or coincidence, and we can't save the family with that. Ten is a much more reasonable test for true power." Mother drew the top card off the deck and held it in front of her face, staring intently at what was there. "Stop whining and begin, Arabella."

Arabella stared at her mother with her jaw hanging open and tears gathered in the corners of her eyes, her mouth opening and closing on no sound at all. Elizabeth smacked her on the back of the head and said, "Start! Don't leave Mother waiting!"

"The Lovers." Arabella's voice came out in a squeaking stutter, and she looked at her mother with pleading eyes. Mother made no indication of whether she was wrong or right. She just set the card face down on the table and pulled a new one from the deck and again focused on it intently.

"Three of Cups?" Arabella said in a shaky voice.

Again, Mother said nothing and drew the next card. And so they went like that through all seventy eight cards in the deck. When they were done, Mother gathered the cards together and began to shuffle them without a word.

"Well?" Arabella asked as she slumped down in the chair as much as her bonds would let her. "How did I do, Mother?"

"You had a few runs of three, but never more than that," she said as she cut the cards. "That's not good enough to convince the Council, so we'll just have to move on to prophecy."

Arabella groaned and her chin drooped to her chest. Elizabeth reached out and pinched the tender flesh on the back of her arm, making her jump and yelp.

"Ungrateful little bitch, stupid slag," she growled. "We've fed you, clothed you, housed you, and protected you for years and you've given us nothing. And now when we ask you simply to not destroy the rest of us right along with you, you can't even put a good effort into it."

"Language, Elizabeth," Mother admonished. "Just because we are trying to force Arabella to manifest her power doesn't mean we have to lower ourselves. We are still ladies and witches."

Elizabeth nodded and stepped back from Arabella, but her lips were still tight and she did not apologize.

"Now, Arabella, we will repeat much the same exercise as we did with the telepathy, except you will try to predict what card I am about to draw. Again, ten in a row will release you from the chair." She laid her hand on the top card and said, "Begin."

Arabella sighed and closed her eyes, letting her chin drop to her chest, pausing for a moment before she said, "Five of Pentacles," in a voice barely above a whisper.

Again, Mother went through all seventy eight cards before she called an end to the exercise. "Three of Wands," Arabella said for the last card and Elizabeth boxed her ear.

"You already said that one, ninny," Elizabeth growled.

"And yet she was right this time, Elizabeth," Mother said as she frowned over the final card.

Arabella shook her head to try to clear the ringing in her ears. "How many did I get right this time, Mother?"

"Never more than four in a row," Mother said in a far-away voice as she shuffled the cards in a mindless rhythm.

"Maybe if we do it again, I'll get even better." Arabella's voice trembled and cracked.

"No," said Mother. "I'm afraid we won't be doing that exercise again just now. Perhaps we need to let you think by yourself for a time. Maybe that will convince you of the seriousness of the situation."

Arabella blanched, thinking of being trapped in the cellar, alone in the dark, and wondering what things might come crawling out of the shadows to harass her in her helpless state. The thoughts of spiders, rats, and boggles made her shiver. "You already have me quite convinced that the situation is serious, Mother," she said.

"I don't know that we do, Arabella," said Mother as she continued to shuffle. "You still show no more talent than a mundane woman, which is to say, none. If you were taking these exercises with sufficient seriousness we should have seen some glimmer of power by now."

"But I do have power, Mother! It's just not traditional power!" Arabella rocked against her bonds.

Mother's hands stilled. "But without a showing of traditional power, the Council will not countenance your presence and the family will fall right along with you."

"Perhaps we should just move on to the final exercise, Mother," said Elizabeth.

Mother pursed her lips. "I had hoped that it would not be necessary. It does have a high mortality rate, which is why it fell out of favor as a training technique."

Elizabeth shrugged. "To save the family, either Arabella demonstrates true power or she dies. There is no other way. We cannot continue as we are."

Arabella gasped and whipped her head around to face Elizabeth. "You would wish me dead? Your own sister?"

Elizabeth regarded her with a flat stare. "I lose one sister or I lose them all. I don't find it a particularly hard choice."

Mother sighed and pinched the bridge of her nose and shut her eyes. "I do not want to do this." Her soft voice carried through the stillness of the cellar.

"Mother, it's the only way," said Elizabeth in a wheedling tone of voice.

Arabella turned her face to her mother. "Mother, please. I don't know what this final test is, but please don't do this. There must be another way."

Mother covered her face with both hands and shook her head from side to side.

"Think of the others, Mother." Elizabeth's soft whisper carried this time. "Amelia and Rowena, Jessamine and Josephine, Vivienne and her unborn babe—would you sacrifice all of them for *her*?"

Mother's shoulders curled forward and she moaned, muffled by the hands over her face.

"Mother, it's the only way," Elizabeth repeated as she squeezed her mother's shoulders. Elizabeth's brow furrowed and beads of sweat popped up on her forehead.

Mother lifted her tear-streaked face from her hands, her eyes glassy and unseeing, and said, "You're absolutely sure? You're sure this is the only way?"

"Yes." Elizabeth's voice was firm.

"Let's get this over with then," Mother said and both she and Elizabeth approached Arabella with grim determination.

Arabella shook her head rapidly and repeated "no, no, no, no" over and over. Mother and Elizabeth avoided her eyes as they each grabbed a side of the chair and dragged it backward across the room to the large wooden tub. They grunted as they heaved Arabella and her chair up onto a hinged platform at the lip of the huge tub. Together in silence they bound the chair down with leather straps, binding her right arm down last, and tested the ropes that ran from the pulley above to the platform. Arabella looked back over her shoulder to see what was in the tub. A broad, flat span of water, black in the dim light of the cellar, lay below her. She could feel waves of cool air rising up from it. She rocked back and forth, trying to somehow find a weakness in her bindings.

"Mother, please," she whimpered. "Please don't do this."

Mother reached and caressed her cheek. "It's to save the family." She stepped back and nodded to Elizabeth, who held the ropes tight in her hands. Elizabeth grinned and let go.

Arabella plunged backward into the pool of water. The icy cold dug into her flesh and she gasped from the shock. Water rushed into her mouth and down her throat. She clamped her mouth shut and thrashed against her bonds. There was already water in her lungs and she had to fight the near-overwhelming urge to cough. Then she was hauled up out of the tub and was upright again. She hacked and gagged, vomiting lungs full of water into her lap. Her body was wracked by tremors as her water-logged clothing clung to her. Water ran into her eyes and she couldn't see. She tried to blink to clear them, but more water just streamed down out of her hair.

"You can save yourself, Arabella," Mother's voice came from her left. "All you have to do is move the water out of the way, or spin the air into a cyclone to clear the water from your face. Or you can call to me or your sister with your mind, or you cause any of the testing implements to move." There was a pause. "Again."

Arabella felt herself start to drop and heard the squeal of the pulley. This time she was prepared and held her breath. The icy fingers of the water tried to make her gasp, but she kept her jaw clamped shut. In her mind, she screamed, "Help me! Help me! Help me!" over and over, begging for her mother or sister to hear her and let her out of the water. Her lungs started to burn when the pulley hauled her out of the water again. She drew in a ragged breath and said in a rough voice, "You heard me. Oh thank you, you heard me!"

"I didn't hear anything, did you, Mother?" Elizabeth's voice came from her right.

"I heard nothing." Mother's voice was cold and harsh, making the dunking water seem warm in comparison. "Again."

Arabella felt the chair pitch backward and barely had time to suck in a breath before the water covered her again. Once more, she cried out with her mind and pushed out the words with every ounce of strength she had. But the water still trapped her. Her lungs began to burn, but this time there was no reprieve. She struggled and thrashed as well as she could, but the ropes were swelled with water and held her tighter than ever. Darkness pushed down on her and Arabella feared losing consciousness. She reached out with her mind for something, anything that could save her. She found the pulley. It was a simple machine, but it was still a machine. Arabella made the sheaves turn and the rope slide and she rose out of the water. She was upright and the fetid air of the cellar tasted just as sweet as the first day of spring.

"What did you do?" she heard Mother say as she sat in the chair panting with her head drooping to her chest.

"I didn't do anything!" Elizabeth howled. "She moved the rope, somehow she moved the rope and now it won't work." Arabella heard the block and tackle jangle and thump, but she held it firm in her mind and saved herself from another dunk in the water. She heard her sister howl in rage.

"It's a machine," Mother said in a soft voice as she looked up at the immobile block and tackle.

"Leave it," she said with a gesture to Elizabeth. "Perhaps if we let her sit with her own thoughts for a while she might come to her senses and leave the damn machines alone."

Arabella's head snapped up and she watched her mother and Elizabeth retreating with the only light in the whole cellar. She tried to beg them not to leave her in the cool dark, alone and soaking wet, but she couldn't force any words past her raw throat. At the base of the stairs, Elizabeth paused and whispered something to their mother. Arabella cried out with joy when she saw Elizabeth walking back toward her with an oil lamp. But her joy was short lived.

Elizabeth clambered up on the platform and dug her fingers into Arabella's chignon and yanked her head back. She pulled a rag from her apron pocket and stuffed it in Arabella's mouth, then took another and bound it around the lower half of her face. She gave Arabella a little smirk, then climbed down and flounced away, oil lamp in hand.

When the cellar door shut, Arabella heard a key turn in the lock and she was alone, shivering in the pitch black. She let her head drop forward again and sobbed, the sounds muffled by her gag, hot tears running down her cold cheeks for what seemed like forever. She cried and cried until there was nothing left inside her. She sat bound and shivering, waiting in fear for whatever came next.

CHAPTER XVII

Wherein a Sister Comes to Arabella

EVEN THOUGH THE DAY OUTSIDE HAD BEEN WARM, PROMISING A sweltering summer, the cellar remained cool, as it had been designed. And the temperature just kept dropping as the sun went down. Arabella sat in the dark, bound to the chair, and could not stop shivering. Above her head she could hear movement in the house and wished she was able to call for help. She chewed on the rag in her mouth in frustration. She worked it with her tongue, trying to push it out of the way, but Elizabeth had done her job well. Arabella twisted her wrists against the ropes and winced at the pain from the raw skin.

When she heard a hinge squeak and the light step of a foot from deep in the cellar behind her, she froze. Every muscle in her body stiffened and screamed at her to run, but she could not. A cold dribble of sweat slid down the length of her spine as she listened to footsteps coming closer. All around her the darkness slowly retreated and she began to make out shadows of the things around her. The light grew brighter as whoever held the source drew near. It was a gentle golden glow, like a candle rather than an oil lamp.

"Arabella?" It was Rowena. Arabella felt all of her muscles relax and she screamed into her gag.

"Oh, *Sweet Lady*, Arabella!" Rowena cried and the light source lowered to the floor as her sister clambered up onto the platform and immediately removed the gag, then began to work on the knots around Arabella's wrists. "What happened? Who did this to you? We need to get Mother right away!"

"No!" Arabella tried to scream, but her voice came out as more of a raw croak. "Mother is the one who did this to me, Mother and Elizabeth."

"What?" Rowena gasped, as she momentarily stopped pulling the rope away from Arabella's chest. "You can't be serious!"

Arabella sagged forward with a groan when the ropes finally released, allowing her to relax from the stiff-backed chair. "I've never been more serious about anything in my life, Ro."

The tears began to fall again and Arabella told Rowena everything that had happened since Elizabeth led her to the cellar door. As she spoke, Rowena finished untying her and helped her down from the platform. Arabella's legs trembled from cold and exhaustion, and they sank to the floor together as Rowena wrapped her arms around Arabella, trying to warm her up.

"And then they left me here alone in the dark," Arabella said with a sob as she finished her story. "Mother thought that if I was alone with my thoughts long enough that I would somehow figure out how to use traditional magic." She buried her face into Rowena's shoulder and wept.

Rowena held her, patting her shoulders and rubbing her back. She shook her head and murmured to herself, "It's like Mother and Elizabeth have gone mad."

"She said I was a danger to the family unless I can exhibit traditional magic because the Council will punish the whole family because of me; all of Blackstone House too." Arabella's teeth chattered and her voice came out shaky from her shivering.

Rowena squeezed her again. "We need to get you warmed up, little sister. Then we can think about what to do. Stay here."

Rowena disappeared into the shadows and Arabella heard the hinges of trunks squeak as her sister opened and closed them. After a few minutes, she came back into the circle of light with an old wool blanket in her arms. It smelled musty and was riddled with dozens of moth holes, but it felt like the finest cashmere to Arabella as Rowena wrapped it around her shoulders.

"This will have to do for now," Rowena said. "After I get you tucked someplace safer, I'll bring you something better."

"What?" Arabella asked as Rowena helped her to her feet. "What do you mean tuck me someplace safer?"

"Well, I certainly can't leave you here to wait for Mother and Elizabeth to come back and torture you more," Rowena said. "And I can't take you upstairs. They are both up there and would just drag you back down here."

"Oh, Ro, what am I going to do?" cried Arabella as she thought about the implications of her situation. She could not go back to life as she knew it, Mother would never allow it. Where else did she have to go?

"We'll think of something," Rowena said, squeezing her again and guiding her deeper into the cellar. "For now, we just have to worry about hiding you for long enough to give us some time to think." She paused. "Ah, this will do."

Rowena guided Arabella behind a stack of old trunks that created a small, lightless alcove against the bare earth of the cellar wall. She helped Arabella sit down and tucked the musty blanket around her.

"I'm sorry, Ari," she said. "But I'm going to have to take the candle with me and leave you in the dark, but don't worry. I'll be back for you." She kissed her sister on the forehead.

Even though she was filthy, wrapped in a moth-eaten blanket, and still soaked to the skin from her dunking, Arabella started to feel her body relax for the first time in the hours and hours since she'd been in the garden.

"I'll be fine, Ro, I know you'll be back," Arabella said, stifling a yawn.

Rowena rose and turned to walk away when Arabella asked, "But how did you get in with the door locked, Ro?"

"Remember the big door in the corner of the garden the servants use to load in large things for storage?" Rowena said as she looked down on her little sister with a small smile.

Arabella smiled back. "But how did you even think to come and look for me?"

Rowena frowned a little and her brow pinched together as she considered the question. "I just had a feeling I needed to come find you. It nagged at me all afternoon, and when I couldn't find you in any of the

usual spots I got worried and started looking in some unusual places."
She shrugged. "I need to go before I'm missed, but I'll be back."

Arabella nodded and settled back into her corner, watching the
candlelight drift away and drowsing from her exhaustion. As she
drifted off to sleep she wondered, had Rowena's nagging feeling been
her own psychic abilities warning her sister that she needed help, or
had Arabella actually succeeded at telepathy and Rowena had heard
her?

Arabella had no idea how long she had slept when she started
awake to Rowena's hand on her arm. She had a large basket perched on
her hip, and a shawl draped over her head.

"It's alright," Rowena whispered. "It's just me. I've brought you
some clothes to change into."

Arabella unfolded her aching body from under the smelly blanket
and allowed Rowena to help her peel off her stiff, filthy clothes.

"Ugh, I wish there was some way for me to bathe properly before I
put on clean clothes," Arabella said with a wrinkle of her nose.

"I know," Rowena sighed. "But you'll be able to bathe once you get
to where you're going, and that will have to do."

"Going?" Arabella's voice cracked. "Where am I going?"

Rowena set her mouth in a grim line. "I sent word to John. I thought
he'd be safe because he already knew some of what is going on." She
blew out her breath. "You'll be going to live with Father."

"Are you sure there's nothing else we can do? Nowhere else I can
go?" Arabella pleaded.

"Ari, any witch on Mother's side of the family would bring you
right back here," Rowena said. "And Father's side of the family would
take you straight to Father, if they didn't drag you back to Mother. So,
you might as well go to Father on your own."

Arabella sighed and her shoulders sagged. "You're right, Ro. I just
hope he doesn't try to treat me like a mundane woman. I couldn't bear
that kind of restriction after the way we've lived all our lives."

Rowena helped Arabella do up her last buttons and then gave her
a quick hug. "Father is a good man, a reasonable man. He'll see the
wisdom in you keeping your freedoms. He married a witch and never
fought to keep her under his thumb, didn't he?"

"And he eventually left her too," Arabella said in a bitter voice.

"Well, Ari," Rowena said with a sigh. "It's got to be better than waiting for another dunk in Mother's tub."

A shudder ran through Arabella's body and she grabbed Rowena's hand. "Which way is out?"

Rowena led her through the cellar and up a short flight of stairs to the old cellar door that led to the corner of the garden. The hinges only squeaked a little as Rowena pushed up on the doors. Moria was waiting for them, muffled in a gray wool shawl, clutching a large carpet bag. Arabella looked up into the clear night sky at the stars and the moon. It was well past midnight and on into the small hours of the morning. The night was silent but for the crickets and the rustle of fabric from their skirts on the flagstones.

"I packed a few essentials for you, enough to last you a few days," Moria whispered as she handed the bag to Arabella. The three women walked quickly around the edge of the garden, keeping to the shadows and heading for the hidden garden gate Arabella had used on that fateful day almost a month ago. "There's also some bread and cheese and cold bacon wrapped up in a cloth on the top. I thought you might be hungry."

They paused at the gate and Arabella caught Moria's sad eyes. "Thank you," she whispered and gave her a quick hug before Rowena hustled her out of the garden.

"Please send word about how you are doing," Rowena murmured as they hurried down the empty alley toward the waiting hansom cab at the end. They stopped just short of the cab and looked at each other for a silent moment. The bay horse in the traces snorted and stamped its foot. The girls embraced each other and held tight for two heartbeats.

"I don't know if I can bear leaving you," Arabella whispered as a single tear snaked down her cheek.

"And I can't bear to see you hurt any further," Rowena said as she put her hand on Arabella's cheek. The cab door creaked open.

"As touching as this moment is," John said from inside the cab. "I think it would be wise if we were gone before Mother discovers the game is afoot."

Both girls nodded to him and after one last quick embrace, Rowena helped Arabella into the cab and shut the door behind her. Arabella didn't lean out the window to watch her home recede away this time.

Inside the cab, Arabella fumbled with the clasp on the carpet bag, digging out the food as soon as she got it open. John watched her with a raised eyebrow as she tore off hunks of bread and cheese and bacon and stuffed them into her mouth, barely pausing to chew.

"I have tea," he said as he held up and old-fashioned earthenware flask stoppered with a thick cork.

"Thank you," Arabella mumbled around her mouthful food, staring at him with wide eyes.

"Do you want to talk about it?" he asked as he handed her the flask.

Arabella shook her head and took a long swallow of tea. "Not yet," she said. "I just want to eat and bathe and sleep in a real bed."

John leaned back and crossed his ankle across his knee. "That may have to wait just a little bit, Ari, at least until you've talked to Father."

"You woke him before you left?" Arabella choked on another gulp of tea.

"I didn't have to," John said with a shrug. "I told you, he's been on a tear with his experiments. He's been up at strange hours of the day and night. He'll want to know why his youngest daughter, the daughter of a witch, is coming to live with him."

Arabella bowed her head and nodded. "I'll tell you the story together then, that way I'll only have to tell it once."

She was silent for the rest of the ride, doggedly applying herself to the food Moria had packed her. John kept his own counsel and watched the city go by with thoughtful eyes.

CHAPTER XVIII

Wherein Arabella Provides Her Father a Demonstration

L ORD ALEXANDER PAUL LEYDEN'S LONDON TOWNHOME WAS NOT A familiar place to Arabella. The summer visits her mother allowed always happened at his country estate. Those visits had been stilted affairs, and Arabella fretted over how her father would receive her as they pulled up to their final destination. John handed her down from the hansom cab on the broad sidewalk in front of an imposing Georgian townhouse. It was not quite as large as her mother's own Gothic Revival affair, but it was still quite impressive.

The wrought-iron gate blocking in the front walk creaked as John pushed it open and waved Arabella through. It seemed like every light in the house was burning, windows ablaze despite the late, or perhaps early, hour.

"Don't your neighbors complain about the lights?" Arabella asked as she followed her older brother up the walk.

John shrugged as he fit his key into the lock and let them into the front hall. "I don't really pay attention to such things." He shut the door behind her and locked it again, then hung up his coat and hat on the already crowded coat tree.

Arabella looked up and around at the pictures of relatives she'd never met crowded next to each other, each frame nearly on top of the next to the point that she could not tell if the wallpaper pattern was flowers or stripes.

She goggled as the massive chandelier above her head hissed softly with gaslight, each crystal drop shimmering in the light. Arabella also watched the magic glow seeping down the arms that contained the gas lines, swirling around the mechanisms that allowed the flame to be brought up or down. Her skin tingled and she longed to reach out with her mind and feel the flow of power.

"What? You've never seen one of those before?" John asked as he stood next to her with his hands in his pockets, rocking heel to toe.

Arabella shook her head as she stared, entranced. "Mother only allows candles or oil lamps. I've seen some gaslight since my power manifested, but it's still glorious to see."

"Well, you'll be seeing plenty more of it," John said as he took her carpet bag from her and dropped it on the floor next to the coat tree. "Father loves every technological advance and installs them as soon as possible." He took her hand and led her down the hall further into the house.

John sighed. "Let's go see the old ox then, and then we can all get some rest."

Her father's lab was at the back of the house, extending across the entire width of the building. Arabella wondered if her parents had fought for the location when they'd lived together, since it occupied the same territory her mother used for her still room. Two broad counters running side by side took up most of the room, and bookshelves covered the walls. Shoved into a corner were two small desks, both piled high with papers and books. In the corner of the room diagonal from the desks was an occupied cot. Arabella's older brother Henry snored away, still dressed in a suit. On the slick black marble surfaces of the counters were most every type of alchemical or scientific instrument available. A brass astrolabe shared space with grisly jars of preserved animals. Slick brown bottles of chemicals, neatly labeled, nestled alongside bundles of herbs. But the far counter held the most interesting contraption of all.

Spanning nearly the entire length of the surface was a perplexing hodge-podge of beakers, open jars, and test tubes, all connected with a welter of wire and glass tubing. Some of the containers sat over flames, while others floated in ice baths, and the liquid shifted from pale blue to dark blue to green, then finally clear. Arabella sucked breath in through her teeth at the sight of all the magic flowing through it. It was so bright it left an afterimage on her eyes when she looked away.

Behind the counter, at its center was her father, Alexander Leyden. He leaned forward with his arms spread wide and his palms flat, shoulders hunched, over the book in front of him. His graying hair, which had once been a dark brown like Arabella's, stuck out in all directions. His tie was loose and his sleeves rolled up. It looked like he hadn't slept in days, or if he had he'd slept in the clothes on his back as her eldest brother did now. He muttered to himself over the book, his brow furrowed, and did not acknowledge the presence of his two youngest children.

After waiting to be noticed for a few moments, John cleared his throat. When Alexander did not react, he coughed and said, "Father?"

"What is it, boy?" Arabella's father said in an exasperated voice as he pushed away from the counter and lifted his eyes. "Can't you see I'm busy?"

"You asked me to bring Arabella to you right after I fetched her," John said in a calm voice.

Father's clear blue gaze, the mirror reflection of her own, fell on her. He said nothing at first, and Arabella began to squirm under his intense scrutiny.

"So I did," Alexander said in a faraway voice. "So I did..." He took off his half-moon spectacles and polished them with a dingy handkerchief from his pocket. He put them back on and blinked owlishly at his daughter and son.

Arabella broke the silence. "It's very nice to see you, sir," she said as she bobbed a curtsey.

"We'll give you a day or two to settle in, Arabella," Father said with a nod as he turned back to his book. "Then you'll need to get to work setting the house to rights and bringing in some new staff." The last words trailed off in a mumble as he became absorbed in the book again.

Arabella flushed to the roots of her hair. "I'm sorry, sir? What do you mean set the house to rights and hire new staff?"

Father looked up from his book with a frown. "It seems we ran off the last batch, something about us being too difficult to deal with. You'll need to hire more."

"Father," Arabella said, balling her fists up at her side. "I'm not here to run your house; I'm here because I need your protection."

He sighed and shook his head. "Of course I'll protect you, Arabella, you're my daughter. I'm not some kind of monster. But you can't expect to just lay about the house all day, like you did at your mother's. You're going to have to earn your keep."

"But I'm a witch!" exclaimed Arabella. "Not some common housemaid!"

"No, my darling, you are not a witch," Alexander said in a condescending voice as he tilted his head to the side. "You can't manage even the simplest of spells, therefore you are not a witch, no matter how much you or your mother might wish it."

"Not a witch, eh," Arabella tightened her jaw and growled, eyes ablaze, the events of the last twenty-four hours igniting a fire in her belly. She reached out with her mind and turned up the flames on every single burner in her father's contraption. In short order, the pale blue liquid boiled over. The green liquid bubbled to the brim of its beaker and foamed away merrily. Father howled and tried to turn down knobs on the burners to reduce the flames, but they would not budge. The sealed beaker with the dark blue liquid exploded, followed shortly by the sealed beaker of clear liquid. Her father dropped into a crouch and covered his head with his arms. John yelped and reached for Arabella, but his hands froze and hovered just over her shoulders, as if he feared touching her would make the destruction worse.

Once Father was sure no more explosions were imminent, he stood and turned to Arabella with his mouth wide open. With a slight smile and a lift of her chin she made a gesture with her hand and turned the flame of every single burner off. The green liquid subsided to a viscous sludge, and what was left of the pale blue liquid sent one last, huge bubble to the surface, where it popped. Whatever had been in the exploded beakers now dripped off the edge of the counter and onto the floor.

"It seems, Father, that while I may not be a conventional witch, I am somehow able to manipulate technological devices," she said. "However, this makes the witches on the Council very nervous and they threatened Mother's position as Grande Dame. Mother seems to think that unless I display some kind of traditional power they will destroy the family and all of Blackstone House. Given that Mother was resorting to torture to try to get me to manifest them, Rowena and I thought it would be best if I came to live with you."

In the corner, Henry sat up on the cot blinking sleep out of his eyes and running his hands through his hair. "What did I miss?" he mumbled.

Father waved his hand to silence him and turned to John.

"Did you know about this?" he demanded.

"I knew some of it," John said with a shrug. "But I didn't know all of it until tonight."

Their father turned back to Arabella and pinned her with a calculating gaze. "Can you control this power reliably?"

"I am still learning, Father," said Arabella. "But every time I use it, I grow stronger and more precise."

He nodded and stroked the stubble on his chin. "It is usually that way with magic. How long have you been working with your talent?"

Arabella thought for a moment. "A few months, since May."

His eyes widened and he grew still. He swallowed convulsively. "Oh my, you're showing quite a bit of control for being so new to your power."

Arabella shrugged and sighed. "Perhaps that is just the way of it with technological witches; perhaps we learn faster than conventional witches."

"One witch is hardly a large enough sample to prove that theory. Perhaps you advanced more quickly because you've watched you mother and your sisters manipulate nature magic your whole life and you absorbed those techniques and knowledge." he *harrumphed*. "I may not know how to cast spells myself, young lady, but I do know how to prove a hypothesis. It could be that you are just incredibly powerful, but we can't know which hypothesis is true until we have a larger sample. Has anyone else shown similar abilities?"

"Not that I know of," Arabella said as she shook her head. "Lilly Ferguson from Dunleah House said something about a schism in the North and that some of the younger witches are more friendly to progress, but nothing about powers like mine."

Henry sidled up to his father and whispered into his ear. "We can use this to our advantage, Father. We can use her to draw some of the more traditional people into the fold."

"I can hear you, Henry," said Arabella as she crossed her arms over her chest and started to tap her foot. "My powers haven't deafened me, and I don't appreciate being thought of as some pawn to be moved about a chessboard for the sake of political influence. I had more than enough of that earlier today, thank you very much."

Henry turned a brilliant smile to his sister. "Of course, you're right, Arabella; how rude of me."

He sounded sincere but Arabella still felt uncomfortable under his predatory gaze. It reminded her ever so slightly of Elizabeth and sent a shiver down her spine. She dropped her eyes and started to fidget.

"Henry, don't be a cad," their father said. "Arabella is right. You don't use family as pawns. Perhaps other people, but not family." He chuckled at his own joke but none of his children seemed to find it funny.

He tilted his head to the side and addressed Arabella. "Although… We have been having quite a time with the Luddites and trying to unite the machinists and technologists as one. You could do quite a bit to improve the situation if you so desired. But of course, that would have to be your choice, my darling." He crossed the room in three long strides and drew Arabella into his arms.

Arabella felt her tension melt away and she relaxed into her father's embrace.

"It's alright now, my darling," he murmured as he stroked her hair. "Everything is going to be alright."

CHAPTER XIX

On an Unkempt House and an Unexpected Visitor

WHEN ARABELLA WOKE, HER HEART BEGAN TO RACE AND IT TOOK HER a moment to remember why she was sleeping in an unfamiliar room on musty sheets. They had obviously been clean when they were put on the bed, but it was just as obvious that no one had aired out this room in quite some time. Arabella lay on her back staring at the thick clusters of cobwebs that clogged the corners of the room thinking about what she should do for the day. She felt unmoored, lost. As much as she had hated her mother's stiff control, at least there was no question about what to do or how to do it. Now, she needed to figure out what her father's house needed and assemble a new staff, with no instructions or template to follow.

Arabella got up and began to investigate her new bedroom. There was a thick layer of dust in the washbasin and water ewer. The empty armoire smelled strongly from the pungent blocks of cedar wedged in the corners. She padded across the floor and pulled open the thick velvet curtains, nearly choking on the cloud of dust that showered down on her. It was early afternoon, judging by the angle of the sun. Her bedroom window overlooked the back garden, which was weed-choked and full of all manner of dead plants. Arabella frowned. It was obvious that there were no garden Fae at work here.

This was nothing like the clean, well-tended house she'd grown up in with her mother. She remembered her father saying the last servants had run off, and she wondered how long it had been since the Leyden men had had proper human servants. It seemed that they did not even have a simple household hob or brownie when a house this size should have been home to a whole clan. She turned away from the window with a sigh and started to form a mental plan for finding servants and setting the house to rights, despite her previous protest that it was beneath her. She made a mental note to also send Rowena a letter and ask her to send over copies of some of the simpler magic charms, ones even a mundane person could manage, for attracting household Fae. Her father and brothers were obviously incapable, and she would not live in squalor for the rest of her life.

With new determination, Arabella set about getting ready for the day, and dressing as well as she could without the help of a ladies' maid. Fortunately, Moria had been smart when she packed the bag and chose the simplest dresses Arabella owned. As she tied her hair back with a ribbon and tucked the stray locks behind her ears, she gave her reflection in the grimy mirror one last look and a wry smile, murmuring, "It will have to do." Arabella's stomach growled and let her know that it would not be ignored for much longer. She set off to look for the kitchen and hoped there might be something in the larder.

The hall outside her bedroom was silent and still, the plush blue carpet hushing her footfalls. There were three other doors, all shut, which Arabella assumed were the bedrooms for her brothers and father. She paused in the middle of the hall, listening carefully, but heard not a single sound stirring from any of them. She paced down the hall, knocking on all of the doors. There was no response. She wondered if the Leyden men were not home at all, or if they were just so deeply asleep that her knocking didn't rouse them, which would not be so odd considering the strange hours it seemed they kept. At the end of the hall, stairs led down to the main floor and to the floor above. Arabella decided that she would investigate the upper floors after she'd found something to eat.

On the ground floor of the house, Arabella peered into the first room to the right of the front door and found the parlor, dark, silent, and as dusty as the rest of the house. Next to it was the library, all dark wood and leather, and again, dust. Arabella crept inside on tiptoe, feeling a bit like a naughty child snooping through her father's private space. She opened the drawers of the desk one by one, finding old ledgers for household accounts and paper for correspondence, but all the ink was dried out. She'd have to get some fresh before she could write a proper letter to Rowena. She turned and looked at the bookcases that lined the wall behind the desk, squinting at the titles in the dim light coming through the filthy windows. Most of them seemed to be focused on science and mechanics. Arabella traced her finger tips over the spines and thought that she should probably read a few of them since a greater understanding of mechanics might lead to a greater understanding of her own power. Her stomach growled again and reminded her that this side trip on the way to the kitchen was not appreciated.

She made one last detour, bypassing the dining room to the left of the front door and checking her father's lab for signs of life. It was just as quiet and dark as the rest of the house, but it was not as dirty. It felt like the only inhabited room in the house. Books, papers and implements cluttered the room, to be sure, but otherwise everything was sparkling clean and dust free. In fact, there wasn't even a trace of the mess from her temper tantrum that had destroyed her father's contraption the night before.

She left the lab behind and found the door to the basement kitchen, and descended into the dark. At the bottom of the stairs, she stopped at the threshold and wished that she had her sister Jessamine's talent for fire magic so that she could just call up a small ball of fire in her palm to light her way. The half windows at the top of the walls were so coated in soot and grime that it might have been full night at the dark of the moon outside instead of an early afternoon full of bright sun. Arabella squinted into the darkness and tried to suppress a shudder as she heard something skitter across the tile floor. She gritted her teeth and stepped into the kitchen, making her way to a large, low shadow that she hoped was the cook's table in the middle of the room. She made it to the table without anything running over her feet and found an old kerosene lamp with a near empty box of matches beside it on the table. There were only two. Striking one of them with trembling fingers, Arabella lit the lamp and adjusted the flame. She held it up high to look around the room, revealing just what she had gotten herself into. If anything, the kitchen was even filthier than the rest of the house. Old, crusted dishes were stacked in a stone sink across the room. Likely only the spiders who had spun the thick webs that covered the ceiling rafters knew how long they had been there. Arabella let out a startled yelp when she saw two sleek, fat rats scuttle away from her circle of light. She approached the gas range that was nestled in the old original broad hearth. She'd never seen one in service and longed to see it working, glowing with both fire and magic. The hinges on the oven door made an ear-piercing squeal as she pulled it open. She thought not even the spiders or the rats knew the last time it had been cleaned. She moved on to the larder. The hasp of the lock hung open, swinging free. It was bare but for a nearly empty sack of rice spread out over the middle of the floor. Both ends had been well chewed by industrious rodents, and what few grains were left probably wouldn't be there for long.

All in all, the kitchen looked like it belonged to a house that had been abandoned for years, rather than one that had people living upstairs at this very moment. Arabella shook her head and decided that she would be taking all of her meals out until she could resolve the servant and house hob situation. Food from this kitchen, in the state it was currently in, could hardly be considered healthy. Holding up the hem of her skirt, she made her way out of the kitchen and wondered if she had enough money in her reticule to stand a hansom cab ride and luncheon at a tea house. She bit her lip and wondered if that would be safe. Would her mother have begun looking for her? Perhaps she should wait for her father or one of her brothers to return, hopefully before she starved.

She had just reached the top of the stairs and was brushing cobwebs and dust off her skirts when she heard a knock at the front door. Arabella froze, struck by the sudden fear of who or what could be on the doorstep. Was it her mother come to drag her back home? Her hand began to tremble. She blew out the lamp and set it at her feet before she dropped it. Silently, she stood, chewing her bottom lip and twisting her fingers together. Maybe whoever it was would go away.

She startled when the knock came again and pressed her palms to her stomach in an effort to calm the butterflies. What if it was someone one of her brothers or her father was expecting? What if it was a package of important materials for an experiment? They would be quite cross with her if she didn't answer the door to take delivery. Arabella decided to wait and see if whoever it was persisted in knocking. If they knocked again, she would answer the door.

The minutes crept by and Arabella started to breathe a little easier, letting her shoulders drop, sure the mystery person on the other side of the door had given up. Then the knock came again. Arabella hesitated, but squared her shoulders and strode up the hall to the front of the house to answer. Setting a polite smile on her lips, she lifted her chin and opened the door.

The words of cheerful inquiry she'd planned died on her lips. Her stomach dropped and she felt as if her entire body had been drenched with ice water. Standing on the doorstep with a feral grin on his lips was Bartholomew Westerfeld in a crisp black suit, vivid green brocade vest, and bowler.

"Ah, good afternoon, Miss Sortilege, I'm so glad I found you at home," he said as his grin grew wider and more menacing. "May I come in?"

"How... How did you know where to find me?" Arabella blurted as she tried to keep her voice from trembling.

Westerfeld chuckled. "There are many people in this city so desperate for money that they will do anything, even watch the house of the most powerful witch in the Isles day and night. I dare say I knew you'd left long before your mother did. And I know where you are, something she doesn't know yet. Then it just took a bit of patience until all the men left the household so that you and I could have a private chat."

A shudder ran through Arabella. "No. No, I don't think that would be a good idea."

"But, Miss Sortilege, I've only come to apologize for the incident at the Garden." His voice dropped to a menacing octave and his thick brows drew together.

"That's quite unnecessary," Arabella said in a quivering voice. "I would quite like it if you would leave now."

"Not before I've apologized." Westerfeld's smile grew strained.

"Say what you must then and go." Arabella lifted her chin a notch.

"Oh, don't be rude, Miss Sortilege," Westerfeld said as he took a step toward the door that Arabella held only partially open. "Don't make me stand on the street and grovel." He shoved a gloved hand at the door.

Arabella shrieked and leaned all her weight into the door to make it shut. Westerfeld threw his shoulder into it and grunted. For a moment, they struggled, but in the end Westerfeld won out and flung the door wide open. Arabella stumbled back with a cry, nearly falling to the ground. Westerfeld strode into the house with a maniacal smirk on his lips. He reached behind him and slammed the door shut. He touched his fingers to the brim of his bowler.

"Alone at last." His voice sent chills running up and down Arabella's spine. She looked around her desperately for an escape route. Westerfeld stood in front of the hall that went to the back of the house, and from there outside to the garden. The parlor and library behind her were both dead ends, with one way in and one way out. Her eyes darted to the stairs. It wasn't ideal, but it just might allow her to avoid Westerfeld long enough for someone to intervene.

Westerfeld took a long stride closer to her, his gears whirring and clicking. "Oh, no you don't. Now that I've got you alone, I'm not letting you run off that easily."

Arabella took another step back with her hands at her sides, fists opening and closing, looking from side to side for some sort of a weapon.

"Come now," Westerfeld said in an oily voice. "Calm yourself. I only want to talk to you, *for now.*" The threat in the last two words made her shudder again.

She swallowed hard and looked away. "What do you want of me?"

"What do I want of you?" Westerfeld echoed with a laugh that turned into a snarl. "You can't give me what I really want. I want my reputation back. I was a rising star before you destroyed it."

"I'm so sorry, Mr. Westerfeld," Arabella stammered. "I didn't mean you any harm, truly I didn't."

"You expect me to believe that, you filthy little witch? You expect me to believe that you came and toyed with my machine, distracting the dillies, with no malice at all? You expect me to believe you didn't do it on purpose?" Westerfeld bellowed.

"Dillies? What dillies?" Arabella frowned and her brows pinched together.

"Stop pretending, you stupid witch!" Westerfeld shouted and shook his fists. "You know exactly what you did and you did it intentionally to destroy me!" Spittle flew from his lips.

"Mr. Westerfeld, I'm certain I don't know what you are talking about." Arabella backed up another couple of steps.

"Yes, you do!" he shouted and pulled a revolver from his pocket. He pointed it at Arabella, his hand trembling so much that the muzzle jittered around in a spastic pattern.

Arabella gasped and her hands flew to her mouth. "Mr. Westerfeld, there's no reason..."

"Yes, there is," he interrupted her and put his other hand on the gun to steady it. "I've lost my reputation, my friends, my ability to make a living—all because of you." The gun stabilized and the barrel aimed straight for Arabella's heart. His lips hardened into a thin white line.

Fear washed through Arabella and her breath caught in her throat. She watched him pull back on the hammer with his thumb, and saw the muscles in his hand start to tense. She closed her eyes, sweat beading on her forehead, and reached out with her mind to jam the trigger of the gun.

When the gun didn't fire, Westerfeld howled and shook it with both hands. He yanked and pulled at both the hammer and the trigger, but neither one would budge. He let loose a roar of inarticulate rage and threw the entire gun at Arabella.

She dropped into a crouch. The gun hit the wall above her and bounced away, leaving a hole in the plaster. It landed on the slick marble floor and slid away into the shadows.

Westerfeld lunged for Arabella, knocking his bowler askew. She jumped up from her crouch and retreated two more steps. When she backed into the wall she nearly stumbled. Westerfeld stretched out his arms to reach for her. As she had done at the Gardens, she jammed the gears encasing his legs with her mind and he toppled to the floor. Arabella kept edging toward the library, pressing herself hard against the wall, whimpering as she went. Westerfeld growled and dragged himself along the floor with his arms, snatching at her skirts.

Arabella cried out in relief when she saw John come through the front door with a paper sack in his arms and the smell of meat pies surrounding him.

"What the devil?" he cried as he dropped the bag and leapt forward. He grabbed Westerfeld by the ankles and began to drag him backward.

"Leave my sister alone!" John roared as he dragged Westerfeld back to the front door. Her attacker clawed at the marble floor and howled the whole way. Arabella followed, but not too close, needing to see Westerfeld gone before she could feel she was safe.

She watched as John pulled him out the door and down the front steps. Westerfeld's head dropped, his nose and chin scraping across the stone painfully with each step. John didn't stop dragging the man until he was outside the wrought iron front gate, where he dropped Westerfeld on the public sidewalk. Westerfeld's jacket was scuffed and torn, the buttons of his vest ripped away and leaving his white shirt smeared with dirt on display. His bowler was missing and a gash above his left eye bled freely down his face. Arabella watched from the front door with one hand on the door jamb and the other over her mouth.

John panted and shook his finger at Westerfeld where he lay on the ground as passersby stood frozen in shock, staring. "Don't you *ever* try to hurt my sister again, or I may not let you live next time."

John spat. Westerfeld flinched and threw up his hand to protect his face. The wad of spittle landed on his shoulder. John spun on his heel and stalked back into the house, leaving Westerfeld where he lay under the stunned gaze of the public.

John leaped up the front stairs, grabbing Arabella by her arm and pulling her inside. He shut the door and locked it behind them.

"It's alright, Ari, I got rid of Westerfeld and he won't try to hurt you anymore." He pulled his sister into a tight embrace. The implications of the whole event came crashing down on her and she began to sob into his shoulder as he patted her hair.

"There, there," he murmured.

"John, it was awful," she sobbed. "He was trying to kill me. He had a gun!"

"He had a gun?" John cried as he held Arabella away from him by the shoulders. "Where is it?"

Arabella sniffed hard and said, "I jammed the trigger with my magic and he threw it at me instead. It's somewhere on the floor in here." She waved a hand to encompass the front hall.

John pulled her close again and swayed with her as she cried.

"Where were you?" Arabella cried as she choked on her sobs. "Where are Henry and Father? I was all alone," she wailed.

"I went out to get us some food, Ari," John said as he rubbed her shoulders. "And Henry and Father are at an Alchemist's Society meeting. I'm so sorry; I shouldn't have left you alone."

It was quiet for a moment as John soothed Arabella and stared off into the distance. "I'm going to call the constables," he said.

"No, please don't!" Arabella cried and clutched at his shoulders. "It will only make him angrier."

"Arabella, we can't let him get away with this," John said as he looked deep into his sister's tear-filled eyes.

"Please, don't," Arabella's voice came out as a whisper. "Maybe he'll leave me alone now that he knows you will defend me. But if we tell the authorities and he's punished again, he'll just get angrier and he might try something worse."

John set his jaw and shook his head. "We should at least tell Father what happened."

"Tell me what?" Alexander Leyden said from the front doorway. Henry looked over his father's shoulder with a shocked expression. "Perhaps you'd like to tell me why are there meat pies all over the hallway floor?"

CHAPTER XX

Wherein a Relationship Is Severed and a Revelation Is Made

T HE LEYDEN HOUSE WAS SILENT IN THE AFTERMATH OF THE RECENT hostilities. Over cold meat pies that had been rescued from the floor, John had insisted throughout the previous evening that the constables still needed to be called, while Father worried aloud if it would be prudent, given some of the people Westerfeld knew. Then John pointed out that Westerfeld was already being abandoned by some of his friends, part of the reason he was so angry with Arabella in the first place. Henry thought it would be more efficient to take care of the Westerfeld problem through less civilized means. Arabella finally gave up on trying to get the men to hear her when none of them acknowledged her and stomped off to bed.

Arabella refused to emerge from her bedroom the next morning and on into the afternoon, despite repeated attempts by the Leyden men to get her to come out. She was profoundly grateful Moria had thought to tuck a novel and a book of poetry into the bottom of her bag. Not that she was able to calm herself enough to read them, but it was nice to have the option just the same. Pacing the carpet again after spending an hour or more staring morosely at the dead garden, Arabella tried to puzzle out what to do. There was a knock at the door. She halted her pacing and stared at the door, refusing to speak. The knock came again.

"Arabella? Darling?" It was Father. "Please answer me, child, let me know if you are alright."

Arabella sighed and rolled her eyes. "I'm fine, Father. Now please go away."

"I'm afraid I can't, dear. I've come to fetch you because you have a visitor."

Arabella's hand went to her throat and she paled. "Who is it, Father?" She tried to keep the quiver out of her voice.

"I really think it would be better if you just came downstairs, darling. Please?" There was a pleading note in his voice that Arabella had never heard before.

"I'm not coming down unless I know who it is," Arabella said.

Arabella heard her father sigh, followed by a soft thump that might have been his forehead against the doorjamb. "It's your mother and sisters, Arabella. They've come to take you to tea."

"*Tea?*" Arabella's stomach dropped.

"Yes, Arabella, tea." A note of exasperation crept into Father's voice. "Your mother said something about this having been arranged last Sunday, and that you had better hurry and get ready or you will make everyone late."

The blood rushed back into Arabella's face and she clenched her jaw. "She just assumes that I will come running when she snaps her fingers?" she muttered to herself as she strode to the door and snatched it open. Father goggled at her as she flounced down the hall with her fists balled up at her side. After a moment, he scampered after her.

As Arabella descended the stairs, her mother, Rowena, and Amelia looked up at her. They hadn't even bothered to take off their hats. John and Henry stood off to the side looking uncomfortable.

"Ah, Arabella, finally," Mother said. "But I'm afraid you'll have to go right back up and change, neither your dress nor your hair is suitable to have tea with House Heads. Rowena, go help your sister."

Rowena started for the stairs but Arabella said, from where she had stopped on the middle of the stairs, "That won't be necessary. I'm not coming to tea with you."

"You most certainly are, young lady," Mother said with a frown. "We are going to discuss you and your delicate situation. Don't be rude."

"This is rich even for you, Mother," Arabella said with a bitter laugh. "You can try to kill me to make me manifest traditional powers and that's perfectly civilized, but if I won't come have tea with people who would rather I were dead, then I am being rude."

Her mother pursed her lips and lifted her chin a notch. "To begin with, I would have never let you die. You are still my daughter, even if you are ungrateful. And secondly, Katherine Wardlow and Theodosia Boscoe have not come out against you — yet. We will need all the help we can get if you, and all of Blackstone House, are to survive, Arabella."

"You can't make all of Blackstone House my responsibility, Mother." Arabella crossed her arms over her chest.

"You are a flower of the Sortilege line, young lady, a scion of Blackstone House, and by Neptune's Beard you most certainly *do* have a responsibility to your House! Now, get upstairs and change this instant." Mother jabbed her finger at the stairs.

Arabella blinked and rocked back on her heels, but she didn't move. "No."

Mother's shoulders dropped and her voice took on a wheedling tone as she tried another tack. "Arabella, my chickadee, I'm only trying to do what is best for you and your sisters. I'm trying to protect you, protect us all, but I need you to come with me so that we can get more Council members on our side before the next session. How do you think it will look if you can't be bothered to answer their questions in person?"

"You just want to trot me out like a prize pig to ensure your grip on the Council, Mother," Arabella's voice low and firm. "Well, I won't do it. You can't have me to use as a pawn in your political games anymore." Arabella turned and headed back up the stairs, passing her father with her chin high and eyes focused into the distance.

"Arabella!" Mother shouted but Arabella did not turn around even as she struggled against a lifetime of conditioning. "Arabella, don't you dare walk away from me!" Still Arabella kept going.

Her mother huffed and shouted, "Arabella Helene, if you do not obey me this instant I will disown you from the Sortilege line, and Blackstone House will no longer offer you refuge!"

Everyone else in the room gasped and Arabella froze at the top of the stairs. She stood with her back to the people below for two long breaths before she slowly turned around and focused a hard gaze on her mother, her hands clasped in front of her to hide how badly they shook. Arabella cocked her head to the side.

"I would think that would solve all your problems, Mother," Arabella said in the same low, firm tone she had used before. Her heart throbbed rapidly, fueled by cold fury. "If I am no longer a Sortilege or sheltered by Blackstone House, then I cannot be a danger to the family or the other members of the House. I suppose I'll be a Leyden now."

Mother's jaw dropped open. Amelia and Rowena exchanged wide-eyed glances, while their father stumbled back onto the banister in shock. Only the young Leyden men didn't share in the general astonishment. John put his hand over his mouth to cover a satisfied grin but could not hide the twinkle in his eyes. Meanwhile, a sly smirk slid up Henry's face and his eyes took on a far-off look, deep in thought.

Arabella executed a slow, deep courtesy without breaking eye contact with her mother. "Thank you for coming to visit my home, Madame Grande Dame. I bid you good day."

And with that Arabella disappeared down the hall without a backward glance.

Arabella paced again, fuming, for twenty minutes, even though it felt like an hour, when another knock came on her bedroom door. "Go away!" she shouted.

"Arabella, it's your father. May I please come in?"

"I'm not going back downstairs," Arabella said. "I'm not going anywhere with Mother, and there's nothing you can say that will change my mind."

"I'm not trying to change your mind, darling," Father's voice was mild. "Your mother has already left anyway. It's been a long time since I've seen her in such a state."

Arabella opened the door on her father, standing out in the hall with a wan smile on his face and three books piled in his arms.

"She's really gone?" Arabella asked.

"She's really gone," he confirmed.

"Fine," Arabella said with a sigh. "Come in." She dropped onto the small bench in front of the dressing table, leaning forward with her elbows on her knees and her chin in her hands, leaving the reading chair by the window for her father. He sat and looked down at the books in his lap, tracing the spines with his thumb and letting his daughter come to him.

After a few minutes of silence, Arabella raised an eyebrow and asked, "So, what are *they*?"

"What are what?"

"The books in your hands."

Father looked up and smiled. "These were your mother's school books when she was a girl. She left them here when…" He swallowed hard and looked away for a moment. "She left them here when she moved away. I've always kept them in case one of you girls would want them." He extended them to her.

Arabella took them with a confused look on her face. "I thought Mother had all of her spell books, even the old ones. She doesn't want any of the family secrets getting out."

"I think if you'll look at the titles you'll see why she left these behind."

Arabella turned and spread the three books over the dressing table to examine them. "They are all very basic," she murmured. She opened one and leafed through the pages at random. "There are so many notes about focus items and animals," she said with a frown and turned back to her father.

"Mother says using focuses is the refuge of the weak witch. She won't even let the housemaids use wands, and she only lets Rowena and the others use stones for certain spells, like shields."

"I know," he said with a nod as he crossed his leg over his knee and leaned back in the chair. "She was like that when she was here, but she hasn't always been that way."

"Even without precognitive powers I can tell you're leading into a family story I've never heard before," Arabella said with a tilt of her head and a small smile.

Father chuckled and said, "Yes, I suppose I am being rather transparent."

He steepled his fingers in front of his mouth and thought for a moment before he began to speak again. "How much do you know about your mother's girlhood and early training, Arabella?"

"Mother doesn't talk about it much," she answered with a shrug. "About all she says is that she had it much harder than we do, that she's being easy on us."

"That does sound like Minerva." A wry smile touched Father's lips and he shook his head. "Has she ever told you about her sisters Leanore and Lorena?"

Arabella nodded. "Not much, just that Aunt Leanore killed herself trying to defeat the blight in Ireland, and that Aunt Lorena was too exhausted and distraught to stop the Catholics from dragging her from her room and killing her…such a ghastly business."

Father nodded as well. "It was an incident that left quite a mark on your mother. She never told you that she was there, did she?"

Arabella gasped and covered her mouth with her hands.

"I thought not," he said. "You mother can indeed be a hard woman, but she does have her soft spots, and one of them is protecting you girls."

Arabella flushed and turned her face from her father, thinking about her recent experience in the cellar. "Maybe that's true for the others, but I'm not so sure about me."

"Not that I'm defending what she did," Father said as he cocked his head to the side. "But your mother was probably doing what she thought would benefit the most people. She's always been very pragmatic."

"Cutthroat is more like it," Arabella muttered under her breath. Silence stretched between father and daughter. Arabella refused to meet his eyes.

"You were going to tell me a story?" she said finally with a bitter sigh as she looked up at the ceiling, blinking tears from her eyes.

"It was 1821 and your mother was twenty-three and pregnant with Amelia. Vivienne was being quite precocious and all was right with the world," Father began. "Your grandmother wanted to send your mother on one last working trip before she had to sequester herself to get ready for the new baby, and so she sent your mother to Ireland with her sisters Leanore and Lorena. I stayed behind with Vivienne and your grandmother." He glanced up at Arabella. She met his eyes with intense interest.

"The last potato blight in the early 1700s had been handily defeated by the local witches, but this one was proving to be a bit more tricky," he continued. "But they didn't expect it to get as bad as it did. Eleanor thought it would be a good exercise for her daughters, but not terribly difficult." he paused, staring off into the middle distance with a furrowed brow.

"What happened, Father?"

"Your mother and her sisters tried everything they knew and they managed to push the blight back in some of the counties, but in

Munster and Connaught the crops were still failing. They eventually failed completely, but not before Leanore drove herself to exhaustion trying to fight it." Father shook his head. "She was such a bright and vivacious young woman."

"I wish I would have gotten the chance to get to know her," Arabella said.

"I wish you had too," said Father. "Not just because it would have enriched your life, but because that would mean that your mother would have never gone through what she did and might have become a completely different woman." He sighed deeply and shut his eyes for a moment before he continued on.

"Your grandmother and I didn't know what happened at first. We hadn't heard from them in over a month, and all of our inquiries came up with no information. When your mother came home, she was in shock, filthy, her dress and shoes near worn to rags and scrap. Her luggage and money were lost. She wouldn't speak for days. She just stared out the window. Eleanor and I were afraid she was going to lose the baby, if she hadn't already.

"Then one night I finally got her into bed and coaxed her to eat some broth, and she actually fell asleep for the first time since she returned home. I tried to stay awake and watch over her, but I wound up falling asleep in a chair next to the bed myself. I'll never forget that night." Father leaned forward with his hands on his knees and covered his face with his hands.

Arabella waited, but he didn't continue. "Please, Father, what happened next?"

Running his hands through his hair, he sat up and blinked tears from his eyes. "Minerva woke screaming, and couldn't stop. She screamed and screamed no matter how much I reassured her she was home and safe, that I'd protect her. I don't know how long she kept at it, but it seemed like hours. At last she stopped screaming, and started crying. That's when she finally told me what happened.

"Your mother and her sisters had run into some resistance in Munster thanks to some of the local Catholics. They'd already run off every witch in the area, except one." Father paused for a moment as he wrinkled his brow. "Mara, I think her name was Mara. Your mother said that she was a skinny thing, surviving only on what she could grow herself on a piece of dirt smaller than this room. None of the locals would give her a proper tithe to keep her. Her crop was failing too. She didn't think she'd make it through the autumn, much less the winter. She was so beaten down, and her plight touched your mother and her sisters. They went to work on a field near Mara's cottage, tried everything but nothing seemed to work. Through it all, Leanore kept pushing herself. Minerva and Lorena tried to stop her when it became obvious she was straining herself too much, but sometimes when a witch sets her will to something there's no stopping her. She either succeeds or winds up dead.

"Finally, Leanore passed out and Lorena and your mother were supporting her between them, carrying her up the road, trying to make it back to the inn where they were staying. Mara had just come from the cottage to help them, when this gang of thugs came down the road. Lorena was focusing so much energy keeping Leanore on this plane of existence that all their defenses fell to Minerva and Mara. Your mother had her shield stones in her pocket and brought up a shield large enough to cover herself and her sisters. But she hadn't practiced enough and couldn't extend it enough to cover Mara.

"The thugs cut Mara away from your mother and her sisters like a shepherd culls a lamb from the herd. Your mother wanted to stay to help, but Lorena knew, what with the weight of Leanore, that if they didn't escape while the thugs were distracted that they would die too. Your mother and her sisters made it to the inn, but the thugs beat Mara to death and left her body in the road as a bloody warning to any other woman who might think about using magic. Your mother told me later that she still carries the guilt for that woman's death in her heart, and always will. I imagine that's part of why she gets so emotional over the Irish problem."

Arabella and her father were silent for a long time, both absorbing the weight of the story.

"That's not the end of it, is it, Father?" Arabella broke the silence with a soft voice barely above a whisper.

"No," he said. "No, it's not."

He paused a moment before he finished the story. "Once they were back at the inn, your mother discovered that she hadn't brought any of her healing foci with her. She hadn't expected to need them and wanted to travel as lightly as possible. Without having a focus for their healing spell, your mother and Lorena weren't able to bring Leanore back from the brink, and she died. Minerva said it was as if Lorena's mind snapped when her twin died. That was probably why it was so easy for the thugs to track them down because her weeping and wailing was so loud. But when the thugs came banging on their door Lorena did have one last moment of clarity. She stuffed your mother into the wardrobe and told her to be as quiet as a church mouse and to think of the baby. Your mother watched through a crack in the wardrobe's door as the thugs raped and beat Lorena, then dragged her away. When your mother crept out of the inn in the dawn hours, she found her sister's bloody body in the road not far from the Irish witch.

"She walked home from Ireland. She stowed away in a cargo hold and fought the rats for scraps to cross the Irish Sea. Even safely back on English soil she still didn't trust anyone, and kept walking until she arrived home. As I held her in my arms that night, she swore to me that none of her daughters would ever be caught at such a disadvantage. Her daughters would be strong and would not have to depend on foci. That was when your mother started to change from the carefree young woman I fell in love with. She became single-minded and driven, and while I'm sure she did what is best for the Sisterhood and England, I'm not sure it was always best for us." Father heaved a great sigh, leaned back in the chair, put his chin on his fist and silently stared out the window.

"I never knew," Arabella said in a small voice.

"Your mother never wanted you girls to know. She never wanted you or your sisters to ever experience that kind of fear." Father turned away from the window and stood.

"I don't know if these books will be of any use to you," he said. "I still don't quite understand what's happening with your power or how it fits in with the traditional way of doing things, but your mother made notes in the margins in her own hand. You might find them interesting." He kissed Arabella on her forehead and began to leave the room. He paused in the doorway with his hand on the doorjamb.

"Oh, Arabella, Henry suggested that we should have you meet some of the more prominent industrialists here in London. He thought that if they saw your power and if we could convince them of your usefulness, they might support witches more. They might lose some of the adversarial edge they've been developing over the last few years." He looked at Arabella with wide and hopeful eyes.

"Of course, Father," Arabella said with a gentle smile. "After all you, John, and Henry have done for me, how could I say no?"

"Lovely," Father said as he broke out in a wide grin. "We'll take you to their regular meeting this coming Saturday."

Arabella looked at her carpet bag where it sat in the corner of the room. "I hope they are not terribly formal. I don't have anything suitable to wear."

"Don't worry, I'll have John go to your mother's house and retrieve the rest of your things. You do have something there that would be suitable for a formal tea?"

"Yes, Father, I have the perfect dress." Arabella said.

"Good then, it's settled." He nodded sharply and disappeared down the hall.

Arabella turned to her mother's old text books with a sigh, hoping that they would contain a charm to bring helpful Fae back to the house and the garden.

CHAPTER XXI

Of Wardrobes, Fae, and Setting the House to Rights

JOHN GRUNTED AS HE HAULED THE LAST STEAMER TRUNK INTO
Arabella's room. "I don't understand how you could possibly
need so many clothes," he said, wiping the sweat from his brow.

Arabella peeked out from behind the open wardrobe door,
where she was putting away her blouses and said, "You don't need
to understand, you just need to accept it. Women need lots of
clothes."

She flounced over to the last trunk and opened it. "Oh, thank
goodness, I was beginning to think that Mother wasn't going to allow
any of my really good clothes out of her house." She began pawing
through the folded dresses, looking for the one she wanted to wear to
the formal tea the next day.

"Well," said John as he touched his fingertips to his forehead. "Have
fun with your mammoth pile of dresses." He turned to walk away.

"Where are you going?" Arabella stood with her favorite hunter
green watered silk dress in her hands. It was the only one that her
mother had allowed her to choose herself. Most of her clothes were
hand-me-downs.

"I've brought all your boxes up," John huffed. "I think I've done my
duty for the day. I was going to go down to the club and play cards."

"Oh no, you don't," said Arabella. "We still have a lot to do today."

"We?" John's face fell.

"There's absolutely nothing I can use in this house to call the Fae. I need you to come with me to pick up the essentials. We won't be able to turn the house and the garden around over night, but we can at least get started. I just need to set this out to air, and hang a few more things up so they don't wrinkle, and we can go." Arabella smiled cheerfully at her brother.

"Why do we need to call the Fae?" John threw his hands up in the air. "We haven't had Fae in this house for years, and we've been doing just fine."

"Just fine?" Arabella's voice rose in shock. "Have you looked around you at all, John? This place is filthy! This house needs Fae more than any other I've seen." She put her fist on her hip and pinned her brother with her sharp gaze.

John groaned and threw his hands up in the air again. "Fine, fine. I'll be waiting in the parlor, just tell me when you're ready to go."

"I would be ready to go a lot faster, and you could get to your card game a lot sooner, if you would help me put my things away," Arabella said with a sweet little smile.

"If I were meant to be a ladies' maid I would have been born a girl," John grumbled to himself as he went to one of the trunks and began to draw out fabric and hand it to Arabella.

By the time they returned in the late afternoon, laden with packages enough that they had to hire a young man to carry some, John grumbled that he would never get to play cards at the club again.

"Stop pouting, and pay the nice young man," Arabella said as she directed their helper to set the packages in the front hall. "I'll finish the rest of the work myself. You can go to your precious club now."

John sighed theatrically. "All the best players will already be involved in games; I may as well keep helping you and just go to-morrow."

"Good, then you can take that statue there out into the back garden." Arabella smiled and gestured to a waist-high Grecian woman holding an empty plate in front of her. John took the statue but he grumbled under his breath as he headed back through the house to the garden.

"Try not to break it," Arabella called after him as she picked up a potted foxglove and placed it on the portico by the front door.

Arabella strode into the garden humming a happy tune, her arms full of bundles. John was standing in the middle of the garden on one of the overgrown paths with the statue still in his arms, spinning in a slow circle with a confused look on his face.

"Where am I supposed to put this, Ari? I don't know anything about the Fae."

Arabella laughed and pointed to the Southwest corner of the garden, farthest away from the house. They trooped over to the weed-choked flower bed there and John shook his head. Arabella set her packages down and immediately got down on her knees and began to pull the weeds from the earth.

John pulled a face. "Isn't that something we should be hiring a gardener for?"

Arabella sat back on her heels for a moment. "We must hire a gardener for the rest, most assuredly, but you should never leave any fairy gardening to the hired help. That's just asking for trouble. Now, go back to the front hall and fetch me the pots of milkweed."

"Which ones are the milkweeds?" John genuinely looked puzzled.

"I already put the foxglove out front," Arabella said with a shake of her head and a fond laugh. "The milkweed will be the only growing thing left."

"Right." John nodded and headed back into the house while Arabella returned to pulling weeds and humming.

"Bring a shovel with you," Arabella called over her shoulder.

By the time John came back, Arabella had cleared a patch of dirt about four feet in diameter and she was wiping the dirt off her hands on a towel from one of the packages. He juggled the two potted milkweeds and a small ash shovel from one of the house fireplaces. Arabella raised her eyebrow.

"An ash shovel? I'm trying to garden, John, not clear the grate," Arabella said.

"Well then find one yourself," John huffed as he put everything down with a clatter. "It's the only one I can find."

"Don't be a child," Arabella said and rolled her eyes. "Just put the statue in the middle of the spot I cleared and then you can dig a hole for each milkweed, one on either side of the statue."

"Since when did this become my project?" John put his hands on his hips.

Arabella sighed. "Do you want to have a neat garden and an orderly house? Do you want clean clothes and shined shoes? Would you like to not have to worry about vermin scurrying around the house?"

John shrugged and pursed his lips, refusing to look at Arabella.

"If we attract the Fae, we get to have all that. It's not all that hard to keep them once they are here. A little honey and bread, an occasional offering of milk or some shiny thing, and they keep your house running right. No housemaid worth her salt will work without house Fae. We must attract them before we can even think about hiring good quality human staff."

John shrugged out of his jacket and laid it over a mossy stone bench, shaking his head. "Fine, I'll place the statue and dig the holes if you'll just stop lecturing me."

When John was done digging and planting, he stood back and wiped the sweat off his brow leaving a long streak of dirt across his forehead. Arabella giggled. He gave her a sidelong look and stuck out his tongue.

"What do we do next?" he asked.

"You don't have to stay for the rest, John," she said. "You can go on in and wash up."

"I've done this much work, I may as well stick around to see the results," he said with a shrug.

"Well, then, sit over there and be quiet." Arabella pointed to the bench where he'd laid his jacket. "The Fae can be skittish sometimes, and I don't want you spoiling things."

John sat and folded his hands in his lap. "You won't even know I'm here."

Arabella snorted and shook her head, then she set to work. She knelt down in the path before the statue with the packages at her side. First she took some bright glass beads, in a rainbow of colors, and laid them on the plate the statue held.

"Those were very expensive, and now you're just going to leave them out in the elements?" John crossed his arms over his chest and frowned.

"What happened to 'You won't even know I'm here?'" Arabella asked without turning her head.

"Fine, be secretive then," John said.

"Men," Arabella muttered to herself and went back to work.

She pulled out two fine bone china teacups and saucers, decorated in a pink cabbage rose and ivy pattern, and laid then at the feet of the statue. She filled them both with a deep purple libation. John craned his neck, frowning more, trying to see what she was doing, but he held his tongue.

She placed a stoneware plate, decorated with a star chart pattern, on the ground in front of her and laid a bundle of elderberries on it. She then pulled a simple box of kitchen matches, and set the elderberries alight. The sweet, pungent smoke wafted up on the late afternoon breeze. Arabella sat back on her heels and watched it.

After several long minutes, John could no longer stand the waiting. "And now what?"

"Sshhhh…." Arabella held up her hand to silence him without turning her head. "Now we wait, quietly." She kept her voice to a whisper.

John opened his mouth to say something, but another voice came from the rustling milkweed to the right of the statute.

"That's some mighty good smelling drink ye have there, Mistress." A tiny, wizened man, hardly more than a foot tall, dressed in rustic clothes peered out from around the green milkweed stalks.

"You may come have some if you like," Arabella said calmly, gesturing to the tea cups while John goggled.

"That's very kind of you, Mistress." The little man bustled forward and pulled a wee wooden mug from off his belt. Dipping up a cup of the elderberry wine, he took a long pull and smacked his lips together. "That tastes just as good as it smells, just what a thirsty fairy needs."

"I'm glad you like it," Arabella said. "You can have more."

"That's very generous, ma'am," he said as he dipped up another mug. "But I have a feeling you're not satisfying my thirst out of the kindness of your heart." He took another gulp.

Arabella smiled. She kept her expression calm, but her fingers twisted in her lap. "I was just hoping that I might entice you or some of your kin to come live in this garden and make it nice again."

The Fae pursed his lips and looked over the overgrown beds all around him. "That would be quite a large job, Mistress. And what could my people be hoping to gain from that?"

"There's some glass beads in the dish there that could be yours." Arabella gestured toward the statue and the little man stood on his tip toes to peer over the edge. "And I can promise to leave you proper offerings — bread and honey and elderberry wine."

The little man nodded and sipped from his mug again. "That is quite a generous offer. I do have a daughter with a new husband and they're already starting a brood of their own. It's getting mighty cramped in my own home garden. Would you want me to send them to you?"

"That would be lovely." Arabella grinned from ear to ear. "Shall we drink to that?"

"Indeed," said the little man as he filled his mug again. Arabella picked up the other tea cup. They touched cups and drank.

"I'll send them by in the morning," the little man said. "Give them a day or two to settle in, then you can talk to them about anything specific you'd like done."

"Thank you ever so much," Arabella said. "I'm very grateful for your help, but there is one more matter I'd like to ask your assistance in."

The fairy man rolled his eyes and groaned. "That's always the way with you humans. You always want one more thing."

Arabella flushed and bit her lower lip, dipping her eyes to the ground.

"Well, what is it girl? I haven't got all night, not if I'm going to get my kin packed and over here."

"It's just that we don't have any house hobs, and we're in desperate need of them," said Arabella. "And I was hoping you might know some who are looking for a new home?"

The fairy man filled his mug again and belched, then said, "Actually, you're in luck, Mistress. There's a house a few gardens over that's just overrun with portunes, shoved in there cheek by jowl they are. Always fighting each other to see who will get to complete the tasks at night. If you just do the simplest things to open your house to the Fae, you'll be overrun by them in no time."

"Oh thank you, that would be perfect," Arabella said. "I've already put the foxglove out by the front door."

"Don't forget the Elfswort and Thyme," the little man said as he tucked his mug back onto his belt. "Thank you for the wine." He disappeared around the milkweed stalks without another word. Arabella heaved a relieved sigh and set to work cleaning up the mess.

"What was that?" John finally exploded.

"Honestly, John," Arabella said as she turned to look at him. "You've got the blood of one of the greatest witch Houses in your veins and you're surprised over the appearance of one of the Little People?"

John blushed. "It's not like I've gotten a lot of exposure to it, Arabella. I was only two years old when you were born and Mother left Father."

Arabella pressed her lips together and looked down at the ground, her own cheeks flushed red.

"I'm sorry, Ari," John said and he stood and went to her. "Here, let me help you clean that up."

John helped Arabella clear everything away, and after that he helped her spread dried Elfswort and Thyme along every window sill and threshold in the house. They put the bread and honey away in the kitchen, then made sure that there were no iron locks on any of the doors.

Arabella settled down to bed that night with a smile on her face. It felt good to be useful.

CHAPTER XXII

Wherein Arabella Braves the Lion's Den
and Meets Clockwork Creatures

O N SATURDAY, ROWENA SHOWED UP PROMPTLY AT ONE O'CLOCK TO help Arabella dress for her afternoon tea.

"However did you manage to get out of the house to see me?" Arabella asked as Rowena tightened her corset. "Mother can't be feeling too charitable toward me at the moment."

"I told Mother I was going to have tea with a friend to try to shore up some more support for us at Council next week," Rowena said as she finished the final knot.

"Next week?" Arabella gasped. "But I thought there was usually a summer break, like Parliament does. I thought we'd have at least until autumn to drum up more support."

"Indeed, that's the way it would usually go, but Elmswell House and Fossdrum House led the charge to meet immediately to deal with the matter of you." Rowena helped Arabella into her hunter green silk dress. "Mother held them off as long as she could, but there's only so far that she can stretch her influence. At least we got Crawmere House and Rowanbry House into our corner when we went to the last tea."

"What did Mother tell them?" Arabella asked, glad she was facing away as Rowena buttoned her up, hiding the sadness on her face.

"Mother said you weren't feeling well, that the stress of having to show your powers again so soon after the episode at home was too much." She finished the last button and patted Arabella on the shoulders. "Katharine and Theodosia were very understanding. I know we can depend on them. In fact, Theodosia just sent word that she managed to sway Philomena Beedlebaugh of Birchwold House to our side. The letter came just before I left. If we can get just one more good sized House on our side, we just might have the majority."

Arabella turned to face her sister. "Why is Mother still doing all this campaigning to help me? She seemed so determined to either control or destroy me before."

"You're still her daughter, Ari, no matter how freakish your power may make you look to outsiders. She still loves you and would defend you until her last breath."

"I have my doubts about that." Arabella's mouth set into a bitter line.

"Well, if you won't believe that she's doing this for altruistic reasons, maybe you'll believe the political ones. Now sit so I can try to do something with that bird's nest you call hair." Rowena gestured toward the dressing table bench and Arabella sat facing the mirror while Rowena began to draw a brush through her hair. "If a witch of Blackstone House gets executed or banished, what do you think that would do to the name of our House? We've not had a single incident of censure for over three generations; our witches have been paragons of virtue and benevolent power in every way. Your execution or banishment would be the first missing stone that would eventually cause the whole House to crumble."

Arabella frowned. "But Mother disowned me. I am no longer part of Blackstone House."

Rowena paused in her brushing and cleared her throat. "Mother hasn't informed anyone of what happened, not even Elizabeth or the twins. As far as anyone who wasn't there is concerned, you are still a daughter of Blackstone House and the Sortilege line. Therefore your precarious situation is still a danger to us and Mother must continue her campaign."

Arabella grew pale and she met Rowena's eyes in the mirror. "That I can believe."

Rowena shook her head as she continued to work on a difficult knot. "Why don't we move on to happier subjects? How is living here?"

"It should be getting better now that I've attracted some Fae to the house. It was in ghastly shape when I first got here," Arabella said.

"Even with only one night to work, the garden fairies and the portunes have already made some lovely progress. I think we'll actually have the place livable by this time next week, and then maybe we can hire some decent human servants."

Rowena nodded and mumbled around a mouthful of hairpins. "What is it like living with the boys and Father?"

Arabella shrugged. "John is just himself. I hardly see Henry or Father because they are always off to one Alchemical Society event or another, or sequestered in their lab. It's almost like they are not here. Oh, except Father gave me some of Mother's old school books and told me a story about Mother." Arabella twisted around in her seat to face Rowena. "Did you know why Mother is so dead set against using foci?"

Rowena shook her head and Arabella relayed the story their father had shared when he gave her the books. The blood drained from Rowena's face and she sank down on the bench next to Arabella with her hand over her mouth.

"That's just horrifying," gasped Rowena when Arabella finished.

She nodded. "I know. It's no wonder Ireland keeps suffering with so much blight and famine if that's the way they treat their witches."

"It's like the earth itself is rebelling against them, and why not?" Rowena shook her head and clucked her tongue against her cheek. She sighed and stood again. "Let's finish this hair before Father complains we will be late."

In the end, it was their father who ran late. It took repeated pleading by both Arabella and Rowena to extricate him from his lab and get him ready to go to tea. Arabella kissed Rowena's cheek and turned to the carriage but Rowena caught her elbow. "Send me a note about how it goes," Rowena said. "Maybe we can use the information to our advantage when it comes times to talk to the Council."

Arabella nodded and the girls waved to each other as the carriage pulled away.

In the carriage, Father was completely absorbed in the journal in his hands, mumbling to himself and making notes in pencil. Arabella tried to amuse herself with watching the city go by, but finally she couldn't stand it anymore and broke the silence.

"Father, what do you think will be expected of me this afternoon?"

He looked up from his journal with a quizzical look on his face, as if he had forgotten she was there and precisely where they were going. He blinked slowly and said, "I imagine we'll have tea, Arabella."

"Yes, Father, I know we will have tea," Arabella said with a sigh. "But you said something about demonstrating my powers and I wondered what might be expected of me so that I can prepare."

"I don't quite know," he said with a frown. "Your brother Henry set this up. Perhaps we can speak with him privately for a few moments before we go in. We're almost there." Father turned back to his journal and closed himself off to any further conversation. Arabella pursed her lips and returned to watching the world go by.

When they arrived at the address of the gentlemen's club Henry had left for them, they found him pacing the sidewalk in front of one of the most impressive buildings in London.

"You're late," he hissed as he handed Arabella down from the carriage.

"Talk to Father about that," she said as her jaw tightened. "He was the one who didn't want to leave his lab."

Henry frowned deeply but he didn't say anything to their father about the hour. "Just come in, everyone is waiting."

As they made their way up the walk, Arabella turned to Henry and asked, "Can you tell me what's to be expected of me today?"

"All you need to do is dazzle them, Arabella," Henry said. "Do the same thing you did in the lab the other night."

"Will there be a contraption I can manipulate?"

"A contraption?" Henry stopped and looked at her.

"The thing you and Father built in the lab," Arabella said, gesturing with her hands to outline the large shape.

"This is a meeting of members of the Alchemist's Society and noted gentlemen of industry, Arabella, not a gathering to perform an experiment." Henry shook his head in exasperation.

"Well, then, what am I supposed to use my power on, brother dear?" Arabella crossed her arms over her chest as cold anger settled onto her face.

"There will be mechanical items, of course," Henry growled as he grabbed Arabella by the elbow and began to pull her toward the entrance where their father waited, having failed to notice that his children had stopped to talk. "Everyone likes to show off their latest toys."

Arabella yanked her arm from Henry's grip and took a moment to straighten her gloves. "All you had to do was say that in the first place. And you don't need to get so cross with me. I've never been to one of these meetings before. I have no idea what goes on."

She put her chin up and kept her back straight as she ascended the steps toward her father, and the butler who held the door open. She paused in the doorway and turned back to her brother where he still stood, fuming on the pavement. "Are you coming?"

Their footsteps echoed against the high hall of dark wood as they proceeded to the library where everyone was gathered. At the door, Henry stopped Arabella as their father entered the room and they heard him greeted with hearty voices.

"Do not speak until you are spoken to, and do as I say," Henry cautioned her. "And try your best to be agreeable, Arabella. Women are not supposed to be here and I've had to call in a lot of favors to get an exception for you."

"Well, if I had known I was to be treated no better than a favored pet trotted out to perform tricks, I wouldn't have come," Arabella huffed.

Henry glowered down at her. "Why do you think I brought you here? We need to get these men on our side, Arabella, and they are not used to dominant women. They don't spend a lot of time with witches. We need to play to their insecurities and assumptions to draw them in."

"I don't see what is so important about impressing these men," Arabella pouted.

Henry shook his head and groaned. "Are you that ignorant about what's going on around you? There's a war brewing, Arabella, a war with the witches and Luddites pitted against the industrialists and technologists. Witches may have saved mankind once upon a time, but they have been losing favor over the last few years as the people want to make their own progress. The witches and Luddites want to keep us in the past. If we can prove to these influential men that magic and technology can coexist then we can get their power behind the witches and save the Houses from falling. I may not have spent a lot of time with you growing up, but I would still rather not see my mother and sisters dragged from their home to be burned alive at the stake."

Arabella's hand went to her throat and the blood drained from her face. "I never…" Anxiety clutched her heart and her head swam for a moment.

Henry sighed and waved her words away. "Just pull yourself together, and do your best to be charming. You are the best chance we have of getting these men on our side." He opened the door and gestured for her to enter.

The air was thick with cigar and pipe smoke, and Arabella did her best to not cough, trying to keep a pleasant smile on her face despite the smell. Huge dark wood book cases, stuffed to the gills with rich leather spines, covered every inch of walls, except for three large windows framed by thick dark green velvet curtains across the room from her. Men of all shapes and sizes, in expensive suits in all tones of black and gray with waistcoats in a riot of colors, gathered in knots talking, smoking, and drinking. Some sat in chairs covered in luxurious ox-blood leather while others stood. Silent butlers ghosted through the crowd offering more drink and tobacco, while whisking away empty glasses and ashes.

She stayed close to Henry's side as he moved through the crowd, smiling and nodding as she went. The men regarded Arabella with curiosity, but said nothing. She felt rather like a bug under a magnifying glass. As they paced through the room, Arabella listened carefully to each conversation. She paid close attention to their facial expressions, a survival mechanism masked as a habit, allowing her to gather as much information as possible, learned from spending so much time with witches who could speak to each other silently with their thoughts.

If anything, her brother's war metaphor was too gentle for the situation. Arabella heard the anger flowing just under the civilized conversation about textile mills ransacked and looms burned, threshing machines wrecked, and riots fomented by Luddite rabble rousers. And the aggression seeped into their feelings about witches — *why should witches receive stipends from the government? Their time had long since past. There were cheaper and faster ways of doing everything a witch did. Or at least there would be, once they could manage to break the walls the witches have erected against progress.* Arabella wanted to cower in a corner, but she swallowed hard and focused on what Henry had said. He was depending on her, their family was depending on her, everyone was depending on her.

Henry stopped and leaned over to murmur in her ear. "This is the man we need to impress the most." he nodded to indicate a plump balding man in a fine black suit with a waistcoat of dusty rose and burgundy in a repeating fan pattern. "His name is William Horsfall and he was nearly killed by the Luddites early on in the movement. He's become sort of a figurehead of the technologist movement. If he will back us, the rest will fall into line."

"But what if we can't convince him?" Arabella whispered back.

"Then we try to convince someone else. We keep trying until we succeed. Are you ready?"

"No," said Arabella as she squared up her shoulders. "But let's go speak to him anyway."

"Good girl." Henry guided Arabella over to Horsfall with his hand on the small of her back, smiling and catching Horsfall's gaze.

"Henry, my good man! So good of you to join us." Horsfall's jovial voice boomed out over the other conversations, but the men turning to look didn't seem upset. Rather, they smiled indulgently at their cheerful figurehead.

"The pleasure is all mine, Mr. Horsfall," Henry said. "It's an honor to be part of such an august group."

"Oh come now, my boy, I keep telling you to call me Will." He clapped Henry on the shoulder. "If you don't start, I'm going to think you don't care for my company."

The two men shared a laugh and Henry said, "Nothing could be farther from the truth, Mr... Will."

"There's a good man," Horsfall chuckled, and then he turned his attention to Arabella. He looked her up and down and she, mindful of what Henry had said, bobbed a courtesy and smiled pleasantly without a word.

"Is this your latest automaton? I've never seen one so lifelike," Horsfall asked and he reached out and pinched Arabella's cheek. Unable to help herself, Arabella yelped and took a step back, her hand going to her rapidly reddening cheek. Horsfall jumped back himself with a look of shock on his face.

"No, sir," Henry said in a calm voice. "This is my youngest sister. May I introduce Arabella Helene Leyden?"

Still mindful of what they were there to do, Arabella covered her shock at her brother using their father's surname for her instead of their mother's, stepping forward again to offer her hand and murmuring, "How do you do?"

Horsfall frowned even as he took Arabella's fingertips in his for just a moment. "I'm sorry, Henry, did you say your sister?"

"Yes, sir, my sister."

Horsfall turned full on to Henry, his reddening face gathering rage. "First you bring a woman here? And then you have the audacity to make it worse by bringing your sister? You do realize that she is a witch, don't you, man?" Every conversation in the room had stopped and every eye was on the tableau of Arabella, Henry, and William Horsfall.

Henry smiled and spoke in a soothing voice that carried throughout the silent room. "I would have never brought her unless it was important, Will. You should know that I would never violate the sanctity of our club without very good reason."

Horsfall started to speak, but Henry held up his hand to head off the interruption.

"Gentlemen," Henry began, turning slightly to take in all the men in the room, beaming at all of them. "We are at the dawning of a new age in more ways than one. Many of you are familiar with the work my father and I have done to advance the fields of alchemy and mechanics. And today I have yet another advance to show you, an advance that is embodied in the very person of my darling sister." Henry turned his smile to Arabella and offered her his hand. Arabella had no idea what Henry was up to, but she took his hand and turned the most brilliant smile she could manage on the men of the room.

Henry continued, "While Arabella may have been born into a house of traditional witches, and as you no doubt know her mother and mine is the most powerful witch in all of England, quite possibly the world, what you may not know is that, until recently, Arabella has not shown one shred of magical power." Arabella felt the blood rising to her face, but she did her best to keep her expression serene. "All that changed just a few months ago. Arabella's power awakened, like a sleeping giant after a long winter. However, her power is not one of the traditional powers we normally think of. Arabella has no mastery of the elements, not healing, nor telepathy or telekinesis. Arabella is a new breed of witch, one that it would behoove us all to encourage and protect, gentlemen. My sister's ability is the power to manipulate *technology*."

The room exploded into a shocked cacophony of voices, but then Horsfall's voice rose above them all. "Impossible! It's absolutely impossible! Magic and technology do not mix," Horsfall shouted.

Henry turned back to him, his smile still in place, and said in soothing tones, "Oh yes, my dear Will, it is possible to mix magic and technology, and we will prove it to you today."

"That's 'Mr. Horsfall' to you, sir," he *harrumph*ed and put his hands on his hips. Henry's pleasant expression faltered for the briefest moment. "Witches are creatures of nature, as everyone here well knows, and we are progressive men of technology and advancement. Witches serve no purpose in our modern world."

A dark-haired gentleman almost at his elbow snickered. "I dare say you didn't call the witch who saved your life from blood loss useless, Horsfall. You readily accepted the benefits of magic then."

Horsfall narrowed his eyes and took a breath to say something when Henry interrupted him.

"I daresay Mr. Pattersby has a point, Mr. Horsfall," he said. "We are all practical men here. If witches can be useful, then by all means, we should not pass that up, wouldn't you say?" Henry turned to the men around him with raised eyebrows.

A few men were nodding and murmuring to each other, and even Horsfall seemed to be calming down.

"Of course, I wouldn't pass up a legitimate suggestion to move our society forward, but you must admit that your proposition sounds completely preposterous," said Horsfall.

"Indeed I do, sir, which is why I brought Arabella with me so that she can demonstrate her marvelous power," Henry said as he clapped his hands together. "Now, I'll just need one of you gentlemen to allow me to borrow one of your wondrous devices, and we can get on with the demonstration."

The men all muttered and looked to each other, but not one of them produced anything that Arabella could manipulate with her magic.

"Oh come now," came Alexander's voice from the rear of the room. "I know half you lot have something you're working on in your pockets, and the other half brought something in a valise to show off."

After more hemming and hawing, Pattersby was pushed to the fore. "You were so keen to help the witch before," said Horsfall. "I think it's time you did it again."

Pattersby blushed to the roots of his hair. "I did bring something, but it's not working quite right. I was hoping that a few of you might have some suggestions to fix it."

"I'll have a look at it after the demonstration, Pattersby," Henry said as he clapped him on the shoulder, then he turned to the rest of the room. "Does anyone have something working that they can offer for the demonstration?"

"On the contrary, dear boy," Horsfall said with a sly smile. "I think a broken thing would be perfect for your little demonstration. After all, if your sister is as powerful as you say she is, it should be no trouble at all for her to make it work. And I don't know about the rest of you gentlemen, but I'd be very keen to know if she can be useful. Fixing broken machinery is certainly useful."

"It's not broken," pouted Pattersby. "I'm just having trouble with the inner mechanisms and getting everything to work in proper synchronization." He retrieved a black leather case, very much like a physician's bag, from under one of the arm chairs.

Horsfall turned to Henry and Arabella with a predatory grin. "Shall we move this to the center of the room so that everyone can get a good look?"

Henry swallowed hard and said, "Of course."

Arabella glanced at her brother, his show of nervousness bringing her own anxiety to a fever pitch.

Horsfall gestured for the butlers to clear the small round table in the middle of the room of its vase of flowers and then bowed to Henry and Arabella. "Your stage awaits," he said with a grand sweep of his arm.

As they made their way to the table with Pattersby trailing behind them, Henry whispered into Arabella's ear, "Can you do this?"

"I have absolutely no idea," she whispered back. "This is why I kept asking what was expected of me, so I could prepare."

Pattersby set his bag on the table and clicked open the latch. Arabella was pale and felt as if she might faint, watching to see what might emerge from the bag while she twisted her fingers together. Pattersby leaned into the bag and gently wrapped his arms around whatever was within. He pulled out a linen-wrapped bundle the size of an infant, handling it just as carefully. With gentle hands, he laid his burden on the table and peeled back the linen coverings.

It was a highly detailed brass owl, laid on its back. Arabella gasped and moved to the table, and for her the rest of the room receded away. There was only Mr. Pattersby and his wounded owl. To Arabella, the clockwork seemed to hum with possibility. It did not have the glow moving around its gears and feathers, as she had seen with working mechanical things, but the potential was there, lying just beneath the surface of the carefully etched feathers.

"It's lovely," she murmured as she stood next to Pattersby, both of them looking down at his creation. "What did you mean it to do?"

"I meant it as an amusement for well-bred ladies such as yourself, Miss Leyden. But in all honesty, I hoped what I learned might lead me to advances in watch making."

Arabella reached out, but her hand hovered over the brass bird and she looked at Pattersby. "May I?"

"By all means." He gestured to his creation.

Laying her hand on the owl's wing with the same gentleness she would a living bird, Arabella closed her eyes and sent her mind down into the mechanical structure. The cogs and gears were waiting to speak to her. They wanted to mesh. They wanted to work. They wanted to sing with purpose, but they were not arranged quite right and they cried out to her. A soft frown furrowed her brow, and without opening her eyes she flicked her wrist to the side and all the hidden latches popped. Without the touch of her hand, the owl's breast swung open, revealing its clockworks. Arabella was so focused on her task that she didn't hear the shocked whispers all around the room, or feel Horsfall's breath as he stepped closer to watch over her shoulder as she worked.

Arabella caressed the air over the open clockwork, sending her mind deeper to see where the problem was. "There," she said, and stabbed her finger down.

If one little gear was shifted slightly to the left, the machine would work as Pattersby intended. Arabella set her fingertip on the gear and let the magic flow. The metal shifted and stretched as she moved it over, other bits moving out of the way, rearranging themselves into the most advantageous configuration. Again, Arabella was so engrossed in her task that she didn't hear the cries of amazement all around her, nor did she hear Horsfall whisper "Good Lord" even though he was quite nearly in her ear.

She drew back her hand and let her palm hover over the whole of the clockwork owl, eyes still shut, and tilted her head to the right with a frown on her face. Although it would now work as Pattersby intended, there was still more that could be done to make the little machine truly marvelous. Arabella dipped her fingers into the chest cavity once more, this time focusing on the cogs that moved the wings and letting a little extra magic flow from her fingers and roost there. With a flick of her wrist, she shut the owl and latched the breast plate.

Arabella opened her eyes and turned to Pattersby. "That should do it," she said. "Shall we try her out?"

"Absolutely," Pattersby said with a wide grin on his face. "I'll just need to get the key so we can wind her up." He started to dig in his bag.

"That won't be necessary," Arabella said as she stood the owl up on its feet. She ran a hand down its back and curled all the springs tight, ready to release and do their job. With her hands on the owl, Arabella smiled at Pattersby, "Ready?" Pattersby nodded, the grin still plastered on his face.

Arabella took her hands away from the owl and it immediately straightened up and its eyes popped open. Pattersby had set the eyes with brilliant cut citrines and they gleamed with an inner fire. The owl opened her wings and resettled them, just like a real bird, and turned her face to where Arabella and Pattersby stood beaming like proud parents.

"That's absolutely brilliant!" said Pattersby. "She's even more than I expected."

Arabella smiled, saying nothing, and twirled her forefinger in the air sending the owl walking around the perimeter of the table so that each of the men in the room could get a closer look it. When the owl at last came back around to Pattersby, she flexed her finger up and down and made it bow to him. He crowed with delight and clapped his hands.

"Are you ready for the best part?" she asked Pattersby.

"What could be better than this? You've made her work better than I even imagined."

Arabella smiled even wider and lifted her hand in the air, palm up. The little brass owl flew. It flew up to the ceiling and made one circuit of the room before taking a few swoops and diving just above the heads of the men gathered in the room. They all laughed even as they protected their heads. Arabella brought the owl to roost again on the table, where it stood like a silent sentinel, its eyes glowing a pale gold.

The room erupted into cheers and men clapped Henry and Alexander on the back. Horsfall turned to Arabella, eyes full of open admiration as he took her hand and kissed the fingertips.

"You have truly achieved a miracle today," he said. "And I would be happy to be your humble servant if you would only bring some of your magnificent power to bear on my projects. That is, if your father and brother won't keep you all to themselves." He laughed as he looked over to where Henry and Alexander were grinning at each other in the midst of being congratulated by members of the Society.

"It was just a small thing, really. So much more could be done. I imagine that using some of the concepts from the Difference Engine and the Distinction Engine could make her at least partially autonomous," Arabella said.

Pattersby turned to her slowly, pulling his eyes from the owl and said, "You, my lady, are astonishing." Arabella blushed and ducked her head.

"Speaking of the Distinction Engine," said a man with a florid red handlebar mustache and freckles dusted across his nose. "Perhaps you can help us with that. Mr. Francis Granville at your service, Miss Leyden." He bowed over her hand.

"Help you with the Distinction Engine? I don't understand," Arabella said.

"There was an incident at the Crystal Palace and some people accused Mr. Westerfeld of faking his machine," Granville said. "We've banned him from the Exhibition until we can investigate the accusations, but so far we haven't been able to prove it definitively one way or the other. We can get parts of the machine to work, but we can't duplicate what Mr. Westerfeld was doing. Perhaps you can come by Monday, say a little after 10 a.m., and see what your formidable talents can show us?"

Arabella raised her hand to her throat and tried to keep her voice from shaking, with only partial success. "Will Mr. Westerfeld himself be there?"

"Absolutely not, not with the ban in effect," said Granville.

"Of course she'll do it," said Henry as he came up from behind Granville and clapped him on the back. "Leydens always stand ready to use their talents to help others."

"Wonderful!" Granville clapped his hands together. "Then it's all settled."

"Not quite," said Arabella. "I'll need my sister Rowena to come with me when I examine the machine."

"What do you need Rowena for?" Henry frowned.

"When we saw the first private demonstration of the machine, I saw the magic in all the parts except for one bit at the center, and when I mentioned it to Rowena she said that that was the only part that looked magical to her. There's something strange going on with this machine, and I need her help to figure it out," Arabella said.

"Something strange indeed..." Granville murmured to himself.

CHAPTER XXIII

Wherein Arabella Returns to the Exhibition

WILLIAM HORSFALL SENT HIS CARRIAGE FOR ARABELLA AND HENRY, drawn by two perfectly matched bays, insisting that such a treasure as Arabella shouldn't have to tolerate something as plebian as a hansom cab. As Henry handed her up into the carriage, she could not help but marvel at the opulence. Supple black leather covered the well-padded seats, and thick cornflower-blue velvet curtains hung at each window. They were tied back with golden tassels but ready to be dropped at a moment's notice should the carriage occupants desire privacy. Henry tapped on the ceiling with the tip of his cane to tell the driver to move forward as he settled into his seat.

Arabella smoothed the light gray linen of her skirt with a nervous hand. "This is so fancy. I'm not dressed well enough for it."

Henry smiled indulgently. "I'm sure you're fine. Horsfall is more interested in your power than your sartorial statements."

"You don't understand," Arabella sniffed. "I wore a plain dress because I thought we would be working, but now I feel like a servant in her master's carriage."

"You may feel that way, but don't act like it, Arabella," Henry cautioned. "Horsfall will smell it and take advantage of you if he can."

"I thought you liked Mr. Horsfall."

"I do, but that doesn't mean I trust him," Henry said. "Horsfall is a crafty man. He hasn't amassed his fortune by not taking advantage of every prospect he can find. The advantage you have over him, my dear sister, is that he wants what you have. It may sound crude, but right now you are Horsfall's favorite new toy, and he'll do whatever he needs to do to keep you in his pocket."

"I still wish I had dressed better," she said with a sigh. She leaned back in her seat and fanned herself, staring out the window through the hot summer haze of London.

When they arrived at the Crystal Palace, Horsfall met them on the sidewalk and handed Arabella down with a smile. "Right on time, my dear. I've already seen to it that everyone except the interested parties have been cleared from the area so that you can work in peace."

"Thank you, Mr. Horsfall. I must apologize for my dress..."

"Nonsense, sweet girl," he said as he took her hand and threaded it through his arm, leading her toward the Palace. "I was just thinking how sensible you were to wear something serviceable rather than fashionable, and sensibility is a quality to be admired." Arabella blushed and murmured her thanks.

"And here we are," he said as they stopped near the entrance. "Your sister as requested. Your brother John was so kind to fetch her so that I could ready things for your arrival."

In contrast to Arabella, Rowena was wearing a much more formal gown along with her witch's robes flowing from her shoulders. Sweat was already beading on her brow line and upper lip from the weight and heat of the robes on top of her dress in the close summer air. Arabella raised an eyebrow and took in the blue-green moiré silk of Rowena's dress and the new, rich gray velvet robes indicating mastery of all magical arts rather than a specialty. Rowena's former purple robes had been a tweak at their mother, her refusal to declare that she would focus on an element or strive for overall mastery. It was obvious to Arabella that since her own defection their mother would no longer stand for any kind of defiance. Rowena blushed.

"Mother insisted that I dress formally since this was a formal request for my services from Mr. Horsfall," she mumbled as she dropped her eyes.

"Actually," said Arabella. "I was going to remark on your robes. Are they new?"

"Yes," Rowena murmured and she lifted her eyes to meet Arabella's. "Mother also insisted that I declare my magical specialty. She said she'd had enough of willful daughters to last her a lifetime."

Arabella stepped forward with a smile and took both of Rowena's hands in hers. "Gray suits you, Sister; my prayers that your robes will darken."

Rowena took in a breath to deliver the traditional response she would give to a Council witch, but bit it back just in time. Despite the recent developments, Arabella was still not a recognized witch in the Council's eyes, and she had no robes to darken to symbolize her growing expertise. Arabella squeezed Rowena's hands, understanding her hesitation.

"Well, gentlemen," Arabella said as she turned away from her sister. "Now that we are assembled, shall we go have a look at Mr. Westerfeld's machine?"

The group had started for the entrance when a breathless voice called from the crowd.

"Wait! Wait! I have something for you." Pattersby came racing up the pavement with a large bundle in his arms. He stopped, panting and nearly doubled over, in front of them.

"Mr. Pattersby, this had better be good," Horsfall said with a frown. "We have important work to get to."

"Yes, sir, Mr. Horsfall," Pattersby said, gulping down air and running one hand through his hair while he tried to juggled his heavy package with the other arm, nearly dropping it. "I just had something I wanted to give to Miss Leyden. It shouldn't take long."

He turned to Arabella and thrust out the package. "I made this for you."

This time it was Rowena's turn to raise her eyebrow at her sister. Arabella widened her eyes a bit and shrugged.

"Thank you, Mr. Pattersby," she began.

"Oh, call me Julian, please," he said.

Arabella blushed. "I'm not sure we know each other that well yet, Mr. Pattersby," she said with an uncomfortable laugh.

"Oh my, you're quite right," Pattersby said, dropping his eyes and shuffling his feet, pulling the package back close to his chest. "I only meant that you needn't be so formal with me. I'm so sorry if I've offended you. I've never been very good at the social graces."

"That's quite alright, Mr. Pattersby," Arabella said with a gentle smile. "Perhaps someday we shall know each other well enough to use given names."

Pattersby looked up and gave her a sheepish smile. "I would like that very much, Miss Leyden."

"Do you think we could hurry this along?" groaned Horsfall.

Pattersby jumped and held the package back out again. "As I said, Miss Leyden, I made this for you." Arabella reached to take it from him, but he said, "Perhaps it would be better if I held it for you while you opened it. It's a bit heavy."

"Something heavy? I'm quite curious now, Mr. Pattersby," said Arabella as she began to undo the knots that held the brown butcher's paper closed.

The string fell away and Arabella pulled back the paper to reveal what looked like a mass of thin brass wire, curling and looping around, with a handful of gears made from all types of metals on top of it. Arabella looked up at Pattersby with confused eyes.

"I don't understand," she said.

"Here, let me show you," Pattersby said, voice edged with excitement as he began to juggle the mass of metal and in the process dropped the paper and string, where a gentle summer breeze plastered them against his legs. He held up the mass of metal and it revealed itself to be a thin mesh, gathered at the top, with what looked like arm holes.

"It's a witch's robe," Pattersby said with glee. "It's not the usual velvet in any of the traditional colors, but you're a non-traditional witch. I just thought you should have some robes of your own, suited to your magic."

"It's lovely," Arabella gasped as she ran her hand down the flexible surface.

"You should try it on," said Pattersby.

"Wait a minute," said John. "You said it was too heavy for her to hold, how is she supposed to wear it?"

"Oh my, I suppose I didn't think of that..." Pattersby's face fell and he looked down on the metal robe in his hands.

"Well, it's a lovely thought in any case," said Arabella. "And the very least I can do is try it on for a few moments." She turned her back to Pattersby and held out her arms a bit. "If you'll do the honors?"

Pattersby slid the robe up her arms with gentle hands and a tender look on his face. He settled it on her shoulders, not taking his hands away for a long moment. When he finally moved back, Arabella sagged for just a moment, her brow furrowing momentarily. The robe fell from the gathers at her shoulders in graceful folds and ended in a small six-inch train on the ground behind her, just like a traditional witch's robe. Instead of the arcane symbols and patterns stitched in thread, Pattersby had attached gears, both small and large to the back and the lapels on the front.

"When did you have time to make this?" Arabella asked, holding her arms out and looking down at her new raiment in wonder.

"I haven't slept since you last saw me," Pattersby said brightly. "Once I was struck with the idea of the robe, sleep was impossible."

"Alright, you've tried it on. That's quite enough…" Henry start to speak but he stopped as Arabella's new robe began to glow with an inner fire that even the most non-magical person could see.

Bright light twisted and whirled up, down, and around each strand of wire. The gears themselves began to shift and climbed over the mesh, using their teeth as legs, until they settled themselves into an interlocking pattern. Then they began to spin. As they spun, more waves of light rippled out over the robe and all the individual twists and links of the garment pulled together to form one thin, glowing, ethereal sheet. Every person on the crowded street stared at Arabella as the light slowly faded away, leaving her with a gossamer-thin metal robe that moved like the finest silk. Arabella spun with a delighted laugh, the robe flaring out and obviously significantly lighter than before. She turned to Pattersby, her eyes wide. He held up his hands in delight and shook his head, his eyes just as wide as hers.

"Once again, you've made my simple creation into something so much more than I'd intended," said Pattersby. "I am honored." He bowed low to her.

The crowd around them began to applaud as Arabella turned in a slow circle looking at all the faces, her own expression one of shock. A small girl child ran up to her and curtseyed. "May I have a witch's blessing, mum?"

Arabella nodded slowly, as if in a dream, and laid her hand on top of the child's head. "May the light of the world settle in your soul." The child clapped and laughed in delight as she ran back to her mother.

Rowena came to Arabella and, taking both of her sister's hands in her own, said, "Brass suits you, Sister; my prayers that your robes will darken."

"And my prayers for yours," Arabella said as their eyes met, hers wide and Rowena's dancing with mirth.

She leaned forward and touched her forehead to Arabella's and said with a smile, "You'd better get used to this, little sister, I have a feeling this is going to be your life from now on."

As they pulled apart, Arabella shook her head and laughed. Still holding hands, the girls turned to face the men regarding them in silent amazement.

"Shall we go in and tend to the task at hand?" said Rowena.

Horsfall sputtered and said, "Why, yes, of course. That is why we're here. Come along, Pattersby. I suppose you've earned the right to watch."

The guards at the door of the Crystal Palace did not demand tickets from anyone in Arabella's party. They just waved them through and bowed. Just inside the door, two constables waited for them, and at a nod from Horsfall they began to clear the way. The crowd was just as thick as Arabella remembered, if not thicker.

"I thought you'd dispersed the crowds," grumbled John. Henry glared at his brother.

"We couldn't clear out the entire building," Horsfall said. "Just the area around the Distinction Engine itself."

As they passed through the noisy hall, all eyes turned to them—one of the most powerful industrialists in all of England, two well-dressed young men, a scruffy inventor, and two witches in high robes. People went silent as they walked by, then the whispers and murmurs grew in their wake.

As they got closer to Westerfeld's machine, more constables barred the path. Horsfall sketched a salute to them and waved his hand to encompass the entire party, and they were let through. Arabella finally took a deep breath. She realized how shallowly she'd been breathing while they'd been in the middle of the press of humanity. Rowena squeezed her hand and flashed her a smile.

Francis Granville was waiting by Westerfeld's machine with his hands behind his back, rocking from heel to toe as he stared at it. All the exhibits previously around the Distinction Engine had been moved to other parts of the Palace. The constables took up positions a discreet distance away so as to provide service without intrusion. The muted roar of the crowd sounded very far away as Arabella focused on the machine that had been both her awakening and a source of danger in the past months.

For all the glorious light she'd seen emanating from the machine in the past, it seemed dull and lifeless now. Nothing glimmered, nothing gleamed. It just crouched in the shadows, a dormant beast of cogs and gears. Arabella frowned as she drifted closer and came even with Granville. There was still some potential in it, but not as much as had been in Mr. Pattersby's owl. The men who had come with her, as well as Rowena, hung back to watch what she would do.

"How long has it been like this?" Arabella asked.

"Silent as the grave since we barred Mr. Westerfeld," said Granville. "But I think it's more important to hear what you think about it."

Arabella tilted her head to the side and squinted, taking another step closer. "There's always been a light to it before. I could always see the magic, but there's nothing there now."

"Perhaps it's because there is no electricity running to it?" said Granville. "We disconnected it because we didn't want it to cause problems."

"No, that's not it," Arabella said with a fierce shake of her head. "Even when Mr. Pattersby's owl was unwound I could still see the potential. There was still a glimmer." She turned to look back at Rowena. "Sister, what do you see?"

Rowena stepped forward and scrutinized every angle with a frown on her face. "The machinery is just as dull as it ever was to me before. But the place where I saw earth magic, here in the middle, is dull now too. Although there is a quality to the dullness that tells me earth magic was once there."

Granville and Horsfall locked eyes and scowled. "It would seem that you were entirely correct, Mr. Horsfall. Westerfeld was trying to pull the wool over our eyes."

Arabella went to the keyboard, which was still extended from Westerfeld's final demonstration, and caressed the keys. Even though the machine now felt cold and lifeless where once it had been full of energy, she could still feel the faintest whisper of mechanical magic. Half-closing her eyes and pressing harder on the keys, Arabella pushed energy and her consciousness down into the machine. As before she felt herself dance along the cogs and gears and then come to an abrupt stop just at the center of the machine. Arabella gasped and her eyes flew open.

"That was the first time the machine has moved in weeks, quite spectacular Miss…" Granville started but Arabella held up her hand for silence.

She paced down the length of the machine to just past the magically dead center. She laid her hand on the machine itself and let her eyes slip half-closed again. Leaning in, she let her power and her consciousness slide along the metal, flowing freely to the brass stylus where she wrote her name on the waiting blank sheet of paper. Arabella turned to the recalcitrant middle and regarded it with a glare. She knelt down on the ground next to it and laid her palm against the flat metal. Frigid waves of psychic energy, so cold they burned, radiated off the machine and she snatched her hand back with a gasp.

Still rubbing her aching palm, she rocked back on her heels and looked up at Rowena. "I need to get your read on this. I can't do a thing with it."

Rowena nodded and knelt next to Arabella, laying her own hand against the machine as she let her eyes flutter shut. She frowned and leaned in, brow furrowed.

"All I can feel is the echo of ancient earth magic, that and…death." She sat back and opened her eyes, removing her hand from the machine. "I'd have to be a crone to tell more about the kind of death. I haven't had that kind of training yet."

"It was so cold it burned," said Arabella with a nod.

"What was Westerfeld doing playing with earth magic?" Henry said as he crossed his arms and frowned. "Men aren't supposed to be able to touch that kind of power."

"There's an access panel here," said Arabella. "We're going to find out exactly what's going on." She hovered her hand over the plate and popped the latches at the corners with a flick of her fingers. Together, she and Rowena grasped the edges of the plate and pulled it away, setting it on the floor behind them. They both gagged at the stench that rolled out of the compartment. Then, again together, they leaned in and peered into the shadowy recess with their hands over their noses.

"Merciful Mother!" cried Rowena.

"What are they?" gasped Arabella.

"Help me pull them out," Rowena said, and together they pulled out a tiny, wizened man, barely a foot and a half tall, with large pointed ears and an exaggerated beak of a nose. They laid him on his back on the floor with gentle hands. He wore torn brown knee britches with miniature leather suspenders, and his collared white shirt was filthy and worn. His feet and calves were bare, and there wasn't a hat on his balding head. Blood caked in dark, dry clots on the ends of his fingers. There was no sign of life in the poor afflicted thing.

"What is that?" gasped Pattersby.

Arabella and Rowena did not respond immediately, but removed two more little men who looked nearly identical to the first, and laid them next to their brother.

"Are they what I think they are?" Arabella sniffed, dashing tears from her eyes.

"Yes," said Rowena. She raised her eyes to the slack-jawed men around them. "These are dillies, a reclusive race of Fae with a penchant for counting and calculations. You rarely see them outside of the country. They usually hang around sheep-herders and help them count their flocks. They don't tend to get on well with the other Fae because they are so different."

"What happened to them?" asked John.

"Judging from what I can see, Westerfeld couldn't get his machine working and he was coming up to the deadline, so he somehow managed to convince these dillies to work the calculations when his machine could not," said Arabella. "The inside of the access cover is coated with iron, which is anathema to all Fae. So once he put them in there they could not open the cover themselves. When he was banned from the machine, he could no longer feed them and they starved to death."

"Good God," Granville whispered.

"Can you tell what clan they are?" Arabella asked Rowena.

With gentle fingers, Rowena pulled back the collar of the shirt on the one nearest her and pointed to a mark tattooed on his collarbone. "This one is of the Tethera Clan."

"That's not the Clan for this territory, is it?"

Rowena shook her head. "The Jigget Clan claims London for their own."

Arabella looked up at Granville. "Where is Mr. Westerfeld from?"

"He's from Lincolnshire, I believe," said Granville.

When Arabella looked at her Rowena shook her head and said, "Clan Covero holds sway in Lincolnshire."

"Where is Clan Tethera from then?" John asked.

"They are from Nidderdale, and I've never heard of one leaving. Even for a dilly clan, the Tetheras are closed and insular," Rowena said.

Arabella shook her head and wiped more tears from her eyes. "He must have feared upsetting the Fae, so he stole them from a clan that would be less likely to report it."

"He's an animal," Rowena murmured to herself as she shook her head, face pale.

"Don't worry, ladies," Horsfall said and both Arabella and Rowena looked up at him. "I'll make sure that Westerfeld is prosecuted to the fullest extent of the law. Such an outrage will not go unpunished."

Horsfall lifted his hand to call over a constable and asked for some sort of fresh linen that could serve as temporary funerary shrouds.

"What shall we do with them?" asked Arabella. "Do we bury them here? Do we call for Clan Jigget, or do we take them to Clan Tethera?" She looked to Rowena for guidance.

Rowena shook her head. "We have to get them back into dilly hands. Fae ways are not ours, especially not for rites such as these. We cannot risk the wrath of the whole Fae nation if we violate their traditions. Westerfeld may have already done enough damage by kidnapping and imprisoning them."

Behind her, Arabella could hear Horsfall hoarsely whisper to Granville, "If he's caused the Fae to favor the Luddite cause, I'll kill him myself."

"I'll take them home with me," Rowena said. "Mother has all the proper materials to call the head of Clan Jigget, and she's very good at dealing with the Fae. She may just be able to save us from an interspecies incident."

All the constable could find were some relatively clean drop cloths that the exhibits used to cover their wares and machines at night. Rowena and Arabella wrapped the dilly bodies as well as they could, and the men helped them carry the tiny bodies with proper respect to Horsfall's carriage so they could begin their journey home.

CHAPTER XXIV

Wherein a Solution Presents Itself

ARABELLA STUDIED THE DESK IN FRONT OF HER. SHE HAD ASSEMBLED every magical testing tool she could think of—a silver bud vase with a peacock feather, a deck of tarot cards, a silver basin of clear water, and an unlit candle. And, as usual, each element confounded her and refused her efforts to perform the most basic magic.

Arabella flipped through her mother's oldest, most basic textbook once again searching for some secret that had somehow escaped her endless scrutiny over the last few days. Two days after the incident with the dillies at the Exhibition, Rowena had come to see her nearly in hysterics. Their mother had been able to soothe the Fae, but was not so lucky in the realm of human relations.

Mother had managed to get Beatrice Paskin of Fossdrum House to come to their home for tea, and to hear her tell it she had almost swayed Beatrice to their way of thinking. But that all changed as soon as Rowena arrived home from the Exhibition and Beatrice saw the dead dillies. She left the Sortilege home more convinced than ever that Arabella's power was a threat to the natural order of things and the witch's way of life. No matter how much Rowena protested that Arabella had had nothing to do with their deaths, Beatrice was convinced that Arabella's mere presence had caused the dillies to die; she was that much of an anathema to the natural world.

The next day the word came, Beatrice Paskin was going to challenge Mother for the position of Grande Dame at the next full Council meeting.

Mother was not frightened of a duel with Beatrice, but word was that Beatrice was going to try to take the seat by political machinations. The story of the dead dillies spread through the witch community like wildfire. Whispers behind fans and gloved hands said Mother was losing ground. She had birthed and raised an abomination that threatened the natural order of things; she was the one who had tried to get the other House Heads to accept her without question. What was the Head of Blackstone House really up to, Beatrice whispered into the ears of the fearful.

"You have to leave the country, Arabella," Rowena said with tears in her eyes as they held hands. "You're in danger. If this gets much worse you may have a pack of witches on your doorstep waiting to kill you! Westerfeld found you and he doesn't even have tracking spells."

Arabella shook her head and murmured, "Where would I go? There is no place in the world they cannot reach through the Sister Councils in other countries."

"You could go to Ireland!" Rowena exclaimed. "The fact that other witches want to kill you could actually be good for you there."

"Are you mad?" Arabella shook her head.

"Not mad, just desperate." Rowena buried her face in her hands and sobbed. Arabella folded her hands in her lap and stared off into the distance. The parlor was silent but for an occasional muffled sob from Rowena.

"I must brave the Trials," Arabella whispered.

Rowena's head snapped up, her tear-streaked fact aghast. "What? No! No, Arabella, you can't do that." She reached out and grabbed Arabella's hands tight. "Please promise me you won't do that. Promise me!"

"Ro," Arabella said with calm resolve as she squeezed her sister's hands. "It's the only way. I have to do this. If I become a full member of the Council I will have rights and privileges. I can no longer be considered an abomination if I've been accepted as a witch. Don't you see? This is the only way to protect Blackstone House and the family, the only way to protect *you*."

Rowena turned her face away and squeezed her eyes shut. "There has to be another way," she whispered.

"There is no other way, Ro."

Rowena turned back to her sister, tears openly streaming down her face. "What if the Trials kill you?"

"Then I'm not a danger to our House or family anymore, am I?"

Rowena's shoulders sagged and she bowed her head. "There's only one session of the Trials scheduled between now and when Beatrice will challenge Mother. It's next week."

Arabella squared her shoulders. "Then I guess I had better start studying."

And so it was that Arabella took over her father's library, keeping a schedule just as strange as her father and Henry, as she tried to somehow trick her mind and body into manipulating traditional magic in the same way she did the mechanical. For all her efforts, the results were the same. The feather stayed still, the cards gave up no secrets, and the candle remained stubbornly unlit. Arabella screamed in frustration and threw the book across the room, hitting the wall right next to her brother's head as he opened the door.

John looked from the book at his feet to his sister across the room, noting her red face, balled fists, and harsh breathing. "If you'll just tell me what I've done I'll do my best to make amends, but you don't have to throw things. However, if it's Father or Henry you're angry with, I'll join you in hurling the whole library. I've wanted to settle things with them for quite some time."

Arabella's shoulders loosened and she shook her head and laughed, her pallor returning to normal. "It's not you, or Father or Henry, this time. It's *these* blasted things." She flipped her hands at the testing implements on the desk.

"Well then, perhaps it's time for you to take a break, dear sister." John picked up the book and walked across the room to return it to her. "You have a visitor."

Arabella frowned and took the book from John. "A visitor? I'm not expecting anyone. I have no time for visitors, John. I have to figure out how to perform traditional magic before I go to the Trials."

John smiled broadly and rocked back and forth on his heels and toes. "Oh, I think you'll want to see this visitor."

Arabella tilted her head to the side and put her hands on her hips. "Just tell me who it is, John. Stop playing games."

Drawing himself up into a formal pose, John said, "Master Julian Pattersby desires the company of Mistress Arabella Leyden. Perhaps

for tea, or a stroll, or however she may so desire to spend her time."
John leaned in with a smile and winked. "He was stuttering at that last
part. I think the poor chap may be smitten with you."

"Oh *my*," Arabella blushed and ducked her head. Her hands crept
up to her hair. "I'm in no condition to receive anyone."

"Well, he's waiting for you in the front hall, Ari. What do you want
me to tell him?"

"You invited him in already?" Arabella's head snapped up. "Now
there's no way I can get past him upstairs and change into something
more suitable!"

"I think you look eminently suitable, Miss Leyden," Julian Pattersby
said from the open door of the library where he stood clutching a large
carpetbag to his chest. "You have such a natural beauty that you could
wear ashes and sackcloth and still shine like a star."

"Oh, Mr. Pattersby," Arabella blushed again. "You are too kind."

"Oh no, Miss Leyden, I only speak the truth. It makes life much less
complicated. You really do shine."

Arabella opened her mouth to speak again, but John interrupted
her.

"If you could step out of the way, Julian, old boy, I'll happily leave
you two to moon over each other all afternoon. I believe I hear a hand
of cards calling my name."

"Unchaperoned?" Julian and Arabella chorused together.

"Oh dear," John muttered as he pinched the bridge of his nose.

"I brought something to show you," Julian said as he jostled his
carpetbag.

"That sounds lovely," Arabella said. "Would the fresh air of the
garden be amiable for whatever it is?"

"Indeed," Julian said with a bright smile.

"So, it's the garden then?" John grumbled as he shuffled after his
sister. "I don't suppose there could be some sort of refreshment
involved? Or am I to die of thirst?"

John lounged under an apple tree on neatly trimmed grass with a
cup of tea Arabella had cajoled from the house hobs, as Julian spread a
cloth over a stone bench recently denuded of moss.

"I've been reading about this concept…electromagnetism," he said
as he smoothed out the wrinkles in the fabric. "And there was no one
else I could think of who would find it as stimulating as I do." His eyes

flicked up to her and back down again as he started laying coils of wire and small stones across the bench.

"There's no one at the Society with whom you could share your interest?" Arabella's voice held a teasing tone.

"No one whose company I find so pleasant," Julian said, then he paused and blushed, looking away. Arabella's laughter rang out across the garden. John groaned as he slumped down further against the tree trunk and tipped his hat over his eyes.

Arabella smiled and perused the bench with her hands clasped behind her back. "What wonders will these bits and bobs reveal?"

Julian picked up one of the stones and held it out to her with twinkling eyes. "Tell me what you think of this."

Arabella took the stone and frowned as it settled into her palm. "It... it tickles. There's something flowing through it."

Julian's smile grew wider. "Now, take this one in your other hand." He handed her an identical stone. "And bring them closer slowly."

Arabella did as Julian asked. Her eyes grew wide and she gasped as the stones shifted in her hands, realigning themselves on their own.

"Like poles repel each other and opposite poles attract." Julian clapped his hands together.

"Poles?" Arabella asked, looking up at Julian with questioning eyes.

"Each magnet, the stones in your hands, has a negative end and a positive end. Like repels and opposites attract. There are so many applications!"

Arabella laughed at the excitement in Julian's voice and said, "What kind of applications?"

"Well, they're already used for navigation since the Earth itself has a magnetic field and they can show us true north, but wait until you see this!" Julian picked up a coil of wire from the bench. He plucked the stone from her left hand and slid it into the coil. "If this works the way I think it will...well, I don't have the words for it but it should be spectacular."

He took the stone from her right hand and replaced it with the stone and coil. He drew in a breath to say something to Arabella, but before he could say a word she cried out.

Energy poured from the coil to race up her arm and all around her body. In short order, she felt like she was vibrating all over. But the energy just kept coming from the coil and the stone, rolling into her like a cresting river, pushing out on her skin until she felt sure she would explode. She dropped the coil to the ground with a clatter. She took two steps back, shaking both her hands vigorously, trying to shake the energy out of her. It didn't work. She started to keen holding her hands up to her face, and that's when she saw them. Tiny lightning bolts wreathing her knuckles, dancing between her fingertips.

"Miss L-l-leyden!" Julian stuttered. "I-I-I'm so s-s-s-orry..." He reached out for her, but she shouted "No!"

Even John was on his feet by now, body tense and ready, but frozen, not knowing what to do.

Arabella's eyes narrowed and she took a deep breath. She spread out her right hand flat and watched the electricity for a moment. She slowly brought her fingers together and a ball of lightning coalesced in her palm. She smiled and lightly tossed it to her left hand, then back to her right. She turned away from the men and hurled the ball down the path where it cracked in the air, blew apart, and left a huge scorch mark on flagstones. Both men yelped and jumped back in reaction to the sound.

Arabella laughed.

She walked a little further down the path, eyes wild and searching, the tip of her tongue running over her lower lip, absently twirling electricity between the fingers of her right hand. She spotted an undisturbed patch of dry grass and hurled another lightning ball at it. It caught fire immediately.

"What do you think you're doing?" John bellowed as he ran past her and stamped out the fire. Arabella just laughed and clapped her hands together.

"Miss Leyden!" Julian ran up to her. "I'm so sorry! Did I hurt you?'

Arabella turned to him and smiled, still clapping her hands together. "Isn't it wonderful?"

"What do you mean wonderful?" spluttered John. "Setting the garden on fire is wonderful?"

"Silly man." Arabella smiled fondly at her brother. "It's not setting the garden on fire, it's setting candles on fire."

"I'm sorry, Miss Leyden," Julian said with a quizzical look on his face as he shoved his hands in his pockets. "But that makes no sense."

"You've just given me a way to survive the Trials, Julian," Arabella said and she stood on her tiptoes and pecked him on his cheek, making his face flame brighter than the grass had.

CHAPTER XXV

Wherein Arabella Presents Herself for The Trials

HOT SUN BEAT DOWN OUT OF A CLOUDLESS SKY AS THE CARRIAGE PULLED up in front of the imposing edifice that was home to the English Council of Witches. John helped Arabella down from the carriage and held her hands in his for a long minute.

"Are you sure you don't need me to go in with you?" he asked Arabella.

Arabella smiled briefly and touched his cheek. "Even if I wanted to, you know I couldn't bring you in, John. Non-witches are barred from the Council building. Besides, this is something I have to do on my own." She turned and squared her shoulders.

John stood next to her with his hands clasped behind his back looking at the massive structure without really seeing it. "Just come home in one piece, little sister."

Arabella snuck a look at him out of the corner of one eye while she fought a smile. "John Ambrose Leyden, are you getting sentimental on me?"

"Absolutely not." He shook his head and stared at his feet. "I just don't want to have to take on the job of keeping the Fae happy if you don't come home."

Arabella chuckled and checked her reticule one last time.

"Do you have everything you need?" John asked.

"Yes, brother dear," Arabella said. "Everything is still right where I put it, just like it was the last fifteen times I checked."

John looked at her with serious eyes and said, "Good luck."

"Thank you," said Arabella, and then she stepped forward before she let fear take a hold of her and stop her.

Arabella mounted the steps, leading up to the wide portico held up by Corinthian style columns, all carved from the same black granite, shot through with streaks of gold and silver. Arabella, dressed in the same dove gray linen dress she'd just worn to the Crystal Palace, felt dwarfed by the huge building. She imagined she looked like a small speck of ash from a dying fire carried up an imposing rock face. She glanced back as she reached the front door, and saw her brother wave to her before he climbed into the carriage to return home and wait for the results of her test.

Once inside, Arabella was immediately overwhelmed. She'd never been inside the Council building and was completely unprepared for what lay before her. The foyer she walked into rivaled the Royal Court, rising above her in studied opulence. The floor was made of a polished pale brown granite, shot through with flecks of gold and darker browns, inlaid with an azure blue stone she didn't recognize, in wave patterns all around the perimeter of the room and the bases of the columns. The grand columns were intricately carved from red woods, broad enough around that it would take five witches, stretched out as far as they could go, to encircle them. Each column was covered in carvings depicting every known species of the natural world along with all the greater and lesser Fae known to witch. The columns soared up to an elaborate stained glass roof depicting all the important moments of the Sisterhood, from the moment they had revealed themselves at the darkest hour of the Black Plague during the Dark Ages, on to the completion of the very building she stood in, almost 200 years ago. On either side of the room was a grand sweeping staircase so broad that three witches could walk abreast comfortably. Marching up the walls of both staircases were paintings of every important witch in the history of the Sisterhood. It was hard to make out the ones at the top, and Arabella wondered if her mother's had been added to the august company yet.

"It's quite a sight, isn't it, dearie?" came a voice at Arabella's elbow, causing her to jump. A hump-backed, snaggle-toothed old woman smiled up at her, dressed from head to toe in black, her rich grey velvet robes trimmed with the crones deep purple satin borders.

"Yes," said Arabella. "I had no idea it was this grand."

The crone cackled to herself. "Most young ladies don't. I assume you're here to be tested?"

Even though that was exactly what she had planned for, a sudden fear gripped Arabella's belly and all she could manage was a pale nod.

"Go straight up the left-hand stair and it's the first door on your left," the witch said, apparently unsurprised by Arabella's lack of voice. The crone patted her on the arm. "Good luck, dearie, I hope to embrace you as Sister later today rather than mourn your bravery."

Arabella gave her a wan smile and began to trudge up the long staircase. Halfway up she turned around. The crone was still where she'd left her and she waved cheerfully to Arabella. She gave her an uncertain wave back and continued up the stairs.

The first door to the left was a plain, unassuming thing. The heavy oak portal had no sign upon it, only a brass knocker fashioned in the shape of a pentacle. Arabella took a deep breath and knocked. The door swung open to reveal a young witch dressed in a plain blue linen dress and the pearl-colored robes of a novice initiate. Arabella stifled a gasp at the sight of her face, however. It was Judith Paskin, the youngest daughter of Beatrice Paskin of Fossdrum House, barely fifteen and just past her own Trials. Arabella remembered playing with her when they were girls, laughing as they chased each other through the gardens of their mother's houses. Judith had been a late bloomer magically speaking, and so it had taken that much longer for her to look at Arabella with pity.

Judith's eyes widened and her nostrils flared, but she kept her voice sure and even. "May I help you?"

"I have come to endure the Trials and join my heart and spirit to the Sisterhood." Arabella spoke the formal words with a lift of her chin.

Judith glanced back over her shoulder and then leaned in close to Arabella. "Are you sure this is wise? You can still leave. I'll tell the Examiner that no one was here and it must have been Hettie playing a practical joke again."

"I'm surprised to be getting any help from you," Arabella said as she blinked.

"My mother may be the Head of our House, but she doesn't always speak for all of us," Judith said as she flushed bright red.

"Thank you, Judith," Arabella said. "But I need to do this. I can't run away."

Her friend nodded once and stepped back to allow Arabella into the room. She drew herself up straight and tall and called out in a loud voice, "May I present Arabella Helene Sortilege, come to endure the Trials and join her heart and spirit to the Sisterhood."

There were two older witches waiting in the empty room. A tall, narrow woman with a hawk beak nose and severe demeanor dressed in black robes of power, and next to her a plump old crone with black robes trimmed in purple, holding a ledger with a quill pen poised above the page. There was one closed door behind them, but otherwise the room was bare.

"Actually, it's Leyden now, Arabella Helene Leyden," Arabella said as she blushed and curtseyed. "Mother expelled me from the House and the family." Arabella's blush deepened when she heard Judith gasp to her left.

The crone with the ledger scowled and lifted her eyes to Judith. "Always get the correct name before you announce, child. It's lucky for you I hadn't gotten to her surname yet." The quill scratched away as she inscribed Arabella's name in the ledger.

The thin witch stepped forward and pinned Arabella beneath a piercing gaze. "I am Parthena Anne Luther of Birchwold House. I am to be your Examiner. Are you certain you wish to set your feet upon this path?"

"I am certain," Arabella said.

"Have you entered this Council of Witches of your own free will?"

"I have."

"Will you accept the consequences of seeking entrance to the Sisterhood should you fail the Trials?"

Arabella swallowed hard. "I will accept the consequences."

"You have been accepted into the Council of Witches to endure the Trials and join your heart and spirit to the Sisterhood." Parthena held out her hand to Arabella. "There is no turning back now, girl. Come with me."

Arabella took her bony hand and Parthena opened the door, leading Arabella to the next room. It was equally plain except for the wooden benches that lined the walls and another closed door on the far wall. Parthena led her to a bench on the right and sat, patting the bench next to her. Sinking down onto the hard wood, Arabella looked around at the other candidates. Directly across the room there were three girls she didn't recognize all crammed together, clutching each other's hands and staring off at nothing in the distance with pale faces. They were identical in their appearance and dress. The same muddy brown hair and fearful brown eyes. The same thin, too-often mended dresses and none of them wore shoes on their filthy feet. Arabella's heart ached for them. They were obviously girls from poor London families sent on a long-shot gamble. It was unlikely any of them would survive the Trials. Everyone in the room knew it, but no one commented on it. Their Examiners sat on the next bench over chatting amiably among themselves, ignoring the barely contained hysteria to their right. Arabella frowned at the witches, wondering how they could be so cold.

Sitting on the bench to her left was one other candidate Arabella recognized. She was Samantha Tibbet, the middle daughter of Emma Tibbet of Aberdean House, just turned thirteen and now old enough to join the Sisterhood. Rumor had it she was already showing prodigious talent, and there was no question of her passing the Trials. Arabella tried to catch her gaze and share a smile, but Samantha turned away and resolutely stared at the other wall with her jaw set. Arabella sighed and sank back into the bench.

Parthena watched the interaction between the girls before she spoke to Arabella. "You're lucky that you've come on a good day. When there are too many candidates the Council tries to rush us through, but with so few we'll be allowed to take our time."

"This is a good thing?" Arabella asked, looking over at Parthena with wide eyes.

She shrugged. "It is if you don't want to be damned for a single failure. When there are too many the Council will sometimes only allow the candidate one test of her own choosing, but with so few of you today, you'll be allowed to try more than one."

Arabella paled and let out a hard breath. "Lucky indeed..." She shook her head a little. "How long do we have to wait before we go in?"

Parthena shrugged again. "It depends how much Council business they need to deal with. If there is a lot, we could be waiting here for hours; if today is light, we could be in there fairly soon." She settled herself more comfortably on the bench.

Arabella took a breath ready to ask another question, but was interrupted when the door on the far side of the room flew open. Framed in the doorway was her mother, Minerva Vivienne Sortilege, in her full regalia, eyes blazing. She strode across the room, her fists clenched at her sides and stood in front of Arabella.

"I did not give you permission to brave the Trials." Her dangerously soft voice skirted the razor's edge of fury.

Arabella stood and met her mother's eyes with a level gaze of her own despite her inner trembling. "I do not need your permission to attempt the Trials."

"You most certainly do," spat Minerva. "You are my daughter and of my House. I will determine when, and or if, you are ready."

"May I remind you, Mother, that you disowned me just last week and removed the protection of both family name and House? Surely you remember something so recent?" Arabella clenched her jaw.

Minerva's head reared back as if she'd been slapped. "You would use that against me?"

"It would seem that you used that weapon first, Mother." Arabella curtseyed. "Or should I say, Madame Grande Dame. I don't want to forget my manners."

"You stupid girl," Minerva hissed, leaning down into Arabella's face, almost touching noses. "Now that you've announced that in front of witnesses outside of the family, I can't protect you or help you once you enter the Council Chambers. You must survive the Trials entirely without any support from family or House."

Arabella lifted her chin. "Isn't that the way it's supposed to be, Mother? Every witch is supposed to be able to stand on her own feet?"

Her mother stepped back, shaking her head as she narrowed her eyes. "Even within the rules of the Trials, I could have provided you some measure of support if you hadn't chosen to publicly repudiate your House."

"And why would you bother to help me, Mother? I'm not one of your preferred daughters. You made it very clear how much of a burden I am."

Minerva's mouth dropped open and tears sprang to her eyes. "You are my daughter, Arabella. All I have ever wanted to do is protect you." Her voice trembled, and then she turned her face to the side and shut her eyes. The room was silent, with all eyes locked on mother and daughter. Minerva took a deep breath and shook her head to clear it. She drew herself up tall and breathed out, long and slow, grounding herself before she opened her eyes, now empty of tears.

She didn't look at Arabella as she turned on her heel and went back to the doorway where she turned and addressed the room.

"You will be taken into the Council Chambers one at a time and administered the Trials," the Grande Dame announced. "You will be taken in the order you arrived. If you need food, beverage, or a comfort break while you wait, your Examiner will assist you. Good luck, ladies, I hope to embrace you as Sisters rather than mourn your bravery." And in a swirl of skirts, Minerva was gone, the door slamming behind her.

The three girls on the bench began to weep softly, leaning into one another. Even Samantha looked frightened as she stared at Arabella with wide eyes. Arabella sat down hard on the bench and let out the breath she'd been holding. Parthena looked down her long nose at her.

"I can't decide whether you're being incredibly stupid or exceedingly brave for going into the Trials without any protection from your House or family considering your delicate situation," she said.

"Probably stupid," moaned Arabella as she leaned forward and put her face into her hands. "Incredibly, spectacularly stupid."

"Perhaps not as stupid as you think," Parthena said, her mouth quirking up to one side.

Arabella spread her fingers and looked at Parthena from between them. "What do you mean?"

"Going in without a House means that should you pass the Trials, your allegiance has not been declared and you get to choose," said Parthena. "If your power proves to be strong, the Houses will be wooing you to join them."

Arabella dropped her hands from her face. "It's not always solely by family?"

"No, child, it's not," Parthena said with a chuckle.

"But who would choose not to stay with their family if they had any other choice?"

"Someone who is looking for something to gain," Parthena said.

Arabella shook her head and frowned, her brow creased in thought. Before she could say anything, Parthena interrupted her.

"I was born into Crawmere House," she began. "But as there are many powerful witches in that House, and the Boscoe line is strong and fruitful, there was not much chance that I could rise in the hierarchy. However," she spread her hands in her lap. "Birchwold House doesn't have as much strength in the talents where I am strongest, so I can have more power within their walls."

"I never knew the Houses could be so... so..." Arabella flushed bright red.

"Cold? Calculating? Come, girl, say what you mean," Parthena said with a chilly smile. "Your mother may have done you no favors shielding you from what really goes on within the Council and the Sisterhood. There are many good women, to be sure, and there are many who truly seek to do what is right, but there are also dangerous women in our ranks. Sometimes the most dangerous thing about them is that you can't tell who they are until they've pulled the knife out of your back. You may not even be aware of the knife sliding in if she is truly talented."

"Are you one of the dangerous ones?" Arabella's voice came out in the whisper.

Parthena's smile got wider. "Only if you cross me, girl, only if you cross me."

The door to the Council room opened again and this time it was Amelia framed in the doorway. She looked across the room at Arabella and shook her head, frowning sadly. Then she squared her shoulders and called out in a clear voice, "Bessie Cooper, I call you to enter the Trials."

The three girls wailed and clutched at each other as they wept. Amelia looked at the Examiners. One with blonde hair got up with a sigh and grabbed the girl to the far right by her arm, pulling her away from her sisters. The girl could hardly keep her feet. She stumbled against her Examiner and wailed. The Examiner grabbed her by her shoulders and shook her hard, then slapped her across the face.

"Don't make this any more difficult than it has to be," she said in a fierce, low voice.

All three sisters stopped crying at once, but for a few hiccupping sobs.

"Are you ready?" said the Examiner. Bessie started to shake her head, but then she bit her lip and nodded. As the Examiner and Amelia led her from the room, she looked back over her shoulder at her sisters the whole way.

"Such a shame," murmured Parthena to herself, shaking her head.

"You mean those poor girls?" Arabella asked, her stomach clenching at the thought of what poor Bessie was facing right that moment.

Parthena kept her eyes on the Council room door as she spoke. "Yes. These poor girls don't come here like the rich daughters of the

Houses, assured that they will pass the Trials and go on to live the comfortable life of a witch. They know their chances of passing are nigh on impossible. They get sent here by their families because the Council will pay a death benefit that keeps the rest of their families fed."

"That's awful! To be thrown away like that for money!" Arabella felt tears well up in her eyes.

Parthena fastened a sharp gaze on Arabella and said, "Would you rather they starved to death? Or perhaps it would be preferable for them to become prostitutes and let them be beaten to death at the hands of their customers...if disease doesn't take them first? Life is not always about clean and easy choices, Arabella, sometimes a quick death in the service of others is preferable to a long and painful life of your own."

The blood drained from Arabella's face, but she said nothing. She knew Parthena was imparting a painful lesson, a lesson she didn't want to learn. But she had the feeling if she didn't learn this harsh lesson life would be infinitely more difficult. She said nothing when Jessamine came for the second sister, Betsy. She watched the plain girl go to her fate and pondered the strength it took to knowingly sacrifice oneself. When Josephine came for the last of the triplets, Beth, Arabella felt anger well up in her breast. These girls should have more of a choice. Beth shuffled out of the room with her head hung low, all her tears spent. Arabella felt tears gather in her own eyes for the three sisters. In the silence of the waiting room Arabella tried to tamp down the swirling feelings of anger, pity, and pride in the strength of the downtrodden. She needed to calm herself or she would not be able to pass the Trials. She could mourn Bessie, Betsy, and Beth after she survived.

Only Samantha and Arabella were left with their examiners when Rowena came to the door and called out, "Samantha Grace Tibbet, I call you to enter the Trials."

As Samantha and her Examiner rose to cross the room, Rowena caught Arabella's eye and silently mouthed, "What are you doing?" Arabella pressed her lips together and shook her head. And then Rowena was gone. Arabella was alone with Parthena in the still room.

Silent minutes stretched on for what seemed like hours, and finally Arabella broke the hush. "Can you tell me what it will be like in there?"

"Did your mother give you practice tests at home?" asked Parthena. Arabella nodded.

"It will be like that," said Parthena. "Except that you will be doing it at the center of the Council Room floor and you will have rather a larger audience than you are used to dealing with. Most witch mothers are very careful about preparing their daughters, at least the ones that have any sense. I'll cast a shield over the testing area to ensure there is no interference in the Trials, for either good or ill."

Arabella nodded. "Do you have any daughters yourself?" she asked.

A soft smile shone on Parthena's face. "Just one so far, I had two boys before her."

Arabella was about to ask Parthena more about her daughter when the door creaked and Rowena slipped through the crack, carefully looking back in to the hall behind her. She shut the door with trembling hands, turning to face Arabella and Parthena with her fists on her hips.

"Just what do you think you're doing, Arabella?" Her voice was fierce and low. She strode across the room and offered her hand to her sister. "We need to get you out of here this instant, before Elizabeth comes to take you in to the Council Chamber. I don't know how long Samantha Tibbet will be at testing."

Parthena stood and inserted herself between Arabella and her sister. "The candidate has already been registered and accepted. She cannot leave without enduring the Trials now."

"Parthena," Rowena said in a pleading voice. "You know Arabella is different. You know I can't just let my little sister be tossed to the wolves."

"Which is why you shouldn't even be here," Parthena hissed. "You're too emotional to deal with this situation rationally."

"But she's my blood sister." Rowena's voice nearly came out in a sob. She hung her head, trying to master her feelings, and then lifted her face to Parthena's. "At least let me have one last moment with her, let me say good-bye in private. Please?"

Parthena frowned, deep furrows forming between her eyes, but she nodded sharply once and crossed the room to stand by the door that led to the Council Chamber. Rowena crouched down in front of Arabella and took both of her hands in hers.

"We can still get you out of here," she whispered. "The Registration Chamber is empty now. If we run, we can go through there, be down the staircase and out the door before Parthena raises the alarm."

"Rowena," Arabella said, trying to pull her hands away, but her sister held them fast. "I can't do that. I have to go through the Trials if I'm going to have any kind of life. I'll be fine. *Trust me.*"

"No, you won't. You won't be fine," Rowena said in a choked whisper, sinking further to her knees. She put her forehead down on their folded hands.

"Rowena, I have a plan. Everything is going to be alright," murmured Arabella, trying to manage a soothing voice.

Rowena's shoulders hitched with a sob and she lifted her head. Her eyes were full of tears that were starting to roll down her cheeks. She spoke in a strangled hiss. "You don't understand. It's not the test that kills you if you fail, it's the witches. It's *us*."

"What?" Arabella's voice rose.

"It was decided long ago that we needed to convince people that handling magic was too dangerous for someone other than a witch. It keeps people from trying to do what we do and spawning abominations." She let go of Arabella's hands and reached up to hold her face. "Please don't hate us. It was done to keep us all safe, the whole world, magical and non-magical alike. We did it because it's what's best for the greatest number."

Arabella shook off Rowena's hands. She stood up and paced to the middle of the room, turning to face her sister where she sat on the floor, tears streaming down her face. "I think maintaining power is more the reason for murder than all this altruism you're babbling about. Why didn't anyone tell me this before?"

"Because we can't, Arabella," Parthena said from behind her. "We are all sworn to secrecy when we join the Sisterhood. The vow that binds us demands our blood should we ever betray it." She turned a hard gaze on Rowena, who dropped her head and sobbed into her hands.

"But I'm not a common girl from the slums of London. I'd be missed," Arabella protested. "Mother won't let them kill me if I don't pass. We just have to show them that technomancy is true magic and they'll come around."

Rowena looked up from her hands and turned her tear-streaked face up to Arabella. "Mother may not be able to control them, Ari. There are too many of them and only one of her. And if you show them technomancy without also showing them conventional magic, they may kill you for that too. There are women in there right now who believe you are an abomination, that Mother should have put you down already."

Arabella turned sheet white. She shook her head slowly. "No, this isn't the way it's supposed to happen."

The door opened again and Elizabeth, with a vicious grin on her face, called, "Arabella Helene Leyden, I call you to enter the Trials."

CHAPTER XXVI

Wherein Arabella Endures the Trials

PARTHENA EXTENDED HER HAND TO ARABELLA AND SAID, "IT'S TIME." She glanced at Rowena with a mixture of pity and antipathy. "You make sure you pull yourself together before you come back into the Council Chambers. If it's as bad as you say, I'll have enough trouble holding the shield without your uncontrolled emotions tugging at the threads."

"Hurry up," said Elizabeth, her eyes sparkling. "I've waited long enough to see you fall."

Arabella stepped out into the hall and searched Elizabeth's face for any kind of sisterly love. There was none. All she saw was hatred and a possible glimmer of madness. "I don't understand why you hate me so."

"Because you exist," Elizabeth growled, her face twisting into an ugly grimace. "I was the last child born before you. Once Mother got her precious prophecy child, she forgot me."

"But Mother loved you and trained you just like all her other daughters," Arabella protested.

"Mother trained me like she'd train any initiate. I've never felt any warmth of love from her," Elizabeth growled. "She kept that all for her favorites. I had a chance to be one of her favorites, her precious youngest daughter. But you had to come along and spoil it."

"I didn't ask to be born," Arabella said.

"Really? Perhaps you should consult the crones about that someday," Elizabeth hissed.

Arabella choked, trying to think of an answer. But all she could think of was hearing her own child-like voice when she fixed the grandfather clock at Blackstone Manor. *Be ready.*

Parthena guided Arabella down the hall and gave Elizabeth a quelling look.

Elizabeth shut the door on Rowena's weeping. "Let's go. We mustn't keep the Council waiting."

Arabella marched down the hushed, high-ceilinged hall, her heels echoing off the marble, Elizabeth on her left, Parthena on her right. She refused to think of herself as a condemned woman being marched to her doom.

Elizabeth stopped before two massive oak doors not far down the hall. Each door had seven coats of arms carved into its surface, one for each of the thirteen Houses plus another that Arabella did not recognize. Elizabeth put her palms out flat in front of her and spoke a word of power. The doors swung in on silent hinges and revealed the Great Hall of the English Council of Witches. Arabella couldn't help thinking that it reminded her of a coliseum.

Elizabeth motioned for Arabella and Parthena to stand behind her as she stepped onto the landing. Broad marble stairs swept down to an open rectangle on the floor, empty now except for a bare altar at the center and a worktable to the right of it. On the worktable was all manner of traditional magic implements laid out in orderly rows. To the right and left, row upon row of stadium seating rose up until it was even with the landing where Arabella, Elizabeth, and Parthena stood. The chamber was broken up into sections for each House, six on a side with the Houses' coats of arms painted on the wall behind them. Straight across from Arabella was the single swath of stadium seating for Blackstone House. Her mother sat at the center on an ornate wood and leather throne, a gift from King Edward III to the first Grande Dame after they saved the Isles from the worst ravages of the Black Plague. Next to her sat the witch who had scribed Arabella's name with the ledger in her lap and quill pen at the ready.

Stationed at even intervals around the edge of the room were twenty-six Guardians, two for each House. Guardians were witches who showed a knack for the more violent aspects of magic. They stood outside the House structure, keeping to themselves and claiming no family except each other. Arabella had rarely seen these warrior witches. She looked now with unabashed curiosity. They eschewed dresses in favor of breeches, flat-heeled boots, and close-cut linen shirts, although they did wear formal robes of rich brown velvet in the Chamber as a nod of respect to the Council. They kept their hair cropped short, like men. Arabella had never seen them without serious expressions on their faces. Perhaps when they swore the Guardian's oath they also swore never to smile again.

Elizabeth held her right fist in the air and brought it down hard three times. A boom sounded through the cavernous room with each motion, as if she were pounding a staff of office on the marble floor.

Her voice rolled out to all corners of the room, carried with the volume and clarity that only magic could provide. "I bring the candidate Arabella Helene Leyden for consideration in the Trials. Will you accept her?"

"Let the candidate come forward." The Grande Dame's voice also carried on the strength of magic.

Arabella stepped to the edge of the stair with a lump in her throat, clutching the strings of her reticule in her hands. The secrets her sister so recently revealed threatened to spin her into hysteria and ruin her chances of surviving the Trials. She swallowed hard, trying to master her emotions and thoughts.

"Candidate, are you certain you wish to set your feet upon this path?" the Grande Dame asked.

"I am certain." Arabella's not magically amplified voice sounded weak and puny. Some of the witches in the stands tittered into their hands. Arabella felt blood rising to her face.

"Candidate, have you entered this Council of Witches of your own free will?" the Grande Dame continued the required tradition.

"I have."

Even from this distance, Arabella could see her mother's jaw tighten and her lips press hard together. Her voice shook slightly as she said, "Candidate, will you accept the consequences of seeking entrance to the Sisterhood should you fail the Trials?"

"I will..." Arabella coughed to cover her tight throat. "I will accept the consequences."

"Are you sure?" Minerva asked. The entire room gasped at the break in protocol.

Arabella squared her shoulders and said in as firm a voice as she could manage, "I will accept the consequences."

Minerva's shoulders sagged and she said, "Candidate, enter the Council Chamber and begin the Trials. I hope to embrace you as Sister rather than mourn your bravery."

Parthena stepped up even with Arabella's shoulder and whispered in her ear, "Time to get to work, girl. It's all up to you now." And they descended the steps together.

At the base of the stairs, Parthena whispered in her ear again. "Go to the altar at the center while I set the shield. I will tell you when to begin."

"But what do I do?" Arabella's heart filled her throat and her mind went blank.

"You perform magic…or you die," Parthena said with a level gaze. "Good luck. I hope to embrace you as Sister rather than mourn your bravery." Parthena gave her a little shove in the direction of the altar as she circled the space and examined the five points of the silver pentacle set in the floor, making sure all was in order with the candles and stones placed there.

Parthena stopped at the top point of the pentacle situated directly beneath the Blackstone House box and turned to face the altar and the rest of the room. "Are you ready, Candidate?"

Arabella looked from the bare altar to the confusing array of magical implements on the worktable. Some she recognized while others were completely foreign to her. "Ready as I'll ever be," she muttered to herself. She turned to Parthena and nodded.

She watched as Elizabeth scuttled along the top walkway. Her sister made her way down into her seat in the Blackstone box next to their mother and their sisters, surrounded by the rest of the witches who made up Blackstone House. Vivienne was missing, of course, still in her confinement at the Manor. Amelia looked sad and confused. Jessamine and Josephine smiled and beamed at her as they both waved. Rowena was still nowhere to be seen.

Parthena began the ritual of the Trials. Raising her arms, she recited, "Danu and Sulis, I call on you to gaze upon your daughters and bless our efforts here."

Dropping her arms to shoulder level she swept them from left to right. The candles at the points of the pentacle flickered to life as her hands passed by. "Hecate and Diana, I call on you to take the measure of this child and judge if she is worthy to serve you."

Holding her arms out at full length, Parthena brought her hands together above her head. When her palms clapped together a dome of rippling, iridescent energy snapped into being over the center of the Council chamber floor.

"The Trials have begun. No witch may interfere until this candidate is judged worthy or fails." Parthena fixed a sharp, but not unkind gaze on Arabella. "You may begin."

Arabella's eyes darted back and forth from the worktable to the altar, her breath short and panicky. "Stop it, you have a plan," she muttered to herself and licked her lips as she turned to the worktable. Her mind went blank. It was hard not to begin hyperventilating again. She placed her palms flat on the table, closed her eyes, and forced herself to blow out a long, slow breath. When she opened her eyes, the first item she saw was a plain white pillar candle. She picked it up and got to work.

She covered the altar with a cloth of clean blood-red linen, setting the candle in the center in its plain silver holder. She returned to the worktable. With trembling fingers she pulled open the drawstring on her reticule and pulled out a folded bit of paper. Witches in the stands craned their necks to see what she was doing. A hushed murmur rolled through the room as witches with a better view reported what they saw to those behind them. Unfolding the paper, Arabella's eyes raced over it, lips twitching as she read over the words she'd recited so many times in the last two days that they'd invaded her dreams the night before.

Surreptitiously, while she made a show of reading the words she didn't really need, Arabella slid her hand into her reticule and touched the now familiar metal coil around the stone. She let the power flow in to her. It took less than a sharp intake of breath. Crumpling the paper, she dropped it on the workbench and blew out another steadying breath. She then turned to face the altar, grim and determined.

The tingling from the barely contained power danced across her skin. Arabella held her hands low to her sides, hoping that no one would notice the electricity arcing between her fingertips. She then cried out as loud as she could:

"All hail Lucina, Goddess of celestial light! You give your light in the darkest of hours, smiling down upon us. Lucina, hear my call and bless us with your light!"

She brought up her right hand and pointed at the candle's wick. The lightning coursed down her finger. The bolt jumped across the air, the crack instantaneous as the wick burst into flame. Arabella allowed herself a smile then. It had gone just right this time. In so many of her practice runs she'd simply exploded the candle instead of lighting it.

The Council Chamber remained silent for a long moment before breaking out into a riotous roar.

Arabella looked to her mother first with eager eyes. She found Minerva smiling with tears gathered in the corners of her eyes. She scanned her sisters. Rowena was still not there. Amelia looked shocked, while Jessamine and Josephine were laughing and clapping their hands. Elizabeth's face grew as dark as the underside of a thunderhead, her white-knuckled fists clenched in her lap.

Parthena and the witch with the ledger also turned their questioning eyes to the Grand Dame. Minerva gave them both a firm nod. How Arabella had done it was most irregular, but she had still successfully lit the candle with no assistance from mundane means. The witch with the ledger recorded Arabella's victory with a smile and a flourish. Parthena gave Arabella a small smile and a wink before stepping toward the center of the pentacle.

Parthena turned sharply on her heel to fully face the Grande Dame, holding up her hand for silence. The chatter died down and Parthena's magically enhanced voice boomed throughout the Council chamber. "The candidate has performed a proper feat of magic. Do you accept her into the Sisterhood, Madame Grande Dame?"

Minerva stood with a beatific smile on her face and opened her mouth to speak the words that would welcome Arabella into the Sisterhood of Witches, binding her to the Sisterhood and the Sisterhood to her. But another voice cut her off.

"That was hardly more magic than a toddler should manage. At her age she shouldn't need chants," Margaret Lodwick said from her seat of power in the Elmswell House box.

Parthena looked at her through narrowed eyes. Frowning, she said, "The amount of magic matters not, only that it was performed."

"How do we know she didn't have assistance?" Margaret said. "After all, her mother is the Grande Dame. She could have twisted things to save her worthless daughter."

"You dare impugn my integrity as an Examiner?" Parthena hissed and she pointed upward. "The shield still stands. On my honor, there has been no interference." Margaret flushed bright red.

"If you are quite finished, Mistress Lodwick," Minerva said in an icy voice. "We would like to conclude our business so that we may commence the celebratory luncheon with our new initiates."

"What about her unholy abilities with mechanical objects?" Beatrice Paskin called out from where she stood at her own seat of power in the Fossdrum House box. Her voice dripped with disgust. "If she is truly able to manipulate mechanical objects, how can we allow such an abomination among our ranks?"

Two spots of color appeared high on Minerva's cheeks. "The order of business before us is the Trials, not any issues with technomancy. The candidate passed the Trials and we must uphold our traditions and admit her to the Sisterhood."

"You want us to admit a foul viper who will destroy us from the inside out?" jeered Beatrice. "Perhaps the rumors are right and you should step down from the post of Grande Dame." The entire Council chamber gasped as one.

"Ladies, good witches all, let us not be hasty with our words or deeds," Charlotte Anwell of Mynydd House stood and added her voice. "I know some of you fear machines and technology, but I can tell you from my experience with the men of the mines and the railroads that magic can work in harmony with technology, and even to our benefit. Arabella's abilities with magic and mechanics can open new doors and ensure the ascendency of witches for generations to come."

"Foul corruption!" hissed Beatrice. "You Welsh witches have been poisoned against the true way, seduced by men and their stinking machines. I warned you that cavorting with those men would bring your downfall. Do not presume to take the rest of us with you." Beatrice shook her fist in Charlotte's direction.

"Watch what you say, Sister." Charlotte's voice was cold and tinged with menace. "Or I will call you to combat so that I may defend my honor and that of my House."

"Peace." The word rattled the room and shook the witches where they stood. Theodosia Boscoe stood from her seat of power in Crawmere House's box. She swept everyone in the room with a fierce look that brooked no argument. "Bickering like school children does not become the most powerful women in the land." Margaret shrank back into her seat trying to look small. Beatrice fumed, while Charlotte maintained a stoic face.

"Thank you, Sister Theodosia," Minerva said. "Now if we can just forget all this foolishness, we can get on with the business at hand."

"As much as I would like to get to the festivities, Madame Grande Dame," said Theodosia. "I think there is one matter that must be handled first."

Minerva frowned but maintained her composure. "Speak."

"While we House Heads have had the pleasure to view Arabella's unique talent first hand," Theodosia began. "Most of the witches in this room have not. I dare say it would be unfair to expect them to vote on something they know nothing about."

"Vote?" Minerva drew herself up and tightened her jaw.

"Of course, a vote," said Theodosia. "We have before us the prospect of a new ability, and we must vote to see if it will be added to the register of recognized talents."

A smile tugged at Minerva's lips, but she clearly did her best to keep a serious face as she turned back to Arabella and Parthena where they stood next to each other. "Ladies?"

Parthena looked down at Arabella. "Well? Is there something you can demonstrate with?"

Arabella nodded and scampered back to the workbench where she had left her reticule. Nearly dropping it at first, she dug inside and pulled out a pocket watch. She then returned to Parthena's side with a smile as she looked up to her mother.

Minerva nodded with a smirk. "Proceed."

Arabella clicked open the watch face and presented it to Parthena on her flat palm. "What do you see?"

"A stopped watch," Parthena said with a shrug. "With all the magic in this room, I'm not surprised."

"You are absolutely certain that it's stopped, completely dead?" Arabella began to grin.

Parthena raised one eyebrow. "I'm certain."

With a pinch of her fingers and a flick of her wrist, Arabella pulled out the strands of magic interfering with the cogs and gears and tossed it in Parthena's direction. Parthena's eyes widened as she felt the surge of power. Arabella held the ticking watch out to her again.

"What do you see now?" she asked.

"It's working." Parthena's voice held a sense of wonder. "And I felt a power…"

Beatrice Paskin howled with rage and leapt forward. "Abomination! Foul creature!" she shrieked. She murmured a word of power and flung a sheet of fire at Parthena's shield.

Parthena shoved Arabella to the floor and directed her energy to the shield. She grunted and gritted her teeth. Her knees trembled, but did not buckle. She held the shield. Several things seemed to happen at once. The other four Examiners moved to the railing around the arena. They stood at the points of the pentacle and joined their power to Parthena's. Immediately, every witch near Beatrice scrambled to get away.

Two Guardians flew over the crowd and took Beatrice down. Tumbled to the floor, Beatrice screamed and writhed, while the Guardians remained calm and implacable. One Guardian held the witch down. The other tied her hands behind her back with a rope made from silk impregnated by iron. Then she placed her hand on the back of Beatrice's head and said a word of power that grated against the skull of everyone in the room. The Guardians then yanked her to her feet, hissing a dire warning in her ear to keep her spells to herself.

Arabella looked up from where she cowered on the floor, amazed that everything had happened so fast.

"Beatrice Paskin," the Grande Dame's voice boomed out. "I relieve you of your stewardship of Fossdrum House." Beatrice tried to scream her defiance but no sound passed the bonds the Guardians had placed on her voice. She was dragged out by her arms, the Guardians' expressions implacable despite her silent screams and attempts to writhe from their grip.

"Witches of Fossdrum House, do you have someone who can act as a temporary House Head until you are able to decide on a permanent one?" Minerva asked.

The knot of trembling witches looked from one to another, not quite believing that they were not going to be cast down along with Beatrice. A slender black-haired witch stepped forward. "I will serve, if it pleases the Grande Dame."

"Thank you," said Mother and she nodded to the ledger witch. "Genevieve Dinwiddie will be the temporary Head of Fossdrum House." Then she turned back to the room.

"Ladies, I know these last few moments have been quite unsettling, but if you will return to your seats we can get back to business." She waited while everyone shuffled back to their seats and settled in.

"Good witches, we have before us the matter of whether or not technomancy, the magic of machines, will be recognized and accepted as a talent belonging to a proper witch. In light of the divisive nature of this issue and the need for swift action, I exercise my rights as Grande Dame and call for an immediate vote." Minerva turned to her right. "Crawmere House, what say you?"

"We say aye, accept the new talent," said Theodosia.

Minerva turned to the next box and said, "Mynydd House, what say you?"

Charlotte's voice rang off the walls. "We say aye, accept the new talent."

"Elmswell House, what say you?"

Margaret's chin went up a notch. "We say nay. Machines have no place in the world of witches!"

Minerva narrowed her eyes, but went on. "Aberdean House, what say you?"

"We stand with Elmswell House," said Emma Tibbet. "We say nay."

Minerva hurried on to the next. "Ashblaen House, what say you?"

"We say nay," said Eudora Goodwin, her voice barely above a whisper.

Minerva shook her head. "What say you, Oakhurst House?"

"We stand with Elmswell and Ashblaen," said Mildred Bowen. "We say nay."

"How stands the count?" Minerva glanced at the witch with the ledger.

"Two ayes and four nays, Madame Grande Dame."

Minerva turned to her left with pleading in her gaze. "Thornfire House, what say you?"

Cecilia Kellar narrowed her eyes and paused. "We say aye, accept the new talent."

"Hazelrood House, what say you?"

Madeline Thurston glanced toward Cecilia, who gave her a nod, and she said, "We say aye, accept the new talent."

Minerva let go of the breath she'd been holding and moved on. "Yewlin House, what say you?"

"I'd say I'd like to have lessons in the new talent," said Selina Mortimer. "We say aye." Several witches chuckled.

Minerva smiled but her eyes hardened as she moved on to the next. "Fossdrum House, what say you?"

Genevieve bowed slightly to Minerva and said, "It is with great regret that I say nay, Grande Dame. Beatrice served us well until this unfortunate episode, and there must be a reason she thought such a thing would be dangerous."

Minerva inclined her head and moved on. "Rowanbry House, what say you?"

Katharine Wardlow inclined her head and said, "We say aye, accept the new talent."

All eyes turned to the smallest House of the thirteen as Minerva intoned, "Birchwold House, what say you?"

"Oh dear, oh dear," Philomena Beedlebaugh said as she twisted her lace hanky and looked to the witches around here. "We… We say aye, accept the new talent."

Minerva's shoulders eased and she said, "Blackstone House says aye. Secretary, how stands the count?"

"Eight ayes and five nays, Madame Grande Dame. Technomancy is now a recognized talent," she said as she pushed her spectacles up her nose.

"Then since she performed both pyromancy and technomancy, I pronounce Arabella Helene through the Trials and accepted into the Sisterhood." Arabella straightened beneath her mother's gimlet eye. "Will you take the oath and join your heart and spirit to the Sisterhood, and abide by our laws for as long as you shall live?"

"I will," said Arabella in a relieved voice.

Minerva inclined her head. "You will take your oaths at your investiture, in one week."

"We are adjourned," the Grande Dame's voice rang out, another boom echoing throughout the Council chamber as she dropped her fist.

Witches began to file out, chattering among themselves, and Parthena drew a closing sigil in the air with her index finger. The shield winked out of existence.

Arabella watched the witches leave, her body still shaking deep within from unspent adrenaline. It seemed too easy, everything suddenly too calm. She turned to ask Parthena a question and found herself face to face with her mother. She froze, not certain of what to expect.

Her mother, Minerva Vivienne Sortilege, Grande Dame of the Council of Witches, leaned forward and drew Arabella into a warm embrace. "Welcome, Sister and Daughter," she whispered in Arabella's ear.

Arabella held herself stiff, tears pricking behind her eyes, not trusting her voice. Opposing emotions warred inside her. She wanted to scream at her mother for the horrors of the past few months, yet at the same time she wanted to melt into her arms, to bask in the warmth of the acceptance she'd always craved. Her mother released her and held her out at arm's length.

"The last of my girls, finally safe in the fold," she said with a fond smile. "I have to go attend to official duties, my chickadee, but I had to tell you how proud I am of you." She pecked Arabella on the cheek and left before Arabella could decide the appropriate response.

She and Parthena stood in awkward silence a moment before Arabella shook off her shock.

"What happens now?" she asked her Examiner.

"We go to luncheon," said Parthena, then she embraced Arabella and whispered in her ear, "Welcome, Sister." Parthena gave her a parting smile as she left.

Again stunned, Arabella stared after her a moment before following. She needed to find Rowena. She needed her sister by her side at luncheon—what a mundane beginning to a magical life.

ABOUT THE AUTHOR

MICHELLE D. SONNIER WRITES DARK URBAN FANTASY, STEAMPUNK, AND anything else that lets her combine the weird and the fantastic in unexpected ways. She even writes horror, although it took her a long time to admit that since she prefers the existential scare over blood and gore. She's published short stories in a variety of print and online venues, and has upcoming projects with eSpec Books and Otter Libris. You can find her on Facebook (Michelle D. Sonnier, The Writer) or at www.michelledsonnier.com. She lives in Maryland with her husband, son, and a variable number of cats. The Clockwork Witch is her first full-length novel.

PATRONS OF THE
CLOCKWORK ARTS

A. Eleazer
Aidan Schneider
Alla Lake
Allison Kaese
Amanda S.
Amy Matosky
Andrew Topperwien
Ann Stolinsky
Ann Wiewall
Anthony R. Cardno
Ashli Tingle
Barbara Silcox
Beth McNeal
Brendan Lonehawk
Bruce E. Coulson
Carl and Barbara
Kesner
Carol Gyzander
Catherine Gross-
Colten
Cathy Franchett
Cato Vandrare
Chad Bowden
Cheyenne Cody
Chris Cooper

Christopher J. Burke
Cindy Matera
Connie Brunkow
Craig Hackl
Curtis & Maryrita
SteinhourYew
Dagmar Baumann
Dale A Russell
Dave Hermann
David Mortman
DavidZurek
Derek Devereaux
Smith
Donald J. Bingle
D-Rock
Elaine Tindil-Rohr
Eric Hendrickson
Erik T Johnson
Erin Hudgins
Gail Z. Martin
& Larry N. Martin
Gavran
Gina DeSimone
GMarkC
H Lynnea Johnson

Isaac 'Will It Work'
Dansicker
Jacalyn Boggs
AKA Lady Ozma
Jakub Narębski
Jasen Stengel
Jean Marie Ward
Jen Myers
Jenn Whitworth
Jennifer L. Pierce
Jeremy Reppy
John Green
Joseph R. Kennedy
Judy Lynn
Judy Waidlich
Karen Herkes
Katherine Long
Katherine Malloy
Kelvin Ortega
Kevin P Menard
Kumie Wise
Lark Cunningham
Linda Pierce
Lisa Hawkridge
Lorraine J. Anderson

Louise McCulloch
Margaret St. John
Maria V. Arnold
Mark Carter
Mark J. Featherston
Mary M. Spila
Max Kaehn
Michael D. Blanchard
Michael Fedrowitz
Mishee Kearney
Moria Trent
Myranda Summers
Nanci Moy
    & David Bean
Nathan Turner
Nellie

Nigel Goddard
Paul May
Paul Ryan
PJ Kimbell
Quentin Lancelot
    Fagan
R.J.H.
Ralf "Sandfox"
    Sandfuchs
Revek
Richard P Clark
RKBookman
Robert Claney
Ross Hathaway
Sam Tomaino
Scott Elson

Scott Schaper
ShadowCub
Sheryl R. Hayes
Stephen Ballentine
Susan Simko
Tasha Turner
thatraja
Tim DuBois
Tomas Burgos-Caez
Tory Shade
Tracie Lucas
Tracy 'Rayhne'
    Fretwell
V. Hartman DiSanto
Y. H. Lee

CPSIA information can be obtained
at www.ICGtesting.com
Printed in the USA
JSHW040258250822
29583JS00001B/21